A BOOGIE DOWN STORY

A NOVEL BY
KEISHA SEIGNIOUS

FOREWORD BY
ANTHONY WHYTE

T0160668

AUGUSTUS
PUBLISHING

A BOOGIE DOWN STORY

Copyright 2007
ISBN: 0-9792816-0-1

Edited by Anthony Whyte
Design & Photogaphy: Jason Claiborne

First printing Augustus Publishing paperback January 2008

AUGUSTUS PUBLISHING

AugustusPublishing.com
info@augustuspublishng.com

F O R E W O R D

Never judge a book by the cover. Readers know for sure that the statement doesn't really hold water. The reaction to the drama has been strong enough for this story formerly titled, The Blue Circle, not to die. It goes down in the Bronx during the early stages of Hip Hop. A Boogie Down Story unfolds during the eighties, at a time when B-Boy music transitioned into the hybrid called Hip Hop music.

The courage it took the pioneers of the music, Cool DJ Herc, Afrika Bambatta, Russell Simmons and Rick Rubin to reshape culture is what Augustus Publishing is currently doing for literature. Hip Hop fiction began with a bang in 2001 when the Ghetto Girls series was born. Augustus Publishing is still flossing Hip Hop Lit, also gave you Booty Call *69. A Boogie Down Story keeps it moving like the #2 train. It's not only a great story but also comes packing street swagger slighted by a twist of that bourgeois feel of an era when everything from mobile phone to Cross Colors jeans meant status, a time when Gazelles, money-clips and British Walkers were coordinated. The music of super deejays Busy Bee, Charlie Chase, and DJ Red Alert. While on the airwaves the sound of Grand Master Flash abounded.

A note for all the real heads, check photos capturing this early period see In Ya Grill The Faces of Hip Hop photograph by Michael Benabib with text by Bill Adler, produced by Jason Claiborne of Augustus Publishing.

The game's still the same, pimping a lot of cute girls, like Keya the best friend of Dawn, who doesn't understand her relationship with the two-timing and dangerous,

Cash. Keya is caught up and nearly swallowed by the life. The drama of saving her is so real between her friends and parents. A Boogie Down Story is hard hitting and moving fast like the #5 express. That's the way the story rolls as the lives of four friends take off unpredictably. Readers will want to go all the way to the last stop.

The altar or death are the choices these friends face in Keisha Seignious', A Boogie Down Story. The backdrop is the early images of Hip Hop dance battles, shoot outs at park jams. Keisha Seignious deftly shows an intense mood of hope throughout the story. She presents it in a really tight capsule aptly titled, A Boogie Down Story.

First introduced as another title, if you guessed it, then you don't care about the adage. Never judge a book by the cover. If you did dear reader, read on and enjoy. Unless you're in the land of dead, a story remains new until read.

ME, MY MAN'S AND THEM
SUMMER 1985

I remember watching many games played on the basketball courts at Magenta. That's where I met Dawn, Keya, and Cash. Up in the Bronx, near Magenta and Gunhill housing was our haunt. We played in the biggest game of our lives. It began in the summer of '85. Break-dancing was the thing and B-Boy music was beginning to take shape in the world of music.

My name is Forster. My boy Cash and I was popping and locking, breaking to the funky beats. We were jamming when the song by Sweet G, Games People Play, came kicking out of the sound system.

> *...Losers cause misery...*
> *Winners go down in history...*
> *Don't run your game on me...*

I was grooving with my eyes on all the cuties in poom-poom shorts. Cash peeped two honeys doing that sexy walk. We slid over for a closer look and slowed down. I wasn't really looking for anything but one hundred percent prime cuteness. My favorite jam came on by D.J. Chuck Chillout and the B-Boys. The E&J brandy pumping in my system had me amped. It was hot and I sang along.

> *I met a girl named Trina...*
> *I didn't wanna leave her...*

I knew all eyes were on me as I got in my zone. The music had me in a groove and I was busy break dancing. I felt a tap on my shoulder. It was Cash.

"Yo man, I was about to really get loose. This better be good," I said pausing in my B-Boy stance. Folding my arms, I awaited the breaking news.

"Forster man, check out those two hotties right there," Cash said.

I immediately saw her. She was light skinned, pretty and wearing a light pink top with a light blue denim short, short skirt. She styled different color fifty-four-elevens, Reebok's sneaks, one pink and the other blue. I had seen her before but didn't know her name. Her friend was a darker shade and equally good-looking. She was dressed in a dark blue sleeveless shirt with a light-blue short denim skirt. Her outfit was complete with different color Reebok's, dark blue on her right foot and white on her left. Each girl wore a ponytail with bangs on the side. They were of equal height about five-foot six, both had arrived with the right assets.

"Cash, I think they're checking for us," I yelled smiling.

"Dag, look at those def B-Boys," one of the girls announced.

From all the pointing and nodding aimed in our direction, it was clear that they were getting open on our style.

"They on our jimmies, Cash."

"Forster, let's go over there and throw game on them."

"Uh-oh, they're coming, Kee."

"DJ, be chill. Stop staring like you petro, or sump'n."

Cash walked right up to the one with the fattest fatty.

"Girl, do you have a map?"

"No why?" She asked stepping back while flirtingly batting her eyelids.

"I'm lost in your beauty, cutie," Cash said setting his trap. Both girls began laughing. The light-skinned honey looked me up and down. I sized her up quickly. She was a dime.

"That was good."

By the time she had responded, Cash was nose to nose in her face. They stood close enough to be kissing. Cash was bold like that.

"I'm Cash and this my boy, Forster."

"Hi, Cash and Forster. I'm Keya and that's my best friend, DJ."

"What the cat got your tongue?" Dawn turned to me and asked while Cash busied himself with Keya.

"Me? Nah, I'm just observing," I quickly answered.

"Observing what?" She asked.

"Just, you know? Checking," I said with ease.

"You seem kind a shy." Dawn said.

"I wouldn't say that. But I'm the opposite of Cash." I said nervously. Immediately I popped my collar. "Do you have a boyfriend?"

"No, I'm not allowed to have a boyfriend." Dawn responded.

"Why, how old are you?" I asked.

"I'm sixteen," she said.

"Word? So am I. My homeboy is sixteen too," I said excitedly. I had to slow down.

"My best friend, Kee is sixteen too," she said still checking me out. "Wow, we are all the same age," Dawn added.

I nodded in agreement feeling good vibes racing through me. On the sound system, Pebblee-Poo rocked that funky joint called Fly Guy.

"Let's dance," Cash suggested.

The basketball game had been over for about two hours now. Fans were still about and we saw players getting their groove on. Keya and Cash had hit it off and were dancing pretty close. Dawn and I shouted in each other ears, while doing a little two-step. I loved the way her eyes smiled and how she put in a little extra hip movement. I smiled when she spoke.

"Where do you live?" She asked.

"I live on Bronxwood. What about you?" I asked.

"I live on Allerton."

"I have a cousin near there," I said.

"How often do y'all come here?" She asked.

"At least three or four times a year. Cash and I live near each other."

"Kee and I live near one another too," she said wearing a calculative smile. "We've been friends for a long time."

"Really, you don't say. How long y'all known each other?"

"Kee and I been knowing each other since the second grade."

"Get out! Cash and I been hanging since second grade too. We've got a lot in common, huh?" I smiled at the coincidence.

"Look at them two," Dawn said pointing at Cash and Keya. They were dancing so close they appeared to be joined from the waist down. Cash was a lucky guy, I thought smiling.

"They carrying on like they've known each other a long time." I observed.

"Um hmm, what're you saying? We aren't hitting it off?" Dawn asked with trepidation.

"We doing our thing," I said cautiously holding her hand.

"Oh, I'm feeling you," Dawn said and squeezed my hand.

"You're all that," I said and saw Keya looking at Cash. She pointed at us. Maybe she wanted Cash to slow down.

"Let's go over there," Cash suggested.

Rock the Bells, by LL Cool J blasted through the speakers and the crowd went crazy-wild working up a sweat in the summer's air.

"How about we go to the store and get sump'n to drink?" I suggested.

We headed to the exit saw two other teens from the neighborhood standing in front of the pizza shop next to the store.

"What up young ones?" A friend of ours named Boobie, greeted us with high-fives.

"What's good?" I said. Cash followed behind me.

"Where y'all headed?" Boobie asked.

"To the Bodega." Cash answered.

"I wanna see y'all later," Boobie said.

"We'll hit you on the hip," Cash said and the four of us entered the store.

"Ladies it's our treat. Get whatever y'all want," Cash announced and immediately Kool Aide smiles appeared on both girls' faces.

"Let me find out, he's rolling in dough." Dawn leaned over to Keya and whispered.

When we got to the park the emcee was making an announcement.

"...the wizard, Grand Theodore, and right about now party people in the Boogie Down, I'd like ten fine females up here to do the Buffalo Gal dance to the song..."

The guys were applauding, encouraging girls to get down in front of the crowd and compete for the prize money. It was another chance for the guys to watch girls shaking their booties on stage.

"I know you two honeys are going to rep, right?" Cash asked Dawn and Keya. The girls looked at each other then nodded in agreement.

"Hell yes," they said at the same time then ran to the front. They were the last two of ten girls to reach the area. The emcee added that there were two judges and the lucky winner would win fifty dollars.

"And there is only one winner. Okay, ladies are y'all ready?" The emcee asked.

The girls screamed: "Yeah." The anthem began and all ten of the girls started shaking their rumps.

...Two Buffalos gals goin' roun the outside
roun the outside...roun the outside ...
Three Buffalos gals goin' roun' the outside...

The girls shook their tails to the sound of the World Famous Scratching Crew, while the guys placed bets on the possible winner. All eyes were glued on Keya's sexy frame. She moved like she had rehearsed the number. Kicking a leg, spun around and squatted while pumping her hips. The crowd went bananas when she jiggled her plump ass. By the time the music stopped; the crowd had worked themselves into this frenzied state. The dancers sweated and water was sprayed to cool the hype.

"It's show time party peoples, let's turn to the judges."

The crowd cheered. "Ahight, let's start with number one," the emcee announced.

"I'm Kandy with a K," the girl said. The audience applauded.

"Alright, that's Kandy with a K. Number two." The emcee continued on with the rest of the numbers and the crowd met each with an ovation.

"I'm T'isha," a cross-eyed girl said and the crowd roared in laughter.

The laughter continued all the way through until a five-foot sexy Latina introduced herself.

"I'm Sheena," she said with way too much attitude but had me caught up until I heard the emcee.

"Ahight moving right along. The last two coming up: Number nine," the emcee continued.

"I'm Dawn AKA D'licious," Dawn said smiling and curtsied.

The crowd was like "Yeah, ma, you surely are delicious."

"Last but not least let me hear your name, number ten," the emcee requested.

"My name is Keya but you can call me Sweet Kee."

"That butt is booming!" Cash shouted and hooted.

"Alright, alright, calm down...chill out. Stick around for the after-party and you'll get your chance later, kid." The emcee said to Cash and that brought laughter to the crowd. "Everyone in the place to be, we in da Boogie Down. We're in the Hip Hop capital. Gimme a break, you know how we do? I need a beat. H-e-e-y yo!"

"A-h-i-g-h-t!" The crowd yelled back. The deejay threw in some Sugar Hill Gang's Rappers Delight mixed with Good Times, by Chic.

"We uptown in da Boogie Down!" There was applause as the emcee said the name where we partied. "And right about now judges you heard their names, now ladies and gentlemen, B-Boys and B-Girls who's the number one rump-shaker? Who's gonna be our Buffalo Gal tonight?" The emcee asked. "I will have to say, girls y'all were doing ya thang. I gotta give it up", the emcee added. Then he turned to the crowd, raised his hands and applauded.

"Give it up for the ladies for being such good sports." The first judge said. The crowd applauded and the guys showed their appreciation with wolf whistles.

"It all boils down to number ten," the second judge announced. Keya's eyes widened, she turned to Dawn and they both started jumping around screaming. Cash and I were cheering loudly. Cash started doing his dance to celebrate. He put both hands in front of his chest and moved them as if he was patting down someone's Afro. His face contorted and he shuffled his feet as fast as James Brown's. I chuckled while he danced around still cheering on Keya. Both judges walked over to the competitors and shook their hands. The emcee handed an envelope with fifty dollars to Keya.

"Congrats shortie," the judge said and shook Keya's hand.

"Good looking, good looking out." Keya smiled. Dawn started to prance in happiness. Cash and I raced over to the girls and gave Keya a congratulatory hug.

"You could shake your grove-thang, huh?" Cash whispered to Keya. I hugged Dawn.

"You were the winner in my eyes," I said with a big grin. She smiled and blushed.

The deejay pumped up the music and a break-dance battle ensued as east Bronx and west Bronx collided.

"Let's go sit on the benches and watch," Keya suggested.

"Cool, with me because my legs hurt," Dawn said. We walked over to the bleachers and Dawn sat down first. I sat next to her and Keya sat next to Cash.

The conversation quickly turned to curfew and what our plans were since we were on point to graduate next summer from high school. With the exception of Cash, Dawn, Keya and I were ready to graduate. Both Cash's and Keya's tongues were already discussing sex. They seemed made for each other. Cash was a hot-ass since the age of seven. I guess we were all happy about who we had paired with.

Gunshots popped off and the party came to an abrupt end. Crowds of people began running and falling over one another. No one could tell who was shooting or who got shot. There were about more than a hundred people in the park. All four of us laid low watching people panicking and screaming. I glanced at Dawn and realized she was in a daze. Then my eyes caught Cash and Keya making fun of people who fell. Dawn and I weren't laughing. This wasn't new to me. I'd witnessed it all the time in my neighborhood, but there wasn't anything funny.

"Forster, let's go. I'm getting scared," Dawn said.

"Let the shooting clear up some more. The shooter could still be trying to hit targets and you know the innocent bystander always gets killed," I said in one breath. Dawn nodded in agreement.

"Cash," I whispered.

"What up, Forst?"

"You wanna leave now or, wait a little longer?" I asked. "The girls are getting scared," I continued.

"I'm not scared," Keya whispered in her defense.

"Well, I am." Dawn countered in a low voice.

"Yeah, we could break-out now," Cash said.

When we looked toward the middle of the courts we saw someone on the floor. I grabbed Dawn's hand. Cash took Keya's hand and we ran in the opposite direction of the crowd. Dawn's heart was thumping really fast. She was holding my hand so tight that my blood was barely circulating through my fingers. We ran at least four blocks before stopping to catch our breath.

"Oh, shit!" Keya blurted out.

"What happened?" Cash asked. We all turned our attention to Keya.

"I left my bag of goodies," she said.

"Kee, you're straight nuts," Dawn shouted still breathing hard. Cash and I

chuckled.

"I'll buy some more stuff from the store." I volunteered while leaning against a light pole.

"Is everybody good now?" Cash asked. Keya and Dawn nodded at the same time. Then everyone turned to me. I held my head down with one hand clutching the pole.

"Yo homey, you ahight?" Cash asked with a look of concern on his sweaty face. I took several deep breaths before I answered.

"Yeah, yeah, I'm good. My asthma is acting up that's all."

"Oh, I almost forgot you're the sickly type," Cash said laughing. Slowly, my breath returned to normal and I regained my strength. I took a swing at Cash in a playful manner.

"Okay, I'm ready," I said.

"Yo Forst, let's head to the store. Then we gotta go handle our biz with Boobie," Cash said.

"Y'all gonna break out on us like that? We haven't even exchanged numbers yet," Keya said as we walked across the street to the grocery store.

"We can do that when we get in the store. If that's okay with you?" I winked at Dawn.

"Yeah, it's okay," she said blushing. The numbers were exchanged and the girls had their goody bags once again. We assumed the girls would be safe from here on to their homes and decided to break out.

"We'll call y'all later," Cash shouted as he and I walked away from the girls.

"Y'all better!" Keya yelled back, while Dawn waved goodbye to me. I returned her wave with a smile.

"Those girls ain't skeezin', they ahight. That Keya is a fast one, Forst. I'll be up in that in no time, homey." Cash was excited.

"Get your mind off the pootang for a moment. What do you think Boobie want to see us about?" I wondered aloud.

"I don't know but I hope he put us up to the hustle on the block," Cash said.

"Yeah, that's what I'm dealing with," I said.

"Running packages and shit for him is not making it right now," Cash added. A look of determination buried deep beneath his scowl.

"Word to your mother! But you know Boobie may not even wanna put us on, cuz he thinks we just little niggas," I said. Cash nodded his head in agreement and continued to ditty-bop down the block.

"Yep you right."

"Boobie stopped us from selling weed, so we can deliver these packages cross town. Maybe he has something better in mind for us." I offered.

"Maybe, that nigga be throwin' shade too, homey." We continued down the road silenced by the noise of the train.

Meanwhile as both girls made their way to the subway station they began discussing the evening.

"Kee, you and Cash seemed to hit it off kind a quick," Dawn said.

"Yeah, well you know me." Keya answered.

"What is that supposed to mean?"

"DJ, you know I've been sexually active for as long as we known each other. You need to get with the program," Keya said looking Dawn up and down.

"I'm not trying to be fast like you," Dawn said playfully shoving Keya.

"A-n-y-w-a-y," Keya said dragging her word to another subject.

"Did you see the knot they both holding?" Dawn asked.

"Hell yeah, I was clocking it like the money was mine," Keya said laughing.

"Do you think that's their allowances?" Dawn asked and Keya looked at her like she was crazy.

"DJ, you know they hustling or something," Keya said.

"I'm not trying to be near no drug dealers," Dawn said shaking her head in disbelief.

"Wake up, what are you so scared for?"

"If a drug dealer have beef with anybody and that person can't get to the

dealer they getting the closest person, and that won't be me."

"Your whole family is scared and they passed that shit right down to you." Keya laughed at herself.

"Better safe than sorry, is what my dad always saying to me," Dawn added, rolling her eyes.

"Whatever, DJ," Keya smiled.

"Let's go to my father's job," Dawn suggested.

"Ahight DJ, we ain't got nothing else to do I guess...?" Keya said sounding disappointed and kept walking.

A few steps later, she turned and smiled because she really didn't mind Dawn's parents.

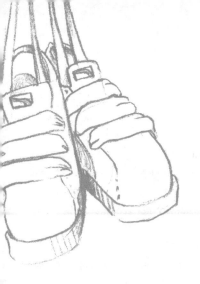

THROWING SALT
ON MY WOUNDS

Keya and Dawn failed to realize that they weren't the only ones who did not have the perfect household. Cash was only twelve years old, when he witnessed a fatally fierce altercation between his parents.

He entered the house and could hear the anger in his mother's voice.

"Don't you keep yelling and cussing, my son's home!"

"Oh, he's only your son?" His father replied.

"You know what I mean? He does not need to hear all of this," his mother said.

She was softhearted and used to help the neighborhood kids whose parents were on drugs or who were too busy to take time out for their children. Two out of the three parents offered to pay Mrs. Wedder but she refused because the love was from her heart.

Cash was cool with all the other children until his mother gave them each an old pair of his jeans. She also gave away boots and sneakers that he no longer wore. Cash was downstairs when he saw them wearing his clothes. He ran upstairs and pitched a fit with his mother.

"Mommy, you know I like those jeans. Why did you have to give 'em my stuff?"

"Baby, you no longer fit those things. I don't think it makes any sense to let them go to waste," Mrs. Wedder said.

"They get me sick," Cash said angrily running back outside.

"That boy better grow out of his selfish ways, or he's gonna be just like his daddy."

Cash was sitting on the stairs thinking of everything his mother had done for him. She helped others and he loved her for that. He was thinking about doing something nice for her, when all of a sudden he heard the scream. Cash opened the door and rushed into the house. His eyes immediately watered and his heart was beating twice the pace. Suddenly he stopped when he reached the kitchen.

"No, no, Sydney. Baby nooo!"

His body shuddered when he heard his father mumbling inaudibly and didn't see his mother. The older man called, Casmere brushed his frightened son aside and rushed out the door. Cash slowly walked into the kitchen and peered around. His mother was nowhere in sight. Sensing something was really wrong he was about to call her name but the noise coming from the street below the window jarred him. Cash rushed to the window and winced as he quickly pulled his head back inside.

He hesitantly stuck his head out the window a second time and saw the small crowd gathered. The boy was speechless and confused. He shook his head as people looking up at the window and pointing.

"He's going to jump". They shouted.

The fire truck was the first on the scene. A fire official covered Mrs. Wedder's lifeless body. Her husband was on his knees when the police arrived.

"What happened?" The officer asked Casmere.

He only nodded his head as the officer continued asking questions. "Can you tell me what happened?"

"Officer, Officer, my name is Miss Carroll. I am a good friend and neighbor." The officer hesitated then waved the woman on. Mrs. Wedder had taken care of Miss Carroll's son whenever she worked late. Miss Carroll dropped to her knees. She was close enough to see that the body covered up was not that of a child. Her tears came immediately.

"Casmere what's going on?"

"My-my- my- wife, she is gone," he said and began crying some more.

"Excuse me Miss, are you a relative?" An officer asked.

"My name is Miss Carroll. I'm a neighbor," Miss Carroll answered. "Officer, where is the little boy?"

"So far sir, we've got nothing," the officer-in-charge said. "The man over there is the husband and he's unable to say much. A neighbor went upstairs to see about their son," the officer continued.

Miss Carroll and an officer were making their way upstairs to check on Cash. Miss Carroll reached the door first. She knocked and called out Cash's name.

"Cashmere, Cash..." There was no response. The officer tried.

"Cashmere this is Officer Gladden. Will you please open the door?"

Still there was no answer from inside. The officer turned the doorknob. To her surprise it opened and she slowly walked in, Miss Carroll followed.

"Cashmere," Miss Carroll called out.

They found him passed out on the kitchen floor. The paramedics were summoned and rushed to Cash.

"He's alright."

His father was taken to the precinct for questioning. The coroner took Mrs. Wedder. Miss Carroll accompanied Cash to the hospital. The hospital was crowded and there was lots of noise. It seemed like this day was the busiest in the emergency room. Miss Carroll sat outside waiting to hear how Cash was doing. The head nurse on that particular floor offered Miss Carroll a cup of water and she gratefully took it.

Meanwhile at the precinct, detectives from the homicide division questioned Mr. Casmere Wedder. He tearfully confessed to killing his wife. Three months later, Casmere Wedder was convicted of manslaughter. At twelve years old, Cashmere Wedder was placed in foster care. It was the beginning of living hell and he rebelled even more. He listened to no one and fought with schoolteachers, counselors and anyone in a position of authority. A social worker once asked Cash if he missed his father. He stared at her feeling like she had slashed him with a knife. Then he walked away saying nothing.

"You can talk to me anytime you feel like it." The social worker told Cash before he had gotten out of earshot.

His attitude and behavioral issues had Cash constantly switched from foster homes. He wound up in a group home. He carried a chip on his shoulders, wanted nothing but rep.

"I won't let anyone get close to my heart again, just for them to be taken away." Cash sat up and stared at the Atari 2800.

It was during this period that we met. We hit it off immediately and I became his brother. He spent no time mourning his mother. Cash was busy getting into fights. He was a warrior who never revealed his true feelings.

Miss Carroll got him out of foster care and brought him home. Cash did his best to follow her tight rules while he was under her roof. Her son, Gabriel was a year older than Cash and liked school. Cash preferred fast money and the streets. One of the rules was he had to complete school.

My parents were there for my sister, Tasha and me. In the relationship with my father, my mother Martha was the abuser. My father, Roland Daniel Brown was her common law husband and received the brunt of her anger. My father wore scratch marks and bruises hidden under his shirt. He would fend off the blows but never struck back.

"You can get the fuck out!" Mother screamed every time she got drunk.

"Come on Martha, the boy is asleep." Dad argued.

"You can kiss my ass, Danny boy, you stupid son of a bitch!" She yelled after taking another long sip of straight Scotch. My father turned up the television in a vain attempt to tune her out. Mother walked over to him and slapped him in the back of his head with an ashtray. I peeked and saw my father holding his breath. He retrieved the remote and sat back down with blood on his shirt. Deep inside I felt dad knew mother had taken part of his manhood. She continuously embarrassed him and did it in front of their friends.

Since then, dad refused to go out with mother. She showed up to school meetings smelling like she took a bath with Jack Daniel. Dad dismissed mother's drinking as hereditary.

"Martha's aunts and uncles all have cirrhosis of the liver. Two uncles died of the disease. Martha, seems to be heading down the same road. If it wasn't for her constant drinking she would be a better mother to Forster."

Mother saw the fear in my eyes when I was five years old and she had erupted, frightening me. She touched my shoulders gently and spoke to me.

"Don't be scared, baby. Mommy will never curse or yell at you. Your father and I are having some difficulties right now. But, regardless of our disputes, I love you Forster. You are my only son. I will never let harm come your way. Do you understand baby?" She stared deep into my eyes and asked. I wiped my teary eyes with the sleeve of my pajamas and nodded.

As the years progressed, I learned to make up excuses so I could drink. If the teacher asked, where was my homework I'd say I didn't get around to doing it and would bring it tomorrow. When I was in school I'd call Cash to tell him he needs to get somebody to go to the liquor store to get me a bottle of Mad Dog Twenty-Twenty. That Mad Dog was like a lethal combination of Cognac and whiskey. When I first started drinking it was strong but after awhile I could drink it all day without feeling a thing. I was a minor and could get anything from the liquor store. I had been drinking since I was thirteen.

A BOOGIE DOWN STORY

THIN LINE BETWEEN FRIENDSHIP AND BUSINESS

"Yo Forster, don't we have to go check Boobie later?" Cash asked.

"Yeah, he wanted to talk to us about something. He really didn't say what." I said stuffing my face with beef and scallions, along with soy sauce from the local Chinese restaurant. I sipped the homemade iced tea. Cash had shrimp lo mien. When we were finished, we walked to Boobie's block. It was like a pharmacy where dust, heroin, weed and crack were sold.

"No prescription required." Cash laughed as we continued down the block.

"Heads are out." I said admiring the amount of clientele.

Boobie was a dealer who was into a little of this and that. He spread the wealth in the hood by recruiting teenagers whose parents were on drugs or who just didn't give a damn. He had become our big brother.

We spotted him half way down the block sporting a beige and brown Izod outfit. Of course he was fussing with one of his workers. It was known though out the hood that if Boobie's money were not right other peoples' lives wouldn't be right. He was dead center in the face of a new worker and chilled when he saw Cash and me.

"We'll finish up this matter later, aight?" He said to the worker, then turned and gave us pounds. "Lil' homeys what's good?"

Cash and I returned the handshake with fingers snaps at the end. It was our way of showing loyalty to the game. Before either of us could say anything, his cellular phone rang. "Pardon me lil' homeys," he said raising his hand. "What's up Lala?" We waited patiently as Boobie chatted to his son's mother. He had her on walkie-talkie.

"Before you come home Boobie, can you bring me some more maxi pads?" She asked him.

"The ones with the wings, right? Ahight, anything else?" Boobie asked. He put away the cell-phone then turned his attention back to us. "Pardon me young ones, that was wifey on the phone," Boobie said. "Always wanting shit from the store."

We both knew that Boobie hated going to the store for anything, much less things for a female. I busted his chops.

"Don't forget the Clairol shampoo." I laughed.

"I ain't goin' to the store. I'm a send someone else to get all that. Forst you know me?"

We were aware of how Lacresia rode that soft spot in Boobie's heart. She had his son. He respected her and even called her homey.

"Women be problems, huh?" Cash winked.

"That's my down-ass-bitch. Let me tell y'all lil' ones sump'n, you need a girl like Lacresia, ahight? Y'all need a girl who's willing to do whatever for y'all. Walk with me," Boobie said. We headed up the block while he kicked his game about how his girl held him down.

We entered the building and walked upstairs. Boobie entered first.

"Y'all niggas get da fuck out! I have business to attend to." He ordered. Two workers immediately walked out. The apartment was where he conducted business. Boobie had seven employees, or workers. He was a boss in these parts. "Y'all could take a seat. Chill out while I go get that and I'll be back," he said walking out the room.

"What do you think he has to show us?" I wondered aloud.

"I don't know, but it better not be no more damn weed," Cash said.

"You are stupid!" I said to Cash laughing.

"Ahight, ahight y'all lil' homies ready for this?" Boobie asked throwing little blue bags on the table in front of us. The bags were small. For about a minute, we both stared dumbfounded at the bags and the contents.

"Okay, okay, what's all this, my man?" Cash asked breaking his silence.

"It's that crack, boy." Boobie smiled as if he was giving away candies to babies.

"So, you want us to sell this?" I asked staring at Boobie as if he was crazy.

"Hell yeah, I feel y'all need to step up to the plate," Boobie said.

"I don't know about this," I said dismissing the idea.

"Nah, we got this," Cash said.

"Don't answer for me. I don't know, ahight?" I said sounding angrier than I actually was. "This shit worst than heroin," I said staring coldly at Cash. He sensed my anger.

"Okay, how's about y'all finish these few bags of weed, and we take it from there," Boobie said interrupting the disagreement.

"Yeah how bout we do that," I said nodding to Boobie.

"Then that's it," Cash said.

"Now Cash, I know you ready but you need your boy with you," Boobie said.

"I ain't trying to be up north doing football numbers on some whim," I said.

"Scared niggas never gonna make spit," Cash said.

"Yeah, I ain't trying to see joints up north, okay?"

"Chill out Cash, listen to Forst," he said while rolling a blunt. "It's not a game. There are three ways out of this. There's jail, death, or you retire from the game. The retirement plan never works out. Get yours now." Boobie held up a brick of dough and set it back down. He puffed and pointed at Cash. "I got your card, I feel you and all. Think on it like your man sez." Boobie puffed as he dragged his glance in my direction. "Forster, everything ain't for everyone. Got me?"

"Yeah I gotcha, man," I said staring back at him.

"Little homeys y'all report to me tomorrow," Boobie said and stood.

When we were out the door, Cash walked down the stairs before me.

"Why you tripping man?" I asked anxiously.

"I ain't tripping," Cash answered calmly.

"This my life. I ain't trying to get killed or go to jail."

"Maintain yourself Blackman." Cash mocked.

"Okay, Scarface, go out in a blaze of glory," I said laughing.

"Nothing or nobody gonna come between us. All I'm saying is that we think about this, and act on it together, alright?" Cash said.

"Cool," I said and pushed Cash on the back of his head. We raced to the train station laughing. I easily outran Cash and jump aboard the Number 2 train.

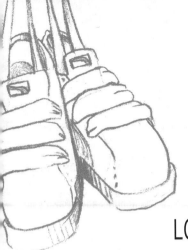

LOVER, FRIEND, MY ENEMY...

Dawn's phone rang at ten thirty in the morning.

"I got it," she said, running in her slippers and pajamas. "Yello," she said playfully.

"Good morning, may I speak to Dawn?" A boy's voice said.

"Speaking, who's this?"

"This is Forster," I answered.

"Hey, what's up Forster?"

"Did I wake you?"

"No, no I'm just watching cartoons."

"What are you doing later?"

"Nothing I'm aware of. I have to wait for Kee to get up."

"Okay, if the two of you aren't doing anything, why don't y'all meet us at around three."

"Cool, I'll call Kee now, she's kinda slow."

"I'll see you later."

"Later," Dawn repeated and hung up the phone. She immediately dialed Keya.

"Hello," someone with a raspy voice answered Keya's phone.

"May I speak to Keya?" Dawn asked.

"Yeah, fool this me," Keya said.

"Why you sound like you have a frog in your throat?" Dawn laughed.

"Later for you, bitch!" Keya said.

"You better not let your mother hear you."

"She isn't here. JB took her and my sister somewhere."

"Why you didn't go?"

"I'm too old to be running around with them. Besides they do kid shit because of my sister. I'm not with that."

"Kee, I'm calling because Forster called me a few minutes ago," Dawn said excitedly.

"What did he say, DJ?"

"He didn't say much. They want us to hang with them."

"Say word?"

"Yes, word. So get your lazy ass ready."

"Ahight DJ, let me go back to sleep for a few more minutes. It's Saturday," Keya said.

"Alright lazy, but be at my house around two o'clock."

"Gotcha," Keya responded. The girls hung up.

The telephone rang at Miss Carroll's house.

"Praise the Lord," Miss Carroll said.

"Hello Miss Carroll, this is Forster."

"Hi baby, hold on let me see if Cashmere is up," Miss Carroll responded.

"Get the phone and watch your language, okay?"

"Yo, what's up?" Cash asked when he picked up the phone.

"What are you up to?" I asked.

"I was busting Gabriel's punk-ass at video games. What da deal?"

"We meeting up with Dawn and Keya around three..."

"For real Forst?"

"Yeah, I done set all that up already, kid," I said.

"Its eleven now. I have to straighten up a few things round here," Cash said.

"Where you want me to meet you at?" I asked.

"Come over here and get me," Cash said.

"Bet that." I replied.

"See you round two-ish," Cash said. We hung up.

Later that afternoon, the girls waited for the boys at the Gunhill Rd. train station.

"I like Forster for some reason." Dawn said sitting on the bench.

"I like his nutty friend," Keya said and they both laughed. "Oh, I forgot to tell you girl, that Mike called me last night." Keya said.

"What he want?" Dawn asked.

"He missed me and he's sorry that his baby momma called my house. I said nigga please and hung up on him." Keya said laughing.

"Kee, I don't know why you be messing with those Willie Bo-Bo's."

"That fool, makes me feel good in bed."

"No you didn't Miss Nasty. I don't wanna hear none of that."

"Later for you DJ, you know I be making 'em wear jimmy hats all the time. I keeps mine. When you get some experience you'll understand exactly where I'm coming from," Keya smiled proudly.

"You're too fresh. I don't want no nasty boy on me," Dawn said.

"Okay, where the hell are they?" Keya asked.

"We'll give them a few more minutes okay, fast girl," Dawn said.

"What is that suppose to mean?" Keya asked.

"Your patience is short, that's all."

"There they go," Keya said when she saw Cash and I crossing White Plains road.

"Hey girls," I said greeting them.

"What's going on, ma?" Cash asked Keya.

"Ain't nothing new," she responded.

"What y'all want to do?" I asked.

"Let's go check-out Skate Key," Dawn suggested.

"I don't mind going skating, if that's cool with everyone," Keya said.

"I don't know how to skate, y'all," Cash said.

"Stop lying," I interrupted.

"Keya, what you really want to do?" Cash asked.

"For real, I want to go skating." Keya said.

"I haven't been in a while," I said.

"We have to take the two-train to Grand Concourse?" Keya asked.

"Nah, no iron-rails. We cabbing it," Cash interrupted.

"Yeah, that's way too much traveling," I said and waived at a cab.

Before we reached the Key we could see the line outside. Cash paid the cabbie and we joined the line already around the corner.

"Dawn I'm paying for you and Cash will handle his," I said and she nodded.

Posses from uptown were in effect along with Club heads from the Rooftop and Union Square.

"Here," I said to Dawn, handing her a folded bill. "Buy something for you when we get inside." I whispered in her ear.

"Thanks," she said and snatched the bill like she never had money before.

"Cash and I are going to talk to those two dudes. We wont be long," I said.

"Okay," Dawn said. Keya pulled Dawn close.

"DJ, did Forster give you money?" She asked.

"Yeah girl, he gave me twenty dollars."

"Cash gave me ten," Keya said.

"It's better than nothing," Dawn said.

The girls wandered over to the snack bar then went and rented their skates.

"I wonder where they getting all this money from?" Dawn asked while lacing up her skates.

"Where do you think, dummy? You're not stupid. Plus we talked about their jobs before." Keya said smiling.

"They don't look like drug dealers," Dawn said.

"Duh..."

"Okay, Cash be acting like he a local drug dealer but not Forster," Dawn said.

"I don't care, long as they ain't selling nothing round me," Keya said.

"That's word to my mother," Dawn said.

The girls joined other skaters around the rink. They held hands while they skated.

B Fats Woppit was rocking. Then Doug E Fresh and the Get Fresh Crew, *Six minutes* busted through the sound system while skaters bounced until the place was steamy hot. When Doug E. Fresh and the Get Fresh Crew performed *The Show* all the teenage girls lost their minds. My favorite line was Slick Rick introducing Doug E Fresh:

> *Excuse me Doug E. Fresh*
> *Have you ever heard a rapper on the mike that's not so*
> *right?*
> *They bite they never write and that's not polite...*
> *Six minutes, Doug E. six minutes, six minutes Doug E. Fresh you're*
> *on...Oh, oh oh on...*

Everyone was partying hard and sang the lines as the Get Fresh Crew ripped up the stage. All the heads sang along.

> *...no no he didn't*
> *excuse me Doug E fresh you're on*
> *Well it started out on 8th avenue*
> *when I made up a name called the get fresh crew*
> *It was me Barry B and my mc Ricky D...*

The party was jumping by the time Slick Rick took the microphone. The crowd went berserk rocking to *La Di Da Da*. The evening was just beginning to rock at Skate Key. Cash and I entered the rink as the deejay spun *AJ Scratch,* by Kurtis Blow. I skated freely, popping and singing along with the song:

> *Up in the Bronx where the people are fresh*
> *There's only one deejay who could pass any test...*

I turned around to see Cash cowardly clinging to the rails around the skating rink. The girls focused on Cash.

"Look at that fool," Keya said to Dawn.

"Why don't you go over there and help him girl," Dawn suggested.

"Forst, you're not gonna help your boy out?" Keya asked as she passed me.

"Why don't you?"

"I will," Keya said to me as she made her way through the crowd, skating easily without falling. Cash was relieved when he saw Keya coming his way.

"Boo, I'm gonna bust my ass," Cash said.

"Not while I'm here, you're not," Keya said.

"Dawn, can I hold your hand while we skate?" I asked.

"Sure," Dawn said.

I was able to skate well enough to keep up with Dawn. Dawn and I made our way off the skating rink. I escorted Dawn to the bathroom. While I was waiting for her I saw an old girlfriend.

"What's up Forster?" Freeda asked.

"I'm good and you?" I answered.

"That's good, I'm alright. You know me."

"How's your son?"

"He's doing okay. He's with my mother right now."

"Yeah, that's all right." I said making small talk.

"Why you don't call me no more, Forster?" Freeda asked.

"Freeda, I'm not going into this with you, because you know why I don't call you." Freeda was so close, her breast brushed slightly against my lower chest.

"You don't miss me?" She asked flirting. I didn't answer and walked around her.

"He still wants you girl." Her friend yelled.

I had busted Freeda with her son's father, after she'd told me she was not dealing with him. All along she had been playing both of us. Freeda was a couple years older than me and had baggage. She had been the one who introduced me to the sensual sex. Before her it was just wide-eyed in and out action. She taught me to slow down, work it in and spank that cat right. You never forget a good teacher. I glanced toward the rest room and Dawn came out.

"I'm ready," Dawn announced.

I was happy that Dawn had not busted me with Freeda.

"What's up?" Dawn asked.

"Huh?"

"What's wrong with you?"

"Nothing. Can we sit for a minute?" I asked. Dawn hesitated.

"Sure," she agreed.

"Am I stopping your fun?" I asked after seeing her frown.

"No Forster, I want to sit with you. What's up?" She asked.

"It's like this," I said taking a deep breath. "Can I talk to you about something personal?" I asked.

"Yeah, aren't we friends?" Dawn asked.

"I just saw my ex," I said.

"Go ahead," Dawn encouraged.

"It's like this, I still have feelings for her, but I don't want to see her anymore. It seems like every time I turn around I see her somewhere," I said frustrated.

"Well, did you tell her how you're feeling?"

"She knows pretty much how I feel, because I don't call her anymore."

"You have to be clear with her."

"Sure..." I said.

"I sure wouldn't want anyone beating around the bush with me. Why did y'all break up?"

"She have dude's son and cheated on the both of us. I caught her messing with dude even when she swore they had broken up," I said too angrily.

"Oh," Dawn said.

My mind was making a mountain of a molehill, when I heard Dawn.

"You still want to be with her?"

I stared at Dawn, shocked by what she asked and saw that she wanted to take the question back. I thought and answered as honest as possible.

"Yes and no," I said realizing that things were getting more complicated.

"Why yes and no?"

"Yes, because of the things we shared during some tough times," I said and paused before continuing. "No, because if she had my back the way she said she did, things wouldn't have gone down the way they did."

"That's a lot on you Forster. Until you make up your mind where you stand, your heart can't catch up."

"That was real deep."

"I try to be," Dawn said with a smile. "Truthfully, you take your time, it's up to you, and you know right from wrong."

"Yeah, thanks."

"If you want to give this girl another chance, you have to forgive her for the things she's done to you, so y'all relationship can progress. My dad told me once a cheat always be a cheat. And once a liar always a liar," she added her eyebrows arched.

"Me too, I believe in that creed. That's why she's my ex-girl," I said. "I'd never lie to you."

"Boy, please!"

"Seriously, Dawn I wouldn't," I said reassuringly. "We are friends and I wouldn't cross you." I added looking deep in her soft brown eyes.

"You promise?" She asked. I put my hand in hers. I waited until she had gripped my hand before I leaned forward smelling her perfume as I whispered.

"I promise."

"One more thing: Where did you get all the money from?" She asked. I didn't know what to say. I smiled and held my head low. I glanced at Dawn for a few seconds before answering.

"I know you know where I got this money so why ask me, huh?" I questioned. Dawn nodded.

"Because it doesn't seem like it fits you, Forst."

"Hold up, shortie, what fits me?"

"School," she said and got up.

"I go to school," I reminded her. "And I plan to go to college."

"We'll see."

"Why you gonna follow me to make sure I go?" I asked jokingly.

"You'll see," Dawn said and grabbed my hand.

We headed back. When we arrived, there was no sight of Cash and Keya. We continued skating and having fun to the rhythm of UTFO and Dr. Ice. The joint was called Leader of the Pack and that's how I felt. Maybe this was the right girl for me. We skated, rocked and rolled till we heard *Five minutes of Funk* .

"I wanna see a flick. What college do you go to?" I asked.

"I attend Monroe College in the Bronx," Dawn answered. Then she asked. "You have money like that? What do y'all parents say about that?" She queried with rabid curiosity. I wondered where this was going because I never mentioned my parents. "Doesn't your mother be asking how you have that kind of money?"

"I don't be showing her my money, girl. I just hit her off with a little and hide my stash." I said and winked. "Can we change the subject?"

"I'm sorry I didn't mean to start butting in your biz. I've been curious since we met."

"It's nothing," I said.

On the other side of the skating rink, Cash and Keya were hiding in the dark.

"Cash, why are you feeling me up?" Keya asked smiling.

"You ain't stopping me, neither," Cash answered.

The two of them cuddled on benches built for tired skaters, where horny teens went to make-out. Cash had a hand up Keya's skirt, his other feeling on her breast. From the writhing of her body he was using his finger to pop her off. Her body convulsed and her hands gripped his shoulders as she reached her second orgasm. Keya wasn't familiar with this. Even though she was sexually active, Keya had never achieved orgasmic pleasures and had never been finger-popped before.

Boys had gone down on her but she had never climaxed. Keya was often frustrated and would relieve herself by grinding her pelvis on the guy's leg while using her own fingers. Cash had done something totally different. Keya didn't care that her hair-do flopped nappy. Her body writhed and her pussy lips were percolating while Cash sucked the nape of her neck. She squirmed and opened her legs wider giving his hand free access. Keya's breath came in short gasps from Cash biting and pinching her exposed skin, He used his middle finger to pop her off. The warm sensation flooding her tingling senses felt so good that Keya didn't want the feeling to stop. His probing hands left her wet and gushy between her legs, her stomach was on fire.

A thought crossed her mind when she ground her hips on his hardness. Keya suddenly became worried that there would be telltale signs from his mouth sucking all over her neck. If her mother saw marks on her neck, that meant sure punishment. His lips felt good but she had to stop now. She pushed him away lightly and Cash knew she was encouraging him.

Lust transported them. Keya grabbed the front of his pants, feeling his penis hard and ready. She swallowed hard with fear. Cash was hard as a roll of quarters. Keya's legs turned jelly and her heart beat came fast when she felt how much larger Cash was than all the other boys she had ever dealt with. Keya glanced nervously at him and saw the twinkle in his eyes as he smiled. He had the softest lips and a gentle touch than any other sixteen year old. He must have a lot of sexual experiences Keya guessed. She was breathing hard. Cash had it going on, she thought. She didn't slow him down.

"Where are those two?" I wondered aloud. Hours had passed since we had turned our skates in. Dawn and I searched for Cash and Keya.

Little did I know that by then Keya had two orgasms and she'd closed her shaking legs to prevent Cash from touching her. He gave up after several attempts then spoke to her.

"What's wrong Keya?" He asked. Keya didn't answer. "Don't be embarrassed about how you feel. Its only natural," he said and kissed Keya on her lips. "Just go to the bathroom and freshen up, you hear?"

Keya nodded, got up and straightened her crooked skirt. Keya had never made-out in public before. She had been a private, behind closed doors only type until now. Keya thought as she hurried to the ladies room. I spotted Cash.

"Dawn's ready to go Cash," I said to him.

"What up money?" Cash asked with a smile.

"Where's Keya?" Dawn asked.

"Oh, Keya, she in the bathroom," Cash answered.

"I'll be right back. I'm a see about my girl," Dawn said and walked away.

"Cool, we'll be here," I said and turned to Cash. "You didn't?"

"I didn't what?" Cash asked trying to play dumb.

"You were making out. Did you give her the finger test?"

"You know what time it is." Cash answered with a pound.

"Them girlies can't handle our finger game, man," I said returning the handshake.

"I had to make sure her kitty-cat was proper."

"Really, she let you?"

"Here sniff my fingers, if you don't believe," Cash said shoving his hand up to my nostrils.

"Get your nasty fingers out my face," I said smacking his hand away. We both laughed.

One of the games we played was finger-candy. Whenever we met a new girl, we'd ask her to put her finger in her vagina and let her taste it. If that finger comes up with a little funk, we'll definitely stop the show.

"She was proper homey. I made her come twice," Cash bragged.

I gave him a pound. Cash and me were always sharing the salacious details of our encounters. We never did this with anyone else.

Dawn went in the ladies room.

"Kee, you in here?" She shouted.

"I'm in here, DJ." Keya came out fixing her hair.

"You little slut," Dawn said playfully. Then she saw Keya's neck. "Oooh, oooh, Kee you got hickeys." Keya rushed over to the mirror and examined the spot.

"Shit, I hope my mom don't notice this."

"What were y'all doing?"

"Nothing," Keya answered.

"Tell that to someone who don't know you."

"What am I going to do about this hickie?"

"Why is your hair so messy if you did nothing?"

"Cut the twenty-one question, DJ."

"I can't believe you were getting freaky at the Key?"

"No, no, knucklehead too many people up in here."

"Y'all did something."

"We were smooching. Are you happy now?"

"Can he kiss?"

"Can he? I'm a have to stay away from that one."

"It's like that? Let's get out of this stink-ass bathroom," Dawn said.

Cash and I were still kicking it outside the girls' bathroom.

"I can't believe you did finger-candy this early."

"I had to test the waters, and besides, I like Keya. She's the female version of me." Cash said winking and smiling. "She's definitely different than the other girls I've been meeting so far." We slapped five.

"Here they come," I warned. Dawn returned with a big smile. Keya looked confused.

"Look what you've done," she immediately said to Cash.

"Damn!" I shouted before Cash could respond.

"Yeah that's the real deal, homey," Cash said and gently turned his head.

"And this supposed to mean what?" Keya asked with her hands on her hips while shifting her weight side to side.

"I meant to put that there," Cash said.

"My mother is going to kill me," Keya said.

"Just make sure she stays on your left side." Cash smiled. Dawn and I started laughing. Keya looked at us like she was ready to fly our dome piece. Cash kissed her hickey.

"It still hurts," Keya said and took a step back.

"Poor booboo," Cash joked.

"It's not funny." Keya was peeved.

"Let's go to the movies." I suggested.

"Are you down?" Cash asked Keya comforting her with a hug.

"Yes I am." Keya answered. Dawn was cheesing because she knew we were going to the movies regardless of their decision.

"Let's be out," I said.

We headed to the train. The movie we agreed to see was only showing at the Metro on 42nd Street in Manhattan. We got on the train, or as my mother called it, the iron horse. The car was empty and the girls sat together. Cash and I sat scheming on the pootang. The ride was quick. Cash and Keya were first off the train. Dawn and I followed close behind. Outside the bright lights of the city caught the girls by surprise.

"Wow!" They exclaimed.

"The city lights are so pretty. Let's walk around first," Dawn suggested.

We headed in the opposite direction from the movie theatre. Musicians were having jam sessions on the Deuce. Large gatherings of out-of-towners flocked to the various street scenes. Artists were busy with easels set up on the sidewalks, three-card mollies were around. Keya dragged Dawn by the hand to a Peepshow booth. I guided them away.

Cash and I were bugging out on the amount of game rooms. So many people were jam-packed on this strip of Manhattan. I heard the different languages and realized many people travel to share this. At the end of the night we walked and talked, laughing giddily the way children do when everything was new. We grabbed a bite at Sbarros.

Dawn snuggled under my arm for most of the night. After posing for our pictures with the PE logo in the background, we went back to the arcade and the four of us had our own Pac-Man tournament. A check of the time reminded us of all the fun we were having.

"Ah man, I hate to leave," Dawn said and we all agreed. Even Cash was smiling and having a ball.

"Let's head back uptown." I suggested. No one resisted. All our teen energy had been drained by the long day on the town. The train was empty on our way back home and we laid out on one another. I checked to see if Dawn was awake. She nodded her head.

"Can I walk you home?"

"Man what are you doing?" Cash asked later after we had walked the girls home.

"What do you mean?"

"Don't start that romantic crap, because she's gonna run and tell her friends and they gonna think all dudes supposed to be like you."

"Why, you scared of a little romance?"

"My mom never got any romance."

"What're you trying to say?"

"Why should I romance any girl? She's for freaking. You a little sucka for love!"

It didn't matter what he called me, I was on a high after my date with Dawn. We headed towards the park.

THE PRESSURE

The months turned into years. Cash and I made plenty dough from crack sales. Boobie had let us in on the new sensation. We were busy chasing papers and the relationship with Keya and Dawn suffered. Every once in awhile I'd check on Dawn to see how she was doing. We'd grab a bite to eat. On one occasion, she mentioned that Keya was having a baby. I knew I should not be surprised but I actually was.

"Say word?" I questioned, caught off guard. I couldn't think of what else to say.

We continued eating in silence. Dawn was a secretary working in a law firm. The girls resided in the Bronx. Cash had moved to Harlem with one of his girls and I had an apartment up in the Boogie Down. 1991 we decided to make our power move. Slinging heavy loads of crack turned out to be very dangerous. I bought my first whip, a red Maxima. Things were going well with one exception; Cash's temper. Over the years he had gotten worse and now that we had money, he was out of control. The telephone rang loud in Cash's apartment.

"Yo," he answered.

"What's good, Cash money?" I asked.

"Same shit. Different day. Forst, come through," Cash said.

"Not a problem. I'll be there in a few."

I lived the single life in my two-bedroom apartment and worked as a chef in an expensive hotel in Manhattan. On my own time I had established another way to get paid. Illegal was only part of business. Cash was down with the flow. I had grown wiser over the years. After high school I went to trade school to get a certificate in order to

become a chef.

I came out of pocket and with government grants I was able to complete school. I flipped the drug money to educate myself. Cash had been in jail for a few months on parole violations. I always visited him. I would talk to him about his actions in dealing with people. His temper was always spilling over into fisticuffs. Guns would be drawn making the block hot and drawing the cops. This slowed down the hustle for everyone.

When Cash got knocked, it gave him time to see the foolishness of wilding on the block. He lost respect on the streets and tried to brush it off. A lot of damage had been done. I was cool, calm and got mad props for being that way. Cash was disrespectful and loud. Things reached a point of explosion where Boobie didn't want Cash to come around his block. It was the end of the game, as we knew it. When I re-upped on my works, Boobie did not allow me to bring Cash. Every guy that glanced Cash's way had beef on their hands. Cash had pistol-whipped a young kid from Boobie's camp. Once Boobie found out, shit hit the fan. He came looking for Cash and found him on the block.

"I created you. You're gonna respect me or I'll smash you. You heard me?" Boobie's rage came spitting from his mouth. Cash was unable to look Boobie in the eyes when he answered.

"Yeah, I hear you, man."

"Yo Forst, keep this punk off my block fore I put couple in him," Boobie said dismissing Cash.

I signaled for Cash to hold his temper. He said nothing but walked away. Cash and I would always go to the block when we needed more work.

"On some real shit Forster, you better check your boy. I'm all for putting it on a brother whenever he tries me. My mans and them told me Cash came over here tripping on some bullshit," Boobie said.

"He was bugging but I'm gonna talk to him," I said.

"Did I not look out for the two of y'all?" Boobie asked.

"No doubt," I agreed. "Cash was the one who talked me into doing what we doing now." I said and looked away as Cash walked on. "But I didn't think he would've changed this much, for real."

"If you don't calm your boy down somebody else will. Even though he's your man, doesn't mean you have to get involved with his bullshit," Boobie said.

"True," I said.

"If he's tripping, you supposed to check him, not ride or die with that B.S. Everyone be complaining about him. I heard he's disrespecting local dealers' babies' mommas. Check your man for real before I make him spare-change."

Boobie was definitely not having it. I left Boobie's block feeling very upset. Cash was making me look bad also. I drove to the park to see what was popping off. Damn! We ain't been here in a minute, I thought as I pulled up. It was fall and only the kids and lovers came to the park at this time of year. I saw two lovers holding hands and I remembered Dawn as if it were yesterday. Immediately I reached for my cell phone and dialed her digits. The phone rang twice before someone picked up.

"Hello," the woman's voice on answered maturely.

"Hello, may I speak to Dawn please?"

"Hey you, this is me," she replied.

"Girl what's really good with you?" I asked.

"Chilling in the crib."

"Guess where I'm at?"

"Where?"

"Be easy, I'm gonna tell you. I'm in the south end of the park."

"Say word. I'm on my way down," she said.

"Ahight, I'll be waiting on ya," I said. I pulled out the bottle of Hennessey, turned it up to my head and chugged half the pint. Drinking when times got hard still seemed to ease my burden, but it appeared things only got rougher everyday. Before leaving, she called Keya to let her know that I was at the park. She was surprised that Keya's mother asked about Keya's whereabouts. Apparently, Keya had not come home since the night before.

"I haven't spoken to her since yesterday. If I hear or see her I'll bring her home myself." Dawn said.

Keya had gone missing before and Dawn had brought her home. Her stomach was busy doing somersaults as she threw on a soft pink DKNY dress with the jacket she had worn to work. Instead of putting on shoes, she slipped on her white Nikes.

I knew that Dawn had feelings for me even though we always managed to keep our relationship on the friendship tip. She saw me immediately when she rushed

into the park. I stood and our eyes locked. From that moment we began to get closer.

"Hey you! Dag, I haven't seen you in awhile," she said smiling. We hugged.

"Good to see you, Dawn."

"My, you've gotten taller. Hmm, and you smell good."

"It's great what little soap and water can do. I'm only kidding, girl. How've you been?" I said laughing.

"Working and attending college, same ol," Dawn said.

"That's the right move."

"How's your homeboy?"

"You talking 'bout Cash?"

"Same one..."

"He's still tripping. You know we changed our steeze over the years," I said and stared at Dawn's reaction. She was still fly.

"I'm listening." Dawn smiled, clearly happy to see me.

"You know he's always had this attitude problem. It's all part of his mother passing away early." I reminded Dawn.

"Yeah I remember. He needs counseling," Dawn said.

"Bust it, since we put other guys on to pitch for us he has changed drastically. Right now, he could fuck it up for everyone," I said and saw Dawn's look of concern. I continued. "People in the drug game is willing to do biz with me, but some be acting funny on the strength of them knowing Cash is my man. Sometimes they act like they don't want to allow me to get work." I glanced at Dawn and realized that her eyes were riveted on me. I tried to explain without my voice cracking. Dawn moved closer and held me.

"Listen, you do what you've been doing holding down your connect in the game. But before things really get out of control, I think you have to give Cash an ultimatum."

"You're right." I did not want to do that. Cash was my brother.

"And if he still wants to wild out, tell him he'll be on his own. I mean, neither of you should be doing it period. But I really can't knock your hustle. Don't let him get to you Forst. You know Cash's going to look out for himself regardless."

"Yeah, I feel you."

"In the end you've got to make sure you look out for you. I know that's your boy and all, but we are supposed to be older and wiser now. It sounds as if he's getting worse. And then one day, God forbid, he's going to get into a pickle with some real live dudes and you'll be caught in the thick of it. Cash knows you have his back, and you know he has yours regardless. It's imperative that you don't get into any unnecessary beef. Y'all have enough to worry about."

I was staring in her soft brown eyes as she outlined the pitfalls of the game.

"You're still very pretty."

"Yeah thanks, but you won't see me if you're in jail, or killed by another brother who gets jealous and wants to take-over y'all spots."

I nodded and listened. In the end she was spitting the truth.

"Dawn, this little thing is turning old, real fast. It ain't for me no more."

"Why isn't it for you now?"

"I got into the game with Cash on a temporary basis. We both gotten greedy and I stayed too long. I'm just not feeling this life no more." I said trying to hide emotions coursing through me.

"Really, I never knew you felt that way?"

"Look, the other day we had a shoot-out. That scared the shit outta me. I can't front. After that, I've been praying. I don't want to be in no jail or shot up, stabbed up, or beaten with no baseball bat. It's not a joke. It's real out here. It ain't like we ain't gotta still deal with the D's bum rushing the show. Now we gotta worry about every Tom, Dick and Harry hitting us up for dough."

"Okay, but you have a mind of your own, right?"

"Yeah, I know but it's like this; that's my man, one hundred grand, and I'm a go all out for my man."

"Does that mean you'll die senselessly for him?"

"I don't see it like that. Cash and I are brothers. You don't let your brother down no matter what."

"What if your brother doesn't give a damn?"

"That's the risk I'll have to take."

"I mean Keya and Cash, you and me all four of us had it rough at some point in our lives?"

"Not you little princess," I laughed.

"Later for you," she said jokingly.

"Definitely me, Keya and Cashmere," I said.

"It sounds funny when you say his whole name," Dawn said.

I thought about it for a second then chuckled.

"It does right? I always called him Cash. Since the first time he told me his whole name." I said looking in her eyes.

"Cash's crazy," she said.

"For real, I don't mind staying in the game for a minute. It's just that Cash's off the wall." I said thinking.

"He's gonna drive you to drinking."

"If he learned to chill, we could retire rich," I said laughing.

"That's not funny."

"I didn't mean it to be."

"Forster, I hope you two get it together. I love you both like brothers."

"Like brother, huh?" I asked.

"Yeah, you heard me the first time," she said smiling.

"Okay, if that's the way it is."

"Not to change the subject or anything, but Kee's out there on the streets," she said getting serious.

"I didn't know."

"I didn't either, her mother told me. She stayed out last night and left her daughter with her mother. Now that's hard to see. We're too close."

"Since elementary days, right?"

"Yep, it's been that long," Dawn said shaking her head.

"You try talking to her. You know them folks at BCW will come and get her daughter."

"I tried talking to her. Even tried helping her with a job, but she's caught up running the streets."

"Why?" I asked staring at Dawn's troubled face.

"I think she's smoking crack."

"Dawn, for real?" I asked.

"Ah, I'm not sure, but it looks that way."

"Lemme know if you find out. If it's somebody I know selling to her, I'll bring that to and end."

"I wish you could."

"You know I got mad props round here." I said then we stared in each other's eyes.

"Yeah, I know." Dawn smiled.

"Enough of them, man. When can we go out?"

"Out like what, a date?"

"If that's cool," I said surprised that she made me nervous.

She stared at me for what seemed like an eternity. I remembered when she used to call me fly and bold. Maybe things had changed. Why was it taking her so long to answer? I anxiously waited for her answer.

"We can go out, but only as friends." She finally said.

"Like friends huh?" I asked not able to hide my disappointment.

It was clear to both of us that her reference to our friendship had rattled me some. Maybe I didn't have it anymore. I had to work harder. Then I heard the worst thing a man with plans could hear from the woman he had plans for.

"I wouldn't want to mess up our friendship," Dawn said and I was stumped for a minute. Then my mind went to work.

"I heard that's the key ingredient in making best lovers," I said.

"Oh really," she said with a smile.

"If we gonna remain friends then why not try to combine both?" I asked.

"Me personally, I'd rather take it slow. I mean, you, Keya and Cash, are my buddies and I would never want anything to mess up that equation."

"Girl, be easy, I'm talking about hanging out. I ain't trying to hit the skins. If things escalate to something other than our friendship, then let it be."

"Okay, we could but don't start clocking me." Dawn agreed.

We wound up chatting up a storm sitting on a bench in the Bronx Park until the sun was about to rise.

"Boy, you had me outside this long. I know breakfast is on you."

"You were reclined in my car with all this warm air. Girl you had a good time in my ride." I said in jest.

"No, it was all good."

"I'll drive you to your crib and take you to breakfast," I offered while starting the car.

Later I kept the engine running while waiting outside Dawn's home. She went inside to change outfits. Her mother was up and cordially invited me to come upstairs. Dawn's mother always had love for me because of my manners. The request was still flabbergasting because Dawn's mother use to warn her about hanging around with me because she thought of me as a hard rock. The reality was that her mother knew we weren't clocking nine to five at that age and must be selling weed. To top it off, Cash and I always had expensive fly gears, from Gucci and Dapper Dan. I went back outside and waited in the car after the conversation with Mrs. Jones. My cellular was ringing off the hook. It was Cash. I flipped open the phone.

"Talk to me, Cash."

"Why don't you holla at ya boy?" Cash asked.

"I'm doing that, right?"

"Where you at Forst?"

"Up here in da Bronx. Why?"

"I was trying to reach you all last night."

"Alright, well you reached me now. What's the deal?"

"Why did you turn your phone off?"

"Cash, stop sweating and chill."

"Forster I'm grown. Ain't nobody sweating you. If you happen to disappear, let a brother know before," Cash said.

"I was with Dawn all night."

"Say word? Did you hit that?" Cash asked excitedly.

"Nah man, it ain't even like that."

"But you've been trying to get at that for the longest. What's up?"

"I know but I think, I'm gonna let nature run its course."

"Man you acting like you scared of the kitty-cat," Cash said laughing.

"I'm not trying to rush anything and mess up our friendship."

"Punk ass!"

"I'll be that and I'll eventually end up with the flyest girl," I said laughing.

"Whatever, man!" Cash said as Dawn came walking out the crib.

"Cash, let me holla at you later."

"Why are you getting off the phone?" Cash asked.

"I'll holla back," I said ending the phone call.

Dawn came out looking lovely in beige pants suit. She had her walk on in a pair of three inch heeled brown boots that complemented her figure nicely. She carried a brown Coach bag and rifled through it as she got in the car. She appeared to be mentally checking off each object in the bag: Cell phone, panty liners, matching wallet and her favorite lip-gloss. I watched as she rummaged through and thought of how sexy she was. I was in deep thought without realizing she was talking to me.

"Earth to Forster, please come in," she shouted from the passenger seat.

"Oh I'm sorry, my bad."

"You're not trying to hear me, Forster?"

"Never that. Where do you work?"

"Lower Manhattan."

"Why, are you going to take me to work too?"

"First we're going to IHOP, and then I'll take you to work."

"Wow!" She exclaimed.

"You can get anything you want. I mean as long as we friends, right?"

"Don't get cute. I know exactly what I want from IHOP," she said.

"What do you want?"

"Hmm, I want waffles with bacon inside of them and a glass of orange juice." She said licking her lips. We both smiled.

"Are you going to be late for work if we stay and eat there?" I asked.

"I have an hour or so before I begin."

Twenty minutes later, we were pulling into a spot in the parking lot of IHOP on Broadway. There were hardly any other cars in the parking lot. That meant no morning rush.

"Let's do it. Wait I'll come around," I said before opening the car door.

She watched me walk quickly around to her side and open the door. Dawn was puzzled at first as to what I would do next. She smiled as she witnessed the gentleman in me.

"Why thank you," she said as I took her hand and helped her out the car. We entered the empty restaurant.

"Two?" The waiter asked.

I nodded and he showed us to a table. We sat down and she ordered exactly what she said she would. The food arrived with the quickness; pancakes and strawberries

on top. My eggs were well done with cheese, Canadian bacon, and a pitcher of orange juice for us to share. Silence slipped between us and hung over our heads as we stuffed our faces. After a couple minutes, we spoke.

"How's your food?" I asked.

"Actually it's really good, thanks," Dawn said as she bit a piece of bacon. "And yours?"

"It's hitting the spot," I said and gulped the orange juice. "I hope your boyfriend don't get mad since we're hanging."

"What boyfriend?"

"I guess you don't have one of those," I said. She smiled and continued eating.

"Where you going after you drop me off?"

"I'm going to catch up with Cash and see what's new for today." I said. Dawn nodded and finished her breakfast. "Will you get in trouble if you arrive a little late at work?" I asked.

"Nah, my boss is really cool."

"That's good," I said.

"Well, I'm done."

"I am too," I said and signaled for the waiter to bring the check. We headed for the car. In the parking lot, I opened the door for her once again.

"So, does your girlfriend let you take old friends to eat?" Dawn asked when I got in the car. I saw her smile before I answered.

"I don't know. I didn't ask her yet." I laughed thinking of the right answer.

"Oh, so you do have a girlfriend?"

"Would you mind if I take an old friend out to eat?" I asked flipping the script.

Dawn made a face that made me think maybe she was considering us an item.

"That's real funny," she said. I started the car and laughed.

"Listen, a lot has changed with me. I'm older and I'm not a player type of guy. If I have a girlfriend, she'll be the only old-friend I'll be taking out, ahight?"

"Okay," she said with a smile.

"Now, don't get it twisted if I don't have a main squeeze I will have a few associates."

"I was considering us, but not only on some friendship tip. I'm willing to lay my friendship on the line, but I feel that's why we will be even tighter. Think about it, we're long time friends and as lovers, man we'll be untouchable."

I jumped on 87 and threw Bobby Brown's Don't Be Cruel in the cassette player.

"Oh, this tape is hot. I lost my copy, but I will buy two the next time." Dawn said. I smiled as the sounds of Bobby Brown brought joy. We made our way through the morning traffic. It made me feel really good to be with her.

"Listen, when I'm finish with Cash, can I catch up with you later?"

"I thought you'd never ask."

"So you've been fronting on me all this time, huh?"

"No Forst, how'd you figure?"

We were near the exit to Dawn's job. At the light I stared at her. She wasn't aware of it until she turned to me.

"You have a beautiful face, Ms. Jones," I said.

"Thank you, Mr. Brown," she said and I watched her blush.

"Well, here we are," I said.

"Wish I didn't have to go in."

"You don't," I said.

"Yes I do," Dawn insisted.

"When was the last time you took off?"

"I never just take off. I take the days that are given to me. The truth is I never had a reason to take off."

"Today you do," I said.

"Really?"

"What's the boss' number?" I asked and flipped the cell phone on. With a sigh of curiosity Dawn gave up the digits.

"What are you doing?" She asked smiling.

"I am calling your boss. What's her name?" I asked.

"Ms. Coward."

The phone rang and a voice answered after the second ring.

"Hello, my name is Mr. Brown and I'm calling on behalf of Ms. Dawn Jones. She

is unable to make it today." I announced in my best business voice.

"Is everything alright with Dawn?" Ms. Coward asked with concern.

"Yes, ah... "

We both laughed.

LIFE'S A BITCH THEN YOU WAKE UP

Keya awoke in the dark Bronx apartment not knowing what day it was. She staggered out of the bed with both hands clutching her head.

"Damn! I got a serious hangover," she said out loud. Keya heard voices in the other room as she searched for her clothes. Her panties were inside out and she found her bra under the covers. Her shirt and pants were scattered under the bed. She didn't bother looking for her shoes. Keya quickly slipped her clothes on and tipped-toed to the front door. Before she could walk out, Keya heard a voice. She froze in her tracks and scurried back to the room.

"Oh shit, what the hell is he doing here?" She whispered to herself.

The voice belonged to her pimp, Mizo. Keya looked out the window to see if there was a fire escape. There was none. Suddenly a light bulb went on in her head. She grabbed her cell phone. I hope Smokey have his cell. If Mizo caught her with Smokey on some personal basis, Keya would get a few lashes on her backside. The call rang though to Smokey's outgoing message.

"Shit, shit, shit," Keya repeated.

Okay Kee, just sit tight, she thought. Hide in the closet, she told herself. Keya sat in the closet and waited patiently.

"Lord, I know I've said this before, but if you get me out of this one I promise I'll change." Keya whispered. Tears were rolling down her cheeks. She froze when she heard someone enter the room.

"Yo Kee, are you in here?" A male voice yelled and her eyes widened.

"Smokey?" Keya opened the closet door.

"What's wrong?" Smokey asked.

"I heard Mizo out there, and you know if he finds me here I am dead meat."

"Don't worry about that cat, no more." Smokey said.

"How am I not going to worry about him? He knows where my mother lives." Keya cried.

"I said, don't worry right?" Smokey caressed her face.

"I'm scared," Keya said.

"Listen, I'm going to drive you to get some clothes and pick up your daughter. Then I'm going to take you to my house," Smokey said.

"He knows where you live."

"This is not where I lay my head. Are you crazy? You think I'm one of those little punks out here, huh? No love, I'm smarter than that." Smokey reassured Keya. They exited his building looking around. Smokey and Keya jumped in his Mazda 929 with tinted windows.

"Get it together, you don't want your daughter or moms seeing you like this. And oh, while you're chilling you need to figure out what your ass is going to do as far as your daughter is concerned."

Keya dug Smokey because he cared, unlike the other tricks that she gave treats. If it wasn't about treats other dudes wouldn't care if she sold her daughter.

"Be quick," Smokey said when they arrived. Keya saw Mizo's money-green jeep parked up ahead.

"Smokey," she said then paused.

"What?" He asked looking around to see what she was looking at.

"That's Mizo's jeep," she said pointing.

"Ahight, put the seat back. I'm a go and ask your momma for you. It'll look suspicious if I just drive off." Smokey said. Mrs. Jordan knew Smokey owned the local barbershop. He walked to the house without looking at the jeep and rang the bell. Keya's mother answered the door immediately.

"How're you doing Mrs. Jordan?" Smokey greeted.

"Hi Smokey, have you seen my daughter? I haven't seen my child since early yesterday. I haven't the foggiest where she's at right now..."

"She's alright. She'll be back home later tonight or tomorrow." The older woman stared at him with a frown as Smokey raised his hands to his lips.

"I don't understand..." she started but Smokey interrupted.

"She told me to come and tell you that she's alright."

"She's alright nothing. Tell her she better bring her ass home."

Mrs. Jordan was visibly upset. Smokey nodded and turned around to walk away.

Mizo checked the situation then suddenly peeled off. Keya made sure that the jeep was completely gone before getting out of the car and running to her mother's house. The older woman greeted her with a wide-eyed stare at the front door.

"What kind of games y'all playing?"

"Ma, I can't explain right now. I just need to pick up my child and some clothes. I'll explain some more when I come back," Keya said dashing past her astonished mother.

"You ain't taking my grandbaby out of here and have her run the streets with you. Better yet, take your stuff and get the hell out. My grandbaby is staying with me," Mrs. Jordan said walking behind Keya.

"Ma, how are you going to fix that to come out your mouth? That's my daughter. I pushed her out, not you."

"You better start acting right. Keya, you look like you need time to get yourself together."

"Ma, move out of my way please." Keya begged, but her mother wouldn't budge. "Ma, don't make me disrespect you, please!" Keya said heatedly.

"Go ahead, what you think you've been doing all along but disrespecting me?"

"That's my child and I am taking her with me." Keya broke down crying. Smokey came over and placed his hand on Keya's shoulder.

"It might be best right now, Kee if..."

"Fuck you Smokey! Getting my daughter is the best thing I need to do right now."

"Look how you're speaking. Look how you look. I never taught you that way. You take off, you don't even call." Smokey helped Keya out to the steps. Keya dropped to her knees wailing.

"Mother, please give me a chance, please." Keya cried.

"Smokey, get this thing off my stoop. Bring her around when she's got it

together," her mother said.

Mrs. Jordan stared at Keya with pity. She grabbed the doorknob and spat before slamming the door shut, then watched from the window as Smokey pulled Keya away.

"When I was younger your mother didn't take me from you, when you were running the streets. Now you're gonna play me with mine?" Keya shouted at her mother. "You wrong."

"And you're right. Smokey you best get this crazy girl outta here."

"I'll be back and next time Smokey won't be with me." Keya said crying her heart out. Smokey pushed her into the car, jumped in and started the car.

"You gonna need more than Smokey when you come back." Mrs. Jordan said with tears in her eyes while hugging her frightened granddaughter.

Smokey drove off and Keya cried for a while before she started to breathe deeply, trying to clam herself. He touched her face attemptting to console her but his efforts were met with Keya's hysterical bawling.

"We're heading to my house. Tomorrow I'll take you shopping to get a few outfits."

He had hoped to cheer her up. Keya's eyes were swollen and blood-shot red. Ignoring anything Smokey had said, Keya pulled out her cell phone and dialed. Dawn's mother picked up the phone. While still crying, Keya asked for her best friend.

"Is DJ in Mrs. Jones?"

"She isn't here Kee. Are you alright?"

"Yes, I'm okay. Please tell Dawn I'll call her back," Keya said then cut her cell phone off.

She glanced out the window watching the world go by and felt nothing but anger. They traveled in a shroud of silence to Smokey's house in Yonkers.

Smokey was very private and hardly anyone knew his real name or age. Even at the barbershop he owned, he was known simply as Smokey. Keya stared at his low eyelids and wondered if privacy was the reason thirty-year old Emanuel Jockton, who had her by seven years, used the Smokey moniker.

"We're here," he announced.

"Is someone in your house?" Keya asked.

"No, I live alone. My mom and two sisters live twenty minutes away. I have a three-bedroom. My sisters be over a lot, so I made sure I have a room for them." Smokey said as they walked into the house. "Make yourself at home."

Keya glanced around and was surprised that he had this huge house. She had never been in a home this beautiful before. The walls of his living room were light gray. Keya wandered through the burnt orange and olive green kitchen. She journeyed to the bathroom downstairs. It had a beige and brown color scheme. Smokey showed her the guest bedroom on the first floor in burgundy, black and white. Keya ran upstairs where there were two bedrooms and another bathroom. She got to the top of the stairs and saw the master bedroom.

This is really hot, Keya thought becoming more familiar with his crib.

"Hi mommy," Smokey said in a sweet momma's-boy tone.

"How's my only son doing?" She asked.

"I'm okay, I have a friend, Keya over at my place," he responded. "And you know she must be a good friend to be over here."

"I know, you don't have just anyone over."

"Right now she's going through a bad time, mom."

"Long as you aren't going to be too involved, then there should be no problems."

"Mommy you know I know better than that." Smokey knew his mother was over-protective of him. "By the way where are my two crazy sisters?"

"They went shopping with your money. You keep spoiling those girls, Smokey."

"Mommy, they're eighteen year old twins, they supposed to be spoiled."

"Boy, since you bought them their own car for graduation, they're never home."

"Speaking of them never being home, are they still going away to college?"

"They both earned scholarships, you doggone right they're going."

"That's good mommy."

"Hmm, hmm, they're supposed to go in September, but the dorm was over booked. The school is making it possible for both of them to be in the same dorm by January."

"Tell them to give bro a call."

"Okay Smokey. Listen, I don't want to keep you, I have to pick up some

material for the church's new robes I'm designing."

"Alright mommy, I'll talk to you later. Love you."

"Love you too, Smokey."

Smokey hung up the phone and called Keya. She came downstairs wearing a big smile on her face.

"What's that lovely smile for?"

"This house is beautiful. If my daughter was here you'd have to kick us out." Keya said and Smokey laughed.

"I'm glad to see you smile after what you experienced today. Why don't we go shopping in the Mall at Cross County?" Smokey asked and Keya's face lit up.

"I'm down," Keya said then put her shoes back on. "Wait, could you please call my mother and ask her to put Te'rena on the phone?"

"No, I will not. You need to cut this crap out and call her yourself." Smokey said handing her a cordless. Keya dialed and her daughter answered.

"Hi Te'rena," Keya said.

"Hi mommy, when are you coming to get me?"

"Mommy will get you soon okay?"

"Okay mommy, do you want to talk to nana?"

"No princess mommy will call nana later. I love you."

"Love you too, mommy."

"Now be a big girl and listen to your nana, and hang up the phone."

"Bye, bye mommy."

"Bye princess."

She thought her daughter was going to cry, but her eyes began to water before she got off the phone. Smokey saw her eyes and gave her a hug.

"Smokey I want to thank you for looking out. This favor will never go unnoticed. If you need me, just call." Keya said while in his embrace.

"Let's shop till we drop." Smokey said. Smiling happily, they headed to the mall.

DEJAVUE ALL OVER AGAIN

"Forster you're hilarious," Dawn laughed. "How're you gonna say that a Mercedes Benz 500Sel should come with a midget?" She was still laughing.

"I feel that a car that costs that much should have a special button on it. When I press that button a midget should jump up and massage my neck." We both laughed. "Where do you want to go?" I asked wiping tears the laughter caused.

"Let's go bowling."

"Good idea," I said making a U-turn.

"I heard they opened a new bowling alley on 42nd Street. Want to go there? Wow! Wouldn't that bring back some memories?"

"You wanted to throw all of this away."

"Forster, cut it out. I got the picture, okay? Yeah, it will bring back a lot of memories. We had fun that night." She sighed.

"Truthfully, that was the last time I really had fun. I think that was the last time I saw Cash having a good time too."

"Really?" Dawn sighed.

"We have many more good times to come, if you allow us," I said while taking a quick glance at her. She smiled.

"Enough of all that mushy stuff for now, whatever year I get enough money I'm going to get me a Mercedes Benz. And I would love to have you in the same seat you're in now when I get it too," I said smiling and touching Dawn's hand.

"Excuse me while I call my mom, and let her know I didn't go to work," Dawn said. She took out her cell phone and pressed the number one. The answering machine

came on. "Hi mommy, I played hooky from work today because of Forster."

"She's in good hands, ma."

"Be quiet boy," Dawn said smiling. "Anyway mommy call me on my cell phone if you need me, love you."

"Isn't that nice, you calling your mommy?" I teased.

"That's right, even when I'm a hundred years old I'll still let my mommy know how I feel. My mom taught me to be considerate. We seem to talk a lot more when we're not at home. She would freak if she called my job and I wasn't there without her knowing first."

"I'm only bugging Dawn, you don't have to explain anything to me. I'm all for good relationships."

"I don't mean to cut you off, but let me check to see if Keya went home yet." She removed her phone from her pocketbook and pressed number two, then send. The phone rang three times before Mrs. Jordan picked up.

"Hi, it's me, did she get back?"

"Yeah, and she was showing out."

"What do you mean?"

"Smokey came here and said Keya was alright. Then all of a sudden, Keya ran up in here talking about she has to get a few things and her daughter. So I told her she could leave but my grandbaby isn't going anywhere with her."

"What? So where did they go?"

"I don't know, but when she returns she better have it together. My grandbaby is not leaving out of this place with her."

"If she calls, please tell her to call my cell, because I'm not at work."

"Is everything alright?"

"Everything is okay. An old friend is showing me a good time." She smiled and looked at me.

"Okay baby, enjoy and be safe. If your friend calls back here I will tell her to call you."

"Is Keya alright?" I asked after Dawn ended the call.

"I guess. Her mother said she came by and left." Dawn did not want to explain the details, but I could tell from the look on her face that she was troubled.

"Are you okay?" I asked.

"That girl drives me crazy. She's my best friend so I'll always care. I'm really gonna have to really take time out and talk to that girl."

"Well love, we're going to park right here and walk a few blocks to the bowling alley. Unless you want me to pay for parking and we'll be closer?"

"Oh no, I'd love to walk. Listen, I am an easy going, not too hard to please female. But all I ask is you come correct."

"My type of gal," I said joking in the square. "I would love to spoil you if you give me a chance," I said and kissed her hand.

"We'll see."

"Come on shortie," I said and walked hand in hand to the bowling alley.

"Yo, stop yelling in my goddamn ear!" Cash screamed.

"But..."

"But nothing! You's a rude ass bitch. I know you see me on the phone."

"I don't give a shit who you're calling. Where in hell were you last night?" His girlfriend, Stacey argued. Cash bit his lip, shook his head and said nothing. "Answer me and I'll leave you alone. And if I'm a bitch so is your mother." She did not realize that she had opened a can of worms. Then she heard a loud noise followed by a loud thud of her chest caving under the force of a fist. She was on the floor, her breath coming in gasps.

"Say that shit and next time I guarantee you'll be picking up your teeth." Cash said with rage. Stacey made a face and Cash slapped the daylight out of her. She covered her face with trembling hands. The palm of his hand wore her down and soon all she was able to do was cry. "Get that stupid look off your face!" Stacey gave him an evil look. "Damn, where my boy at?" Cash asked while waiting for the outgoing message to end. "Yo Forst, where you at? Call a brother back I got something important to tell you."

Cash grabbed his shirt and left. Any other time Stacey would've tried to stop

him, but not this time. She was tired of him disrespecting her.

"Can you come and get me the hell out of here, now?" Stacey asked her friend, Renee.

"Girl I'm not going to leave Spring Valley to get you then you'll turn around and call Cash to pick you up," Renee said.

"I'm tired of his shit Renee, this is it," Stacey said crying.

"Okay Stacey, get what ever you need ready now, I'm on my way," Renee said.

"How many days are you staying up here?"

"For as long as you allow me. Just please come," Stacey said.

"I'm on my way," Renee said then hung up.

Stacey hurried and grabbed as many outfits that would fill the small suitcase. This was not the first time she had run out on Cash. It had reached a point where she left and he wouldn't bother looking for her. Eventually, she called and he would whisper sweet nothings and she'd be back home. Today, things will be different she thought, waiting for her friend to arrive.

"Cash, what're you gonna do?" Justin asked.

"We gonna have to go without Forster." Cash answered.

"How's ace-boon not gonna be around when you getting ready to do this?" Justin wondered aloud.

"Later for Forst, let's roll out."

"Where is the meeting?" Justin asked.

"On Utica Avenue in BK," Cash answered.

"Okay, I know where that is." Justin answered.

"I got my joint. Just, you got yours?"

"Cash it's me Just, I never leave home without."

Justin raised his shirt showing the nine-millimeter that was tucked in his waistband. Cash jumped on the FDR and rode to Brooklyn with the rhythm of Eric B and

Rakim blasting. They crossed the bridge jamming to Paid In Full and slapping fives to the rhymes.

It's been a long time since I left you
without a fresh rhyme to step to...
Thinking of all the weak show you slept through...
Times up, sorry I left you

The two friends were going to buy guns from some Jamaicans they hardly knew. It was a hook-up from a friend of a friend. Cash and Justin had been doing business for a couple of years. It took about an hour. He stopped at a gas station and flirted with the store clerk then got so weeded he missed his turn.

"Ahight, enough joking 'round. Pull over by the grocery store coming up, Cash."

Cash drove into a deserted parking lot. They saw a dark blue Jetta parked on the opposite side. There were men with dreadlocks waiting. Cash took another pull of the weed and they exited the car.

"Hey mon," the man greeted in a coarse voice made thicker by his accent.

His partner stood silently with his dreadlocks covering his face. Justin kept his eyes on the silent, longhaired dread. Cash gave the man a pound and the man returned it. The dread then gave a signal to the other men. Cash and the dread had done business before. The other men left without searching Cash or Justin. They had no idea what was going down. Cash was running his mouth making everyone feel at ease. They conducted business while sitting in their car. Everyone seemed relaxed. Justin kept lookout. The car keys were still in the ignition. The other men stood outside, not far away.

"Man, what you got for us today blood-fire?" Cash asked.

"You say that around my man who just left and you and your partner's brains would've stained these streets." The dread said with a phony laugh. "Alright, let's get this over with," he said opening his dash and revealing guns of all types.

Cash's eyes lit up as if he had found a pot of gold. He sat in the front and Justin sat in the rear. Cash produced the dough. The guy reached over to get the guns. All of a sudden there was a boom. Cash grabbed as many guns as he could carry then jetted to his car parked a few feet away. He made it to the car and turned to see were Justin was. Two Jamaicans from the posse closed in. Cash knew the guns he stole

didn't have bullets so he pulled out his own gun. He hesitated then it dawned on him. He had forgotten to load the clip. Worst, he had left it home. Justin? He looked at the empty gun and shook his head. If it weren't for me rushing and trying to get in touch with Forster, then Stacey getting on my damn last nerves, I would've remembered the clip, he thought.

The posse waited. They took cover behind another car close to his. Cash saw them in his side mirror. The silence was deafening. Everyone was ready for something to ignite. Justin held his gun in his hand and tried to escape by breaking the window. He fired twice out the window trying to cover his path. Outside the dreads waited for him to move. When he did, they pumped lead in him. "No-o-o!" Cash screamed and peeled off. The dreads started bucking, hitting the car. Fortunately, they missed. Cash was so shook, he drove like a bat out of hell, taking lights, jumping curbs and screeching around tight corners.

Cash realized that these guys were more cold hearted than him. When he was out of danger, he began to cry uncontrollably.

"Just man, I'm sorry," Cash repeated.

His thoughts did laps through his cranium for the rest of the evening. He drove trying to clear his head. Cash dialed my number; no answer. Who could he talk to now that everything had gone wrong?

The ill answer came from somewhere deep within. He puffed hard, letting the weed go straight to his head. "It's all because off that stupid bitch, Stacey and her shit!" He exhaled. "All she had to do was to keep her damn mouth shut."

Cash threw away the roach and tears ran down his cheek. "Rest in peace, Just." The words tumbled from his dried lips amidst the tears. Cash jumped on the highway to the Boogie Down.

He was safely across the toll bridge. Making sure no one was following, he called my number and left a message for me to meet him at the park. Cash put all the stolen guns in a shopping bag on the floor of the passenger side. He wiped his eyes and checked the rearview mirror, trying to maintain his composure. The car zigzagged, but Cash maneuvered it safely.

"My man," Cash mumbled on the long fateful ride home.

Flashes from the bullets being pumped in Justin's body was not hallucination. This was real. The nonstop replay of the incident kept his mind busy he did not hear the loud sirens of the police. He sat up straight in the car and looked through his rearview mirror. Bars crossed his mind. Shook, Cash exhaled loudly when the lights of the police drove by.

Slowly he began to get his thoughts together. Cash reached for his cell phone and dialed my digits. The outgoing message was loud and clear. "Yo Forster that's my word, your ass better be in the park in an hour." Then he called home completely unaware that Stacey was gone. He hung up when the answering machine picked up. "Where is everyone?" Cash yelled and banged his fist on the steering wheel. He hit Manhattan and drove with the swiftness across the bridge to the Bronx. Cash was home free but he couldn't carry the weight of Justin's body.

"Yeah, boy-e-e-e! Who's the man? Who's the man?" I shouted in the bowling alley.

"You were lucky," Dawn said slapping me on the butt.

"Don't hate, congratulate, ahight. Give me my reward woman," I said laughing. "Remember, whoever lost the first game has to give the other a big wet juicy kiss. And pay for the order from the snack bar." Dawn's cell-phone rang. She answered immediately.

"Hello there, Ms. Hooky-player." It was Mrs. Jones.

"Hey mommy," Dawn said.

"Dawn, are you okay, sweetheart?"

"I'm okay, mommy. It feels good to play hooky." Dawn laughed.

"Where's that crazy Forster?" Her mother asked jokingly.

"He's standing right here acting like he's the man."

"Why? Where are y'all?"

"We're in the bowling alley and I let him win, mommy."

"Oh yeah? Is that's why you're laughing? Cause you's a liar." I said checking my cell phone. I realized that I had turned it off. I promptly turned it on. "Dawn, excuse

me a sec." I said when I saw all the messages. My ex called to talk about nothing. I heard Cash's messages. "Oh shit!" I said after listening. I quickly closed the phone. "Dawn, we've got to go." I said urgently.

She ended the phone call with her mother. I grabbed her hand and rushed over to get our shoes from the clerk.

"What's the matter? Something wrong?" Dawn asked.

"Cash called me numerous times so something's wrong," I said.

We hurried to the car and peeled out. I dialed Cash's number. He explained that he went and dropped the guns off at his man's. We lost the signal without me really knowing where he was.

"Forster what happened?" Dawn impatiently asked.

"Cash called me a few times crying."

"I didn't know he had tears."

"Exactly what I'm thinking." My mind was speeding. "I'll take you home. I gotta get up with Cash."

"Please be careful Forster. Do not get yourself in any trouble."

"My middle name is trouble," I said laughing.

Dawn seemed pensive. I couldn't blame her, Cash attracted trouble like stink on shit.

"All I ask is that you keep me posted, please."

"Don't worry. I'll call as soon as I know something."

I dropped her off and raced to Magenta Courts. I sat in the car, my stomach twisting in knots. The minutes felt like hours. Finally, Cash pulled up, rushed over and pushed me.

"What's wrong with you, homey?" I asked.

"Where you been all day, man?" Cash asked.

"I was chilling with Dawn."

"You got your head so far up her ass, Forst. You not being around cost Justin his life."

"Wait, hold up. Be easy." I cautioned as Cash got inside the car. He disregarded me and jumped right into his story.

"Justin and I went to buy some gats off these dreads out in Brooklyn. The deal went bad," Cash said.

"How did the deal go bad, Cash?" I asked. Something in the back of my mind told me that Cash and his shady friend, Justin had been up to no good.

"The dreads tried to play us, man," Cash said after awhile. He wasn't looking directly at me.

"Stop lying Cash. It's me Forst, I know you better than that, man."

"Ahight, ahight, fuck it! Here's the real; we were trying to jack 'em for the guns, but they were too many of them. The posse moved in on us. They had us outnumbered and out-gunned."

"Did you get shot?"

"Nah, man, I'm ahight, I'll be alright. But...ah Just...he ain't here." Cash said barely getting it out his mouth.

I saw his eyes watered and gave him a hug. Cash cried like a baby for the first time ever. Cash was hurting. He wiped tears from his eyes.

"Don't worry man, it'll be alright. We'll go by his mother's house and hit them off with some dough, ahight?" I said trying to make sense.

We both stared out the window avoiding each other's eyes. Someone had to be responsible for all this, a cost had to be paid. For fifteen minutes deep breathing was all that existed. I decided to speak.

"Cash on some real shit, you need to evaluate your situation, man."

"Nigga you know me, don't come sideways at me like that."

"Cash, I'm your man for real. But, I'm saying that was some straight street bullshit. You gots to chill."

"I don't want to hear the 'I told you so'. Let my mistakes ride. I don't need to hear all that yang outta you right now." Cash impatiently shouted.

"I'm not trying to point fingers. You're my brother. I'm just glad you ahight."

"It happened so fast, Forst. We had this shit down to a science. I called you at the last minute. I know you didn't wanna fuck with Justin like that. But on the strength, I thought you would've been down. I wish I could take this whole day back. The day started off bad. Stacey started working on my nerves and I couldn't reach you. Then Justin and I couldn't communicate when shit jumped off."

"Did any of them get your plates?" I asked.

"Nah, I had them off, till I left the area."

"You wanna ride on these cats?"

"Nah man, I'm a stay outta BK for a minute."

"So man, where you going from here?"

"Forst, I don't wanna be alone. Can I crash at your crib?"

"Not a problem."

"Follow behind me." Cash got out the car and I called Dawn. Her phone rang for a minute before she picked up.

"Better not be anybody over there occupying your time." I jokingly said and Dawn laughed.

"I'm so glad to hear your voice." She sounded cute when she was happy.

"I'm glad that you're glad that you hear my voice," I said.

"Boo, is everything cool?"

"Cash gonna spend the night at my crib."

"He needs your help, right?"

"Yeah, I guess I'll catch you on the rebound."

"Yeah, maybe next time."

"Not that I wanna hit the skins. I mean I do, but not now. Let me just shut up."

"No continue, this is interesting," she said.

"I just had such a great time with you that I didn't want our time to end."

"Isn't that sweet?" Dawn cooed.

"If you want, I'd love to continue this summer love tomorrow."

"Summer love?" Dawn repeated.

"We met back in the summer. Did we not?" I asked and she chuckled.

"Yes, I guess summer love is right. Where are you?"

"In my own car, minding my own biz and I'm on my way to my own home. Wait up, love. Cash is pulling up alongside me," I said just as Cash started to shout.

"Yo, let's stop at the Crown's Chicken over there before we head to your crib."

"Sounds like a plan." I said returning to the conversation.

"Sorry 'bout that. Cash's hungry."

"Are you hanging out late tonight?"

"Who me?"

"Yes, Forster Brown, you."

"Nah, I ain't going nowhere, I'm a chill in the crib. Are you going to work tomorrow?"

"Yes, I am. I feel bad because I didn't go yesterday. Don't get me wrong, I enjoyed the time with you. But I love my job, and my boss is a friend. I can't do her bad."

"Ahight, that's all good. Let me pay attention to the road. I'll holla."

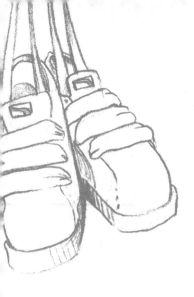

PIMPING AIN'T EASY, HO-ING AIN'T EITHER

Dawn heard the telephone ringing while chilling in the crib. She walked quickly to answer it.

"Hello," she said.

"Hey DJ!"

"Where are you, Kee?"

"DJ, it's a long story. But where have you been?"

"Forster stopped by yesterday and we talked for hours. We talked until the sun came up. After that he took me to breakfast then he took me to the front of my job and you know what, Kee?"

"What? What?"

"I took the day off and..."

"Get out! DJ you actually took a day off?"

"Kee, you should see how he looks. He's the bomb now."

"While you were having the time of your life, I was running for mine." Keya deadpanned.

"Huh, say what?" Dawn was stunned.

"I was at Smokey's, I swear. He's my boo. We had been blazing mad weed and drinking from the night before. When I got up I was hung-over and dazed. I got up, dressed and was ready to leave. Then I heard Mizo's voice. And girl, didn't I feel like shitting in my pants? If Mizo knew I was there, he would've whipped my ass. Then start beef with Smokey."

"Dramas..."

"I was lucky, Smokey didn't blow me up."

"I bet he didn't. I wouldn't neither if I was getting goodies for free."

"It's not even like that DJ and you know it."

"You're too sensitive. I don't know if I like Smokey for you. And I damn sure don't like what you have got going on with Mizo. That man is a pimp and he's gonna get you hurt."

"DJ, Smokey is trying to get me out of that situation as we speak."

"Honestly Kee, where are you?"

"I'm at Smokey's place up in Yonkers."

"Yonkers?"

"Yeah, you think Smokey is using me, huh?"

"I thought he rest in the Bronx?"

"I did too."

"I may be wrong, but you need to be careful. My god- daughter needs you."

"She's with her miserable grandmother."

"Where's Smokey now?"

"He's downstairs going through his mail."

"Downstairs? He has a house like that?"

"His crib is the shit."

"Say word?" Dawn exclaimed.

"Word girl, his crib is huge."

"I didn't know Smokey the bandit, had it like that?" Dawn laughed.

"He wants me and Te'rena to live up here, DJ."

"And what did your mother say?"

"She doesn't know. But she'll probably bug out. Better yet, Smokey is gonna have to drive my mother up to his house so she could inspect it."

"I don't blame your mother, you be wilding out."

"DJ, you're always coming outta your face with some shit!"

"Huh?"

"You swear you all high post, right?"

"I know you're not trying to trip, Kee? I don't do nothing but support and help you. You know when I'm playing." Dawn paused when she heard Keya huffing. "If I'm bothering you Kee, hang up. You're my friend and it's my job to see how other people treat you." Dawn heard Keya sobbing. "Don't get all sensitive on me now, Kee."

"DJ, I just had a rough day, and I miss my baby."

"Don't let the man see you sweating," Dawn jokingly said.

"Please, he's downstairs. He took me shopping."

"Say word?"

"Word girl," Keya sounded better.

"I see I can't judge a book by the cover. But he's still in the fast life. So be careful. Plus you my girl and I got your back, Kee."

"I know DJ. Sometimes I wish I was as mentally strong like you."

"You are. I'm strong in some areas you're weak in, and you are strong in some areas that I am weak in. Most of our childhood friends that we thought were closer than we are haven't spoken in years. So the next time you think I'm being hard on you...it's because I am." Dawn and Keya laughed.

"DJ, you're a true friend."

"Listen, crazy ass I have to get up in the morning. Be sure you call me tomorrow." Keya knew being tough was Dawn's way of showing she cared.

"I'll check you tomorrow, DJ. My boo's here," Keya said.

"Come here and try on these clothes for me." Smokey brazenly requested from the stairway. Smokey noticed her expression. "Did I say something wrong?"

"No, you didn't, Smokey. I just didn't like how my best friend be hating on me."

"Dawn? She doesn't seem like the hating type."

"Anyway, what is it that you want me to try on?" Keya asked with her hands on her hips.

"This dress," Smokey handed to her.

"Oh you like this one because it shows a lot of cleavage, huh?" Keya asked. Smokey laughed and ran to answer the phone.

"Speak," Smokey said.

"It's me Boom. What's good for tonight?"

Smokey knew exactly what Boom was talking about. They planned to hit Mizo once Keya was out of the way. Keya was unaware that Smokey was putting a hit on Mizo and only partly due to her situation. Mizo came to Smokey's house because one of his

hos' sold work for Smokey. Smokey felt violated.

"Listen up man, let me hit you up in half. I'm handling business right now," Smokey lied. He had been watching Keya shimmying into the tight, red dress while she listened to his conversation. "Where were we?" Smokey asked after he hung up.

"Who was that?" Keya asked.

"That's my boy. I'll get up with him in a minute."

Keya looked in the mirror and checked out her frame in the dress. She glanced at Smokey for his approval. The look on Smokey's face made it obvious that he had something else in mind. Keya's curves fit perfectly in the tight red dress. Smokey came up from behind and rubbed his hand over her curvaceous body. He pushed her head forward while raising her dress. He had been turned on by her actions.

"Damn girl, you know what Smokey like, don't you?"

Keya bit her lips without answering. She enjoyed the slapping sounds made when his thighs hit her ass. She felt him all the way inside her. Everything fitted tight like a hand in a glove. Their bodies melted into one, her warm tight hole and his long strokes throbbed deep inside her. He pulled her hair as he rode.

"Yeah, that's it, give me your thick sausage." Keya screamed.

Smokey grunted loudly. She knew he liked his member referred to as a sausage. That made him wild. Keya worked his beef sausage like it was served on a plate with eggs and cheese. Smokey pulled her toward him while she leaned forward. He exploded in her so hard that his right leg shook violently.

"Oh shit, oh shit, girl, you're dangerous." Smokey said and slapped Keya's butt. "Now I gotta go and buy another dress like this." He laughed.

Early that morning Smokey left the house to meet with Boom, his friend and partner in the drug game. They went downtown and took care of Miz. Later they spoke as Smokey drove.

"Ahight just take care of it. I'm going to head home," Smokey said.

"I'll be ahight, Smokey. I'll go check it out in the morning."

The drive home seemed longer than normal. It gave him a chance to clear his head. He had never been so afraid in his life. Maybe it was because he had never bodied anyone before. He was nice with his hands, it had to be done. His man's life was in danger. How am I gonna sleep with this shit on my mind? Smokey wondered as he rode home. I'll have to take my ass to church, he thought. Smokey drove to the garage and switched cars as usual, before heading home. When he arrived, the house was quiet. Smokey walked upstairs to his bedroom trying to calm himself down before he saw Keya. She lay wearing black bra and panties. Smokey went into the bathroom and took a long shower. Keya opened her eyes when she realized the shower was on. She saw the light in the bathroom and fell into a deep sleep now, knowing Smokey made it back home safely.

Smokey exited the shower and went downstairs. He poured a glass of Gin, then he saw the Kool Aid and drank it as chaser. Smokey smiled. He couldn't remember the last time he had done something like this. Thanks to Keya he found himself sipping punch with a few slices of lemon the way she liked it. Smokey appreciated having her around. The bed was warm and her soft body made him even happier to be home. He pulled her close and spooned.

"You're wifey material. I missed you," Smokey whispered in her ear.

FALLING OUT

"Mommy, where are we going?" Te'rena asked. Keya and her daughter were a block away from Dawn's building.

"Te'rena, we're going to see your godmother." Keya answered.

"Oh, we're going to see Dawn? But mommy, this is not her home."

"I know honey. We're going to surprise her at work," Keya said.

She dialed Dawn's job from a nearby payphone.

"Russell and Friedman, Ms. Jones speaking. How may I direct you?"

"You can direct me to lunch with Te'rena," Keya said.

"Kee, where are you with my goddaughter?"

"We're downstairs from your job, Ms. Jones," Keya said.

"Let me grab my purse and I'll be right down."

Keya and her daughter waited patiently. Neither of them knew that I was coming to surprise Dawn for lunch. I spotted Keya before she spotted me. We had not seen each other for years.

"Look at little Keya," I said pointing to her daughter. Keya seemed puzzled.

"Say word," is all she could say. Keya stared at me then we hugged.

"What's good shortie?"

"What you doing here?" Keya asked.

"I came to surprise Dawn for lunch," I announced. Keya saw the bouquet of flowers.

"That's nice," Keya said. Dawn came down right after.

"Hi," she said hugging her goddaughter and Keya. "Mr. Forster what a surprise," she said hugging me also. I kissed Dawn's cheek and handed her the flowers.

"This is one of the best days I had so far." Dawn said with a huge smile.

"Listen, I didn't know Keya was coming, so I'll catch up with you later."

"No, please don't leave," Keya jumped in. "Why don't we all eat together like old times?"

"Sounds like a plan," Dawn said.

"Cool with me. Where would you ladies like to go eat?" I asked.

"McDonald's," Te'rena shouted.

"No baby, let's try Chinese. I haven't eaten that in a while." Keya said.

By the time we reached my car, we had already agreed that lunch would be Chinese. I held the car door for Dawn and she reached over to let Keya and Te'rena enter through the rear.

"Babe, you know a good Chinese joint around here?" I asked.

"Yeah, a couple blocks down. It's the real deal too. Not the usual cat and dog."

"So Keya what's going on with you?" I asked while looking at her through the rearview mirror.

"I'm trying to stay on the right path for my daughter's sake." She answered.

"I hear that." I said then turned the volume a little higher. "I also came all the way down here to ask you a question," I said looking at Dawn.

"So ask away," she said.

"If it's alright with you, I would like for you to accompany me to a long night stay at my house?" I asked. Dawn blushed. Keya got up in our business. She didn't know the half. When Dawn nodded I wanted to pump my fist and yell. It felt like I had just hit a home run. But instead I smiled. I was cool.

"We'll talk about it after lunch," I said holding her hand.

"Ladies, lunch is on me." I announced as we were seated.

"Mommy, I have to tingle," Te'rena said.

"Excuse me y'all, we'll be right back." Keya said and rushed her daughter to the bathroom. I was alone with Dawn flirtingly staring into her eyes.

"Your lips remind of strawberries, can I suck on them?" I asked. Dawn landed her soft wet lips on my lips. "We'll continue this later when I pick you up."

"Cool, I can't wait," she resounded.

 We smooched until Keya and her daughter rejoined us. The waiter came as soon as they were seated.

Keya told the waiter what she and her daughter wanted to drink. I ordered drinks for Dawn and myself. This caused Keya to raise her eyebrows while looking at us.

"Oh y'all know each other like that?" She asked smiling.

"Fo' sho'. Dawn's going to be my wifey one day." I said steadily gazing in Dawn's eyes. I saw her blushing.

"You keep saying that." Dawn said.

"I know what I want to eat," Keya interrupted.

I signaled for our waiter's attention. He came back pad in hand ready to take our orders. I ordered the Peking duck with rice for Dawn and me. Keya ordered the House special lo mien with pork fried rice. She shared the meal with her daughter.

"Keya what's up? It's been a minute since I seen you, girl. How you been?"

"I know. I've been good. What's up with your boy, Cash?"

"He's chilling. Matter of fact, he's at my crib right now."

"Word," Keya smiled. "Can you call him now?"

I did not hesitate to get Cash on the speed dial.

"Yeah," Cash answered.

"Yo, you up?"

"Not really why?"

"I got someone here who wants to speak to you."

"Where you at?"

"I am at lunch with Dawn and someone who wants to say hi to you," I said and gave Keya the cell phone. She cleared her throat.

"Hello," she said changing her voice.

"What's up, baby-girl? I heard you had a baby and all," Cash said.

"Yeah, her name's Te'rena, she's here with us," Keya said sounding happy.

"So when am I going to see you?" Cash asked.

"When do you want to?"

"Get my digits from Forster and we'll take it from there."

"Ahight, sounds like a plan," Keya said then handed the cell back.

"Yo kid, I'm a holla at you after I drop Dawn off at work."

I ended the call and realized that Dawn had been staring at me the whole time and seemed mesmerized. The food came quickly and everyone dived in. After the meal, Dawn returned to work and I offered Keya a ride uptown. She gladly accepted.

"Thank you guys for the great surprise. I don't know what I did to deserve this, but I appreciate it," Dawn said.

"Girl any time," Keya responded.

"I'll be back to pick you up." I paid the tab and left a tip.

They all thanked me as I drove Dawn back to work. Te'rena had dozed off. Keya wore a smile as she admired her daughter.

"Thanks a lot, Forster," Keya said.

"He has been real nice," Dawn said.

I opened the door for her. I escorted her into the office building. Keya and her daughter waited in the car. I gave Dawn a kiss as she stepped away.

"Thank you again," Dawn said blowing me a kiss.

"Ahight Keya, where are you heading?" I asked.

"Where you headed?" Keya questioned.

"I'm going to see what Cash is up to."

"What, your mommy's gonna beat you if you don't come straight home?" Keya joked.

"It ain't like that Kee. I live alone."

"What, I'm not good enough to see the inside of your crib?"

"Nah, it's not that."

"So what is it?"

"Nothing," I said. She knew I was trying to brush her off. She stared at me. I ignored her. What is this broad trying to imply? I thought to myself. I felt Keya was flipping the script since Dawn was out the car. I could feel her eyes searching my face looking for an opening. I kept my mouth closed.

"We could drop my daughter off to my mom and hang out, unless you've got something else to do." She suggested.

"Yeah, I have a lot to do today."

"What aren't we still friends?"

"Nah, it's just that I won't feel right if my girl ain't with us."

"Oh, y'all together like that? DJ never told me."

"Which deejay?"

"No, no, I call Dawn DJ and she calls me Kee," Keya said smiling annoyingly.

"We're keeping it on the down low, but it's popping."

"Oh shoot, fine as you are I wouldn't keep nothing on the low."

Keya cut her eyes. I turned the music up, and increased speed. I needed to get Keya home and away from me quickly. After that she kept quiet. I dropped her and Te'rena off at her home. I wasn't going in the house, so we hugged and she kissed me on the cheek. I gave her Cash's digits.

"Forst thanks for everything. You're a good guy," she said. I got back in my car and sped home. I had to get Cash out of my crib. My cell phone rang. It was my honey.

"Hey baby..."

When I reached my place, I opened the door to the crib and found Cash asleep.

"Wake up sleepy." I shouted and suddenly Cash jumped up.

"Why you wanna do that for?" Cash asked. I had forgotten he hated for anyone to wake him.

"Yo, a few hours ago, my man called and told me that pimp-daddy Mizo, got bodied last night," Cash said getting up.

"Say word?"

"Word up, Forst," Cash said.

"Who he shitted on?"

"I don't know. Whatcha think this eyewitness news or sump'n?"

"Yeah, I know you always keep your ears to the streets."

"This ain't no bull. I heard he owed everybody money, Boom, Smokey and who knows who else?"

"You think one of them body him?"

"I know Boom ain't no joke. But his man Smokey is about his BI. He ain't involved with shit like that. But you can't put nothing pass dudes these days. Stick up kids out to tax," Cash laughed.

"That's fucked up. Pimping ain't easy. He was a good pimp," I said.

"What you mean he was a good pimp?"

"He kept his hos' upkeep well," I said counting off with my hands. "And he wasn't too hard on them," I said finishing with zest.

"Okay, what that's got to do with him strangling other peoples' pipeline?" Cash asked. He never gave me a chance to answer, before saying. "I'll tell you like this, good or bad pimp, if it was my dough he shorted?" Cash swiped his hand across his neck.

"Cash, you need to check all that violence. You need a hug or sump'n?" I offered with my arms opened. Cash laughed and pushed me away.

"You stupid," Cash said and went to the bathroom.

"Are you going to see Justin's family?"

"I'm not going to no funeral. I just can't, Forst man. That night keeps replaying in my head all the time." Cash shouted from the bathroom.

"I gotcha ya my brother, I'll be there with you. We have to hit his peeps off."

"I don't know," Cash said then he thought it over and added. "Let's take care of that tomorrow."

"Tomorrow, then it'll have to be after work."

"Ahight, that's cool."

"You know who I was thinking about when I gave Keya your number?"

"Who?" Cash asked.

"Stacey," I said.

"That dumb broad is in Spring Valley. She left a message on my damn voicemail. And truthfully she could stay her dumb-ass out there." Cash said walking into the kitchen to get a drink. "Yo, how's Keya looking? That butt still booming?"

"Yep, she's looking kind a good," I said and thought about it for a minute. "Her daughter is pretty just like her."

"I'm a go home and pray for some more of that kitty-cat."

"Cash, when were you hitting that?"

"Way before we started making money in the game. That big butt girl is too freaky for me and she's got too much game. You know how I do? I need to be in charge of a bitch."

"Man, what I told you about disrespecting our black beauty queens?"

"Forst, some of these so-called black beauty queens ain't nothing but tricks and ho's," Cash said with a loud laugh.

"Hurry your ass out my house."

"On some real shit, tomorrow after work we need to meet up and go to Justin's mother house. I don't want to step up in that piece solo."

"I told you I got you, right?" I said.

I gave Cash a pound and walked him to the door. Then I started moving furniture around and picking up clothes strewn over the floor in an attempt to clean up. I knew the next time I returned Dawn would be with me. I pumped the radio volume feeling good about doing the chores. Cash did not pick-up after himself. He was mad lazy, he left cups and a plate of food uneaten next to the bed. I was a neat freak.

A few minutes later the phone rang. It was Cash.

"Check it, Justin's wake's tomorrow."

"Don't worry, Cash I'm going with you. Does his mother know you were with him?"

"Hell no! You think she would want to see me if she knew I was with her son? I want to be a part of their lives. I know Justin would like that," Cash was very emotional. I dropped the phone feeling helpless. That's my man and it hurt him to witness another friend's death. I thought about Justin's demise while cleaning. No matter how he lived, his family would mourn.

There were a few hours to spare before picking up Dawn. I lit candles my sister had given me for Christmas. The aroma of mountain berry engulfed the apartment. I left a candle in each room. My romantic side lured chicks. In the bedroom I had new sheets and pillows. I kept my box of condoms on the left side. It was the side I slept on. Just then the phone rang.

"Yes," I answered with attitude.

"Is everything alright?" Dawn asked.

"Yeah boo. What's good?"

"Forster, I can't make it."

The news hit me hard. I paused to recover from the blow. Then searched for something appropriate to say.

"Can't make it?" I repeated and glanced around the bedroom.

"Cannot..."

"Why not?"

"Are you upset?"

"Not really upset, but I was really looking forward to having you over." Unable to hide my disappointment, I sounded pitiful. There was silence over the phone.

"Psych!" Dawn shouted. I sat down when I heard her childish laughter.

"Girl you had my stomach rolling on pins and needles." I laughed with relief.

"When are you planning to get down here?"

"Matter of fact, I was about to head your way this minute. You know? Try and beat that mad evening traffic."

"Call my cell when you're downstairs."

"Sure thing suga plum."

"Gotcha sour apple."

"Why I gotta be all that?"

"Don't trip. That's my fave...I love sour apples."

"Give me a kiss."

"Fo' sho," Dawn said laughing because she knew that had fast become my favorite request. I sucked my lips together pretending to blow a kiss.

"Oh no, Forst, I want mine in person."

"Hmm, that's what I'm talking about," I said. I could hear her giggling.

"Call me when you're downstairs, crazy boy."

Dawn was sitting at her desk fixing her make-up while reminiscing. She heard through a friend of hers how freaky I was in bed. Dawn at first was disgusted because she liked me like that, but didn't want the friend to know just how much. My sexcapades had secretly made her even more curious. Even though neither of us mentioned sex, Dawn sensed it would be on like popcorn. A call from her boss broke up her thoughts. She jetted from her seat after realizing that her boss had called more than once.

"Dawn, I won't be in tomorrow. If you want you can take the day off too with pay." Her boss suggested. The smile on Dawn's face spread from ear to ear.

"Thank you soo much." Dawn cooed. "Let me finish up those e-mails and documents, so that when we return there won't be much more to do."

"Thanks, Dawn."

She felt like running out of the office and clicking her heels together. Instead her smile widened. She was ecstatic and couldn't wait to let me know. Half an hour later the telephone rang.

"Russell and Friedman law firm, this Ms. Jones. How may I help you?" Dawn answered.

"Hey, girl," Keya said.

"What's up Kee? Where are you?"

"I..." There was a long pause.

"Kee, are you there?"

"It's about Mizo. He's dead, DJ."

"What? Are you all right?"

"Not really. I feel fucked up about it."

"Why? He was really mean to you."

"Yes and no. But I feel bad because I knew..."

"Not here girl, talk to me when I get to Forster's." Dawn interrupted.

"You're going to his house?" Keya asked surprised.

"Yeah girl, I know I'll have a blast." Dawn was excited.

"Did y'all do the nasty yet?"

"No crazy. I don't get down like you. But I hope it goes down tonight."

"Have fun."

"I heard Forster is freaky in bed." Dawn whispered.

"Don't let that boy rip you from your frame." Keya chuckled.

"Hush your mouth, fool. He will not, because I got sump'n for him."

"Okay, when was the last time you had sex, girl?"

"Almost a year ago," Dawn answered.

"You're a virgin all over again." Keya laughed.

"Anyway crazy, Kee, I'll call you before I'm settled in. If I don't girl, don't worry I'll be in good hands. I'll talk to you later."

"Don't forget to rock his world, girl. And one more thing, do not swallow." Keya laughed and they hung up.

Dawn finished her work and decided to wait for me downstairs. Five minutes later, she was outside anxiously shifting her weight from side to side. She was ready to get her freak on. A year was too long. Ten minutes later, I pulled up. She was looking pretty, fly out front. I reached across the passenger seat and opened the door for her. Dawn got in and I kissed her full on soft lips.

"Ooh," she said and fastened her seatbelt then examined me. "And why isn't your seatbelt fastened?" She asked.

"I don't do seatbelts."

"You better buckle up when you ride with me, Forster baby."

"Ahight, just for you," I said buckling the seatbelt. I glanced at her to see if she was satisfied. Judging from the smile on her face, she was. "We're going to pick up some stuff at the supermarket, if that's okay with you. I mean, unless you want to eat out?"

"We'll go with your plans."

"Okay. I'll pick-up breakfast food, dinner for tonight, and dessert," I said.

"What about lunch?"

"I'll give you money for lunch."

"Guess what? I am off tomorrow."

"Word?"

"Word up, baby."

"I am not going to work tomorrow either, but I have to go with Cash to his man's funeral."

"What time?"

"In the evening."

"All right...ah who..."

"Cash's man, Justin. You could stay at my place or accompany me to the funeral?"

"I'll go. Cash's your boy," she said. I held her hand and jetted to the expressway.

"Do you need to stop at your crib?"

"For a hot minute." Dawn answered.

"Ahight," I said shaking my head and turning up the music. Dawn heard her cell phone ringing through the loud music. She pulled it from her pocket and I turned the volume down.

"Hello."

"Are you busy, DJ?" Keya asked.

"No Kee, I'm riding uptown in the car with Forster."

"I know who murdered Mizo."

"You do?"

"Huh uh."

"You mixed up in that, Kee?"

"You know me better than that, DJ. I don't get mixed up in dumb shit."

"Oh, your hustle is not dumb?"

"Why are you trying to put my biz on full blast? See DJ, you think the whole world revolves around you. It's your way or no-way, huh? I'm really tired of you and your bullshit."

"Kee, why you blowing everything out of proportion?"

"You're the one who started this. I call you all the time to confide in you and you hold it against me. Don't get cute." Keya screamed.

"First of all, if you're living like that you're endangering your damn self and everyone else around you."

"Whatever bitch!"

"Then whatever bitch!"

The call ended abruptly. I kept both hands tight on the steering wheel but my mouth was agape when I heard Dawn shouting at Keya.

"You ahight?"

"Yes, let that bitch think whatever she's doing wont hurt anyone. She's got a daughter," Dawn said. I put my hand on her lap.

"Calm down, honey. I learned that in life that you can continuously give your friends good advice, but that doesn't mean they listen. Don't worry about her. She's grown has a daughter. You can still love and support her. But some people don't want even their best-friends to criticize their life," I said.

"Yeah, maybe you're right. It's just hard not to say anything when you love someone like a sister. I know she's much better than what she's putting herself through," Dawn said teary eyed. I offered a tissue and a shoulder.

"We're going to have a good time. Don't worry, ahight?" I assured her and she nodded. She was angry and didn't want to speak. "We're going to make a pit-stop at Path Mark and pick up whatever you want me to cook," I said consoling her. Dawn smiled and wiped her eyes.

Cash heard the cell phone ringing off the hook. It was an unknown number.

"Who dis?" He answered. There was a long pause. He was about to hang up when he heard a voice.

"It's me, Stacey."

"What do you want?"

"I want to come back home."

"Oh, you want to come home?" Cash repeated. "Bitch stay the hell where you at. I sent all your shit to your brother's place." Cash hung up. Stacey sobbed. She knew the relationship was over. He wanted his cake after eating it. She was not with that and she had to worry about him on the streets messing around. She had genuine love like the song: It's so hard to say goodbye to yesterday. They had to shoulder pain. Stacey was great company but he never shared his secrets with her. Tomorrow, Justin's funeral would take place. A good man shot dead. No one could bring him back. Doubts and regrets seeped in. Cash knew his boys would always represent. Having Stacey around would have helped to ease the pain. Instead of sitting in the crib pouting, Cash decided to go out.

He went to visit Justin's family and dropped money off. Cash didn't call me. He wanted to go on his own all along. The short visit went on for hours. The family showed him mad love in return. Cash was kicking it with a female cousin of Justin's. She was a little older than him and from way back had tried to push-up on him. They exchanged numbers and Cash kept it moving. There would be no chasing the kitty-cat today. Cash mourned the loss of his man. Occasions like this left him with thoughts of his mother. She was on his mind and in his dreams. It was a twenty four-seven thing and the weight was not easy for him. Having a woman in his corner was becoming important to Cash. He told me his mother spoke to him in his dreams. It was only then that Cash could find peace. Cash was sitting around with Justin's family when his cell phone rang.

"Excuse me," he said to another cousin of Justin's. The number was unknown, but he answered it anyway. "Speak on it."

"Hi stranger," a familiar voice greeted.

"What's up with you, ma?"

"Oh, you know who this is?"

"Girl, I still reminisce on your sweet juices, from back in the days when Doug E Fresh and the Get Fresh Crew rocked at the Keys," he said and she laughed. "Yes I know who I'm speaking with, Miss Jordan." Cash laughed.

"I must have left a good impression on you."

"Why you saying it like that?"

"Easy, I'm just saying I know the girlies must be feeling you and all." Keya said harmlessly diffusing the confusion.

"See, you trying to make a thug blush."

"I want to make the thug do more than that." Keya flirted.

"Say word?"

"Word up, money-grip."

"Who are you trying to be some kind a thug princess? You ain't ready, shortie."

"My middle name is ready." Keya said and they both laughed.

"I heard you got a daughter." Cash said interrupting the laughter.

"I do. She's so pretty, she's my whole world. Whatever I do, I do it for her."

"I heard that. Even if it means trickin'?" Cash asked. There was a pause before Keya finally answered.

"Why would you say sump'n like that?"

"Why not?"

"Yeah, I'd sell my body for my daughter. I mean I was shitted on in the beginning but it's all good. God's gonna help me."

"Why is that all good?"

"That problem is deep-sixed."

"Yeah, right," Cash said jokingly.

"My belief is in my prayers. I believe I can turn my life around. I'm not saying it's an easy thing, but it can be done. I am trying for my daughter and myself to keep it on the straight and narrow." Keya said.

"I hear that," Cash responded then said something that quickened her pulse.

"Keya, I'm here if ya ever need me."

"That's nice to know," Keya replied.

"Yeah it's real. How's your girl, Dawn?"

"That bitch be on some B.S. She needs to get herself some dick." Keya answered.

"Why you on that hater-aid?" Cash asked.

"DJ I mean Dawn acting shady and right now I'm not even trying to feel her."

"Go back. Who's DJ? Your man?"

"Oh please, DJ is what I've been calling that bitch for years."

"Oh it sounds serious, what happened?"

"Nah, nah she was acting brand new in front of your boy. She started coming out her face trying to knock my hustle. So, I was like; 'yo DJ, why you trying to play high post in front of dude?'" Keya went on.

"I feel you. It's like she knows how you get down and shouldn't discuss your biz in front of anyone else." Cash said.

"Absolutely," Keya responded. "See I'm upset and surprised. DJ don't be biting her tongue she sez whatever she wants. But she knows she shouldn't be discussing my biz in front of no one, no matter who it is. You feel me, Cash?"

"I feel you."

"I'm sure she's gonna say sump'n to Forster that I might not want him to know. But I can't stop that. It's life and people will piss you off. Most people feed off gossip. Like I ran into an ex of mine, and he was like I know everything about you. I looked at him like he was stupid. I tell people exactly what I want them to know. Feel me?" Keya asked.

"Am I? You're hitting everything right on the nose, Ma. It's like with other dudes. I feel the same way. Dudes see me, but don't be knowing me. They fear me but dont see that I'm a nice dude. Knuckleheads always want to test me. Then once I'm tested, it's on. There goes that Dr. Jekyll and Mr. Hyde. I get gorilla on you so next time you'll think twice. I have two brothers. One is Forster. I'm not the type to put his life in danger over my beefs. I'll handle my biz. And my other brother is Gabriel. His head is all into college. I wouldn't dare bring him into any war. But if I call him, he'll come running. Believe that, he's a soldier. I get frustrated because it's like I should have someone other than that fake-ass father I have now. Yo Kee, people have no idea what runs through my mind. I respect you doing what you gotta do and the others that don't; later for them." Cash said.

"I'm feeling you," Keya stressed.

REAL LUV?

"How's my hosting skills going so far?" I asked.

Dawn nodded and nestled her head on my exposed chest. We were lying with our bodies entwined. My fingertips traced my name, her name and the L-word on the smooth, satiny skin of her back.

"Sex was unbelievable. Wanna go another round?" Dawn giggled.

"Most definitely," I smiled.

"Noo, I'm just kidding. Maybe later Forst, I'm a little sore. It's been a while."

"I heard that," I said.

"But I got to say this, I...feel like I crave you, when I'm not near you."

"What do you actual crave?"

"Truthfully, everything; your mouth, your touch, your lips and now that you got me sprung, what's between your legs. Your eyes hypnotize me and I love the way your hands caress my spine, spreading joyous delights along my thighs. Explosions occur within me every time you move your hands. My needs get quelled. And by the way, you do me oh so well, my fine man." Dawn let go a sexy chuckle when she was finished.

"Damn girl you got it going on. Is that poetry, or what?"

"I do a little spoken-word thing. That was fresh off the dome with your influence." She said and I kissed her softly on the forehead.

"But was it true?"

"Forst, I'm saying it, right?"

"True, true," I said rubbing the exposed flesh of her sweet brown booty.

"My word is my bond. That and my rep is all I have until you prove me wrong." Dawn said tickling me.

"Stop playing before neither of us can leave this bed." I laughed and kissed her hands.

"Yeah, well we have to be there for Cash at his friend's funeral. Let's get ready."

I fixed breakfast and ate. Dawn jumped in the shower and dressed. Then she ate and made the bed. The phone rang.

"Answer that for me," I shouted from the shower. I know Dawn loved being able to answer a bachelor's phone.

"Hello," she said.

"Yo, who this?" A gruff voice asked.

"You called. Who do you want to speak to?"

"This Cash. Is Forst there?"

"This Dawn. What's up, Cash?"

"What's good, ma. Is he getting ready?"

"Yeah, he's in the shower right now."

"Ahight, tell him to hit me when he's in the ride."

"I got you," Dawn said. Then both lines went dead.

"Who was that?" I called Dawn into the bathroom.

"You're welcome," she said and even with the soap on my face I could see her smile.

Dawn left the bathroom and made a call. Minutes later, I walked out the bathroom with a towel wrapped around my waist, carrying Cocoa Butter cream. She caressed my chest and pinched my nipple. I wanted more but she abruptly stopped.

"Ahh...what's the deal, baby?"

"That's what you can look forward to when we return." She smiled and walked away.

"In that case, we'll be right back. I'm not having blue-balls," I said rushing to get dressed. "You're a tease!" I shouted from the bedroom.

"But you like me, don't you?"

"I'm feeling you a lil' sump'n, sump'n. Are you about ready?"

"Ready as I'm going to be," Dawn said wrapping her arms around me. I was shirtless wearing jeans and white Nike's, putting on deodorant and looking at myself in the mirror.

"We're going to be in and out, because Just was no saint. You feel me?"

"Whatever you say, you're the boss," Dawn replied.

I hurried into a wife-beater and fixed the deuce-deuce in my pants, then threw on a black shirt.

"Hey, what's that for?"

"Dawn, don't worry."

"How can you say don't worry when you're packing a gun to a wake?"

"You know what?" I lifted the mattress and put the gun back. This reaction brought a smile to Dawn's face.

"I know what?" She asked.

"Don't smile, you know you're right," I said shaking my head.

"Where I'm from, you don't need a gun to attend funerals."

"It's a protection thing, you understand?"

"A protection thing? No I don't understand."

"Call it security but it's a long story."

"Well, you can start explaining now and we still have a car ride to go," Dawn said then slapped my butt on her way to the living room.

"Let's go, girl."

"Yeah let's go Mr. Bad-man."

"You got that one," I said locking the door. I was on the phone with Cash as soon as we got in the car. Cash's voicemail came on. "Yo Cash I'll be at the funeral in a minute," I said and hung up.

"Did you call his home?"

"Nah, I called his celly."

"We're not far, so you'll see him, soon. Forst I really don't like funerals."

"Who likes them, Dawn? The people who run the funeral parlor."

"I'm only going because of you."

"Are you going somewhere with this, Dawn?"

"Do you mind if I stay in the car, Forst? My stomach feels queasy."

I stared at her briefly then turned my attention back to traffic.

"Ahight, I'm going let you live. But you have to wait until the wake is over. The funeral is actually tomorrow and I'm not attending that. I'm giving Cash my time today. Two days is too much for me."

"I'll be here when it's over," Dawn said politely. I gave her a long hug.

"We're lucky to get parking right across the street from the parlor," I said.

"Yes, I could see you from there." She smiled.

"You may have to keep the car running, Dawn."

"Why would I have to do that?"

"Come on Dawn, you know how gangstas roll. A drive by may happen. I mean..."

"Oh, is that supposed to make my stomach feel better?"

I laughed and exited the car. Dawn reached over and playfully tried to hit me.

"See you in a few," we both said at the same time.

Dawn sat in the driver's seat with the window rolled down. She appeared on edge as she stared at all the folks that went into the parlor. I greeted the chick and then pointed for Dawn to come over to me. Dawn seemed confused.

To her surprise it was Keya. Dawn was shocked, she didn't know that Keya hooked up with Cash. Keya looked and waved then escorted Cash inside the funeral parlor. Dawn looked perplexed. She wondered why Keya couldn't come over. Dawn did not budge either. She waited and caught up on sleep.

Later, everyone slowly began walking out.

"Thank God, it's finally over." Dawn whispered.

Within minutes the crowd had cleared. Cash, Keya and I came walking toward the car. Dawn got out greeting them. She gave Cash a hug.

"What's up, Kee?" The girls walked away talking while Cash and I stood watching the happening for a minute. "What you have a problem with me now?"

"DJ, you know we've been girls way too long for that."

"But you know I always say what's on my mind."

"If I wanted my business on the radio, I would've done it myself."

"Kee, you act like no one knows your business."

"Anyway, DJ I'm not standing here to talk about the past. So what's up with you and Forster?"

94

"Forster is my boo for-real."

"Y'all look cute together. Girl you always get the cuties," Keya said hitting Dawn on the arm.

"It must be in my blood," Dawn laughed.

The girls continued. Cash and I along with other members of Justin's family were shaking hands extending hugs and chatting on the pavement outside the funeral home. All of a sudden a black, four-door sedan with dark tinted windows crept in our direction. Keya was flapping her gums. Cash and I were not paying attention.

"Forster, look out!" Dawn shouted and pointed at the slow moving car.

I whirled around and saw what the alarm was about. A sigh of relief escaped my throat. Cash did not move.

"What's up, Cash?" Boobie greeted extending his hand. Cash nodded, said nothing and turned away. Boobie was a bigger man than Cash was.

"Oh, it's still like that?" Boobie asked ignoring Cash's nasty treatment.

"I have nothing to say to you," Cash said.

"What have I done to you?" Boobie asked to Cash's back.

"Anyway," I interrupted. "Let me introduce you to my future wife," I said and signaled Dawn. She and Keya walked over. "Dawn this is Boobie. He's like a big brother," I said proudly.

"It's nice to meet you Boobie," Dawn said.

Before I could introduce Keya, Cash grabbed Keya's hand and pulled her away.

"What up Cash?" I offered but they kept walking away.

"Forst, let him go," Boobie said.

"Nah, I came here out of respect for this nigga and he's going to bounce on me without saying nothing. Yo, Cash get your ass back over here."

Keya got in the car and waited. Cash came walking back wearing a mean, screw-face. I hurriedly left Dawn and Boobie talking.

"What's up with you, Cash?"

"I just don't drop to my knees for no fake ass gangsta," he answered acidly.

"What's that suppose to mean?"

"Why you call me back, Forst? I'm out, man!"

"You can front all you want. Boobie was the one who helped us and you won't

give that man respect."

"Are you finished, Pastor Brown?"

"Ahight man, bounce," I said then rejoined Dawn and Boobie.

"Leave him alone, Forst. He'll get over it. We'll see where he'll re-up on supplies."

"Whatever, man. Me and my girl's out."

"Speaking of girl, Dawns a fine honey, kid. You better keep up with her 'fore a pimp like me scoop that ass," Boobie said smiling in my face. I could tell he meant what he said.

"You can dead all that. Ain't nobody taking my girl."

I didn't like the way Dawn and Boobie had been up in each other's faces. She looked like she was in the midst of contemplating whatever Boobie had put in her head. Dawn and Keya huddled before Cash finally dragged Keya off. Boobie and I shook hands and went our separate ways.

"Thank God there was no shoot out at the wake," Dawn said.

My mind was racing, taking me somewhere I didn't want to be. I concentrated on steering the whip instead of my problems.

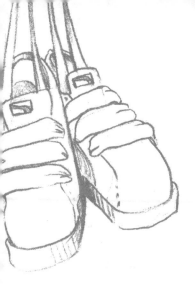

THE BETRAYAL

Weeks had gone by since me and Cash spoke. The reason was the same; Dawn. Our relationship had blossomed now that we had added romance to friendship. Dawn and Keya still kept in touch. They were trying to regain the closeness they once had, but the love was drying. That was what Dawn shared. We were closer and she was proving to be a rider. I was whipping around and decided to call her at the office. It was like I couldn't do without her. I needed her all the time. The phone rang twice.

"Hello, this is Russell and Friedman how may I help you?" Dawn answered.

"Hey sugar." I greeted.

"Hi, what's up I'm..."

"Did you go to lunch yet?" I asked.

"No, I'm helping my boss. She has too many clients and is backed-up. I'll probably be staying late to help her."

"You realize this is the third time you've done that. You've been putting your job before us lately." I complained.

"How so Forster?"

"I'm saying lately you've got no time for us."

"What about all those times you've been in meetings and you were unable to call me for hours? I didn't complain because I know that's business. All I ask is for you to do the same. And besides I never really stay late. As far as you calling me on your breaks, I told you before, I'm at work. Sometimes I just can't talk to you as long as other days."

"Don't get so amped. It's not that serious. Its just biz like you said."

"It is serious, for it to be coming out your mouth."

"What time are you getting off today?"

"I don't know Forst. Call me in an hour and I'll tell you."

"Love you," I said trying to quell an impending argument.

"Wow, I love you too Forster."

"I'll call you later."

"Be careful, because you aren't living for yourself anymore."

"Why are you preaching?" I asked.

"Boy, just call me later," Dawn said.

"I got your boy, right in my hand."

"Nasty boy!"

My phone rang shortly after. I assumed it was Dawn calling me back to give me the time to pick her up from work. "Yeah," I answered softly.

"Nigga don't be sounding sweet on the phone with me." It was Cash.

"Aw man, it's you. What's good, Cash?"

"What's going on, Forst?"

"You know maintaining. The biz, the job, I have two now."

"Word? Where you working now?"

"I mean Dawn's full time, hard work, kid."

"Yeah, I hear you."

"What's good, Cash? I've been calling you for the longest."

"I've been out of town man taking care of biz."

"Why didn't you tell me you were leaving?"

"I did that on the humble. I've got too much on my mind. Yo man, Keya told me she's pregnant."

"You serious, Cash?"

"Don't get all excited. I told her to get rid of it." Cash deadpanned.

"Why did you tell her that?"

"Yo Forst, I don't want that trick having no kids by me."

"Why aren't you using protection with the trick? She's good enough for you to hit without protection, but not good enough to have your child?"

"I thought you knew me better than that? No ho is causing me to lose my life to the virus. Bitch was running tracks for Mizo's camp."

"Cash, anything could've transpired when she was out there on her stroll."

"You right Forst. It was the pussy. I wasn't thinking."

"Dawn still make me use rubbers. I wanna hit that raw."

"That's how it was. She got that sweetness, that ill nana. Man she had me going, ya heard. Too bad she gotta get rid of that. She better!"

"What, you gonna beat it out of her if she don't?"

"No fool. I ain't an animal like that. I'll pay someone else to carry that weight." Cash laughed.

"That's not funny man."

"I ain't worrying."

"Hold on fool. Someone else is on my other end."

"Holla at me later, man."

"Okay," I said and answered the new call. "Hello."

"Forster," an unfamiliar voice answered.

"Who is this?" I asked.

"Its Keya don't get mad. I took your number out of Cash's phone."

"Why are you calling me?"

"To ask you please talk to Cash?"

"Why don't you holla at your girl?" I said referring to Dawn.

"I don't want to hear DJ's mouth."

"Cash has a mind of his own and there is nothing that I can do. Besides I'm not the one to get in anyone's business," I said without hesitation.

"I thought we peeps, Forst?"

"Yo, it's not like we're not. But in a situation like this, I can't help you. I am not some kind a talk show host or sump'n like that," I said as calmly as possible.

"It's like that, huh?" Keya asked sounding frustrated.

"Like what?"

"All y'all is dogs. I'm sorry we had this convo. I just thought you were different that's all."

"Yeah, well if men are dogs then women are fleas."

"Forster Brown who're you calling flea?"

"If the collar fit then wear it."

"You got some nerves. Don't make me have my man do you up sump'n."

"Yeah go ahead, he already diss you. Listen ma put your hand in a goodie-bag find another trick. I ain't the one," I said and hung up, then called Dawn. She picked up the office phone.

"Russell and Friedman law firm, how..."

"Your friend called me wilding-out. Talk to her and tell her to put all that extra bull in check," I said heatedly cutting her off.

"What happened? Hold on my cell is ringing. Maybe that's her." I could hear her cell phone ringing. "Hello?"

"DJ you better tell your little boyfriend sump'n cuz he obviously don't know who I be. He better ask somebody. I ain't none of his little skeezers from the block."

"What happened?"

"He tried to play me when I asked him to talk to Cash for me."

"First of all, Kee, why were you calling him?"

"Why not? Is he your friend only?"

"No, that's not it, but he's my man now. The game done changed. And it's not like you and him cool like that anyhow. I'll handle this when you pick me up," Dawn said ending the call.

"Yeah, I can't wait till you check her," I said then hung up.

Dawn went back to the cell phone conversation. "Where was I? Are you still there, Kee?"

I hung up and headed to pick up my paycheck. I made a pit stop at the liquor store to get a fifth of Henney. After dealing with them two I needed something to relieve my stress.

Cash opened his eyes when he heard the phone beeping. There were messages. Before he could check them, he heard knocking on his door. Cash went to the door and opened it. It was Keya.

"What're you doing here?" Cash asked as she walked in. He closed the door and admired her sexy behind. On one side he wanted to hit that again, but Cash no longer needed this headache.

"What kind of question is that? Fool don't you know I'm pregnant by you?"

"Yeah, but you already know my decision. And I hope you're coming here because you need money to get that abortion." Cash said pouring grape juice. Keya faced him and stood biting her lips with her chest heaving trying to hold back the tears. Cash pulled his phone out and checked his messages then addressed Keya. "What the fuck you tell my man?"

"I called him just to find what's up with him and my girl, DJ." Keya lied.

"Why then is he telling a whole 'nother story on my voicemail?" Cash was angry.

"I don't know. We had got to talking and..."

"Bitch, how you get his number?" Cash moved closer as he asked. Keya opened her mouth to answer and Cash slapped her face. She dropped her handbag and slapped him back. He felt the sting to his face and realized she had also scratched him. Cash punched her dead in the mouth. Keya went buck wild defending herself. Cash put a hurting on her, then tossed her out. She fell in a wrinkled heap outside in the hallway. Keya put her hands to her face. She could feel the swelling around her eyes. She wiped the blood coursing from her nose and mouth. Her clothes were ripped. She got up and started hurling curses at Cash. He slammed his door.

"I'm gonna have the cops take you out in 'cuffs you heard me? You lil'-dick, small-time-crack-pusher, no good piece o' shit. You..."

Inside, Cash sat on his bed listening to her rant. He called me. Keya was kicking and hollering outside his door when I answered.

"Yo Forst, I got your message a few minutes ago. What happened?"

"Ahight, bust it. Keya calls me telling me to talk to you about her getting an abortion and all this other bullshit. So, I asked her how she got my number. Then I told her to call Dawn, since I wanted nothing to do with the situation. She went crazy and all. Telling me she'll get her man to come do me and all this rah, rah, rah woofing."

"She and I was just thumping like dudes."

"You were fighting? Why Cash?"

"I slapped the bitch cuz she shouldn't be searching all up in my phone. I don't

play that shit. It ain't like she bought it or paying my bills or nothing."

"Cash, you can't be hitting on no women, man. That's wrong." I said with a sick feeling. I knew Keya.

"She deserved a beat down. I don't give a what! Ain't no woman putting they hands on me without getting an ass-whipping."

"Whether you like it or not, Cash she's pregnant. You just can't beat on her."

"Right now she's in the hallway beasting her ass off. Do you hear her ass?"

"I'm on my way over there," I said and hung up.

"Go home to your daughter. You ain't nothing but a deadbeat mother," Cash shouted through the door.

"At least my daughter has a mother, you faggot," Keya snapped back.

Cash punched the wall. He did everything possible to restrain himself from going out the door and opening up another can of ass whipping.

"Dumb broad, you don't know who your baby-father is. You better go on Jenny Jones with all that drama, you backwards ho!" Cash was furious but he did not want to hit her again.

"I'm soo sorry that I played myself with you. You ain't worth spit. Don't worry, one day you'll get yours, Cash." Keya cried.

"Yeah, whatever talk all that trash but you still want this no-good nigga right?"

"Fuck you!" Keya yelled and walked away. Cash knew she was leaving because her whining faded the further she got. As soon as I came through the door Keya saw me coming and ran into my arms.

"What the hell?" I gasped for air while staring at her face. She cried hysterically. "Come with me upstairs Keya," I said.

"I'm not going up in his house. That dick will get his," she said angrily.

"Ahight, be easy, Key."

"He don't know who I be knowing. He don't know..." Keya was still crying her face was in bad shape.

"Listen, we won't go to Cash's house. I got other peeps up in here," I said calmly. I took her to one of my boys' apartment upstairs. He escorted Keya to the bathroom and she cleaned herself up some. "Wait here a minute. I'll be right back."

I ran downstairs to Cash's place and banged on the door. Cash probably thought it was Keya. He looked through the peephole, saw me and opened the door.

"Man that crazy ass bitch, Keya just left," Cash said. I shoved him hard in his chest. Cash almost fell backwards.

"Chill nigga. What's that for?" Cash asked getting ready for a fight.

"I saw Keya's face. What's wrong with you? You bugging or sump'n? I let a lot of your ways slide, but beating on a woman that's something else. You need to show these women respect as you would your mother or Miss Carroll. I don't care if you get mad either. That girl has to be around her daughter."

"What you working for save the hos' foundation? Save yourself."

"Save myself, from what? I should probably save myself from you, right? I can't believe you let off on her the way you did. Home-girl's face is a mess. She could easily press charges on your dumb ass. And the fact that she's pregnant will really send you away on some bullshit."

"Forst, you probably plugged that shit in her head, right?"

"Come on, shut-da-fuck-up. I ain't mentioned nothing like that to her. You need to check yourself before you wreck yourself," I said and walked out the apartment.

"That nigga don't know me. Get out before you get clapped. Go ahead keep changing hos' into housewives," Cash said as he slammed the door

I ignored him and went back to see Keya. My man had given her an icepack for her puffy eyes which were now bloody red.

"Kee, I'm sorry that he did this. But you know how he is? Why you gonna go to his place, knowing he's gonna be mad at you?"

"You know how I always felt about Cash? And when we started again, I thought things were cool. When he was in the heat of the passion, Cash kept saying he wanted me to have his baby."

"Yeah, he was probably wet from the alcohol or weeded or sump'n," I said and my friend who owned the apartment started laughing. "No, I'm not trying to be funny." I said to him. "Listen Keya, you been on the streets so you know how it is. Don't believe everything a man tells you. And let me tell you this, when we have liquor in our system we're liable to ask you to marry us. It's when we sober that's when it really counts."

"Forster, I apologize for what I said to you earlier on the phone. I was mad that's all. Dawn got herself a good catch and I was jell. Especially with the two of you knowing each other as long as we have. I guess I wanted something like that. Who

wouldn't want that?"

"All that is forgiven, Keya. Let me call her before she flips. Do you want me to take you somewhere?"

"Yes, can you please take me home?"

"Not a problem." I said waiting for Dawn to answer the phone.

"Russell and Friedman law firm. How may I help you?"

"Hi baby, how is your day going?"

"It's okay. How are you?"

"I'm all right, things got a little bit crazy. Cash and Keya had a fight."

"What? Is she alright?"

"She's right here. Do you want to speak with her?"

"Yes, put her on." I gave Keya the cell phone.

"Hello DJ."

"Kee, what happened?"

"DJ, I'm pregnant."

"Are you really?"

"Yes, I think its Cash's."

"You think its Cash's baby?"

"Damn DJ, what you two are twins or something?"

"Kee, I'll call you when I get off of work."

"You want me to put Forst back on?"

"Yes, please."

"Yeah shortie, what's up?"

"I'm leaving at my regular time. My friends are stressing me out."

"Can I help you relieve some of that stress tonight, suga?"

"When are you going to let me stay home?" Dawn laughed.

"You don't need to go home."

"Tell that to my mommy." She was still laughing.

"I'll call you after I drop Keya off."

"Yeah, you do that," Dawn said and ended the call.

"Yo man, I owe you one for allowing us up in here," I said to my man.

"Thanks a lot for all you've done to help me," Keya said.

"It's nothing. Be well, my peeps," he said. Keya and I left.

I allowed her to hold my arm as we walked to the car. She leaned against me resting her head on my shoulder.

"Thank you for coming to my rescue, Forster." She whispered.

"You're welcome," I said and felt her hot breath against my neck. I helped her in the car and drove her home in silence. After dropping Keya off I sat in the car trying to figure out why she was always making passes at me. It's nastier now that she was pregnant. She could never be my steeze.

Everything had changed since me and Cash put workers on these blocks. It all happened in a smash. Workers kept getting locked up. Boobie advised me these younger cats weren't like the real hustlers from back in the days. The game had changed. These new jacks were all about flossing to impress shorties. Boobie knew I was trying to get out of the game, but besides Lacresia, he didn't trust anyone else. He was telling me that too many new jacks were singing to the cops. Now all the narcs had his name on their lips. He was trying to get Cash and I to stay on together. Getting back on the grind and being on the streets were no longer options for me. Because of my connection to Boobie, I had to go and kick it with him myself.

"Yo Boobie I'm ready to put my hands on these little dudes, man. They out there playing shortstop and cutting off my flow. It's like a nigga can't make it to home plate."

I expressed my feelings to Boobie. I was reluctant to discuss them with Cash. He was too irrational and might pistol-whip all our workers. Then no one would want to work for us.

"Listen man, all you gotta do is drop some of them and be careful who y'all hire, cool? Get rid of the ones doing badly and keep the real soldiers. That's all there is to it." Boobie suggested.

"I feel what ya saying. Truthfully though, I'm not with all of this hustle anymore," I said. Boobie gave me a look from under the rim of his Polo shades but said nothing. I continued.

"I'm thinking nine to five for now and maybe for the rest of my life. I'm having issues with these cats and it'll be a matter of time before I gotta pull out the strap."

"I hear you. But you know that's for 'em college cats. Well at least that's how I see it. Either way that's backward hustling," Boobie said and gave me pound.

"That's one man's story."

"I'm saying the drug game is all I know. I got my GED for madukes. I ain't never worked for anyone and I ain't about to start. Feel me, Forst?"

"I'm chilling like a pigeon right now."

"I was meaning to ask you about the shortie I met the other day."

"Who? Dawn or Keya?"

"Dawn, Dawn fuck that skeezer, Keya," Boobie said puffing on his weed.

"Dawn's my boo, for real," I said and passed on the blunt.

"How sure are you?" Boobie continued puffing.

"I got that handcuffed man. She's on twenty-four seven lockdown. Believe that." I laughed.

"Forst, you's a crazy dude."

"I'm going to talk to Cash about these little workers. I don't know how it's going to turn out, because dudes uptown ain't pitching for him, unless it's through me and I'm about to quit the game."

"Good, now I can get some money off these streets," Boobie said. We both laughed.

"Yeah we're taking a little cheddar out your mouth, huh?"

"It's all good, lil' hustling goes a long way. There'll always be that dough."

"True, listen Boobie, I'm out. I'll tell you what's going down," I said and gave Boobie a pound. I slid off to see Cash in his crib. We had to talk about this street thing of ours. I rang his doorbell and he greeted me as if he was anxious.

"Where you been, man?" Cash asked opening the door. I could feel hungry eyes measuring me.

"I'm here right? That's all that matters. Clear these cats out your crib. We got to talk." I requested. Cash didn't hesitate.

"Y'all roll out for now. I'll catch up with y'all later," Cash said while waving his gun around.

"These dudes only fear you, there's no respect for you. They waiting for you to slip then they'll try you," I said after watching them running out the door like it was a raid.

"Long as they know how I get down, they could fear me, love me or hate me. Best believe none of them will step to me unless they wanna come up missing," Cash said picking up trash off the floor. "I just left Boobie."

"Fuck that fake-ass gangsta."

"C'mon Cash, I don't get down like that. I was telling him about the workers."

"Why the fuck are you going to that snake about our business?"

"No matter what, that nigga helped us get on. Anyway he was telling me to keep the workers holding it down for us on the streets. And let Shah and his crew go from the Polo Grounds."

"Boobie's telling us what to do?"

"He ain't telling us what to do. I'm saying it cuz they the weakest ones we have. I'm tired of this bullshit anyway."

"Tired of what? Getting money? I ain't."

"This you Cash. It's not me. I don't have time babysitting no dudes over money. Any of them could drop a dime on us at anytime and you know it. Especially with you putting guns in niggas' faces and all. How do you expect niggas to feel?"

"I don't give two spits how they asses feel. Long as they sling my packs we good. It's biz. I ain't here to win no friendship contest. It's about money."

"That's the difference from the eighties to the ninety's. Older cats like us don't give a shit. Boobie treat all his soldiers like they his little brothers. There wasn't all this disrespecting and shootings. You're walking on thin ice as it is. Now, you got the other leg sliding on banana peel, Cash. You can't even go nowhere without your strap."

"Damn skippy, Forst. I'm staying strapped and be ready for a cat to test me," Cash said kissing the muzzle of his nine-millimeter.

"Everything is a joke to you, huh?"

"This ain't no joke. How about my moms? These streets raised me, Forst. I'm a product of this fucked up environment. It ain't as lovely for me like it is for some of these little dudes. They don't realize how good they got it. Even with one parent they're better off than me. I'll do anything just to have my mom. One parent is better than none. Well, let me rephrase that. One caring parent will do me just fine."

"You have Miss Carroll, Cash," I said feeling his pain. Cash was my man but we were also close as kids coming up. His eyebrows shot up when I mentioned the name, but he said nothing. "She had to step up, took you in and gave you a chance."

"It's not the fucking same. I don't have my mother. How many times do I have to repeat that to you man. You my ace boon how you not gonna know that." Cash shouted. Tears rolled down his cheeks. Sensitive thug, I thought about giving him a hug but he continued in rage. "It hurts real bad Forst. You don't know until you lose your mother."

"Maybe that's what you should be doing, letting these young cats appreciate who they have in their life."

"I don't even know how to be a parent. Sometimes I wanna kill peeps cuz I hate that they could smile and I can't."

"Man, I just got the craziest idea. You ready for this?"

"I'm listening," Cash said wiping his eyes.

"Let's eliminate all the weak ones. Keep our little soldiers out there hustling and we do our research on helping teens that are having problems in school, homes or whatever. So what you think?" I asked. Cash stared at me like I was crazy.

"You are bugging the fuck out my brother." Cash said dismissing the idea, but I was persistent.

"Why I gotta be bugging? Who better to tell them what the streets are about than us?" I asked. Cash looked at me as if I was totally out there visiting Mars.

"Forst, are you fucking with that white lady? Or sucking that clear glass dick?"

"My mom use to drink and abuse my dad. You think I'm the only one who experienced this? You think you're the only one who lost a parent or two for that matter? Think about it Cash. We could change a lot of young kids' lives," I said with confidence.

"You dusted, Forst?"

"Nah, man. We all have a purpose on this earth. I'd like to give back all the knowledge I've got so others won't make the same mistakes. How many dudes around our age have we seen or heard killed out there on these streets?"

"For you, I'll think about it. Right now you have to go. I need to get on these toy soldiers for my money," Cash said giving me a pound.

"I'm being real serious. I'll do my research and you, you better back me up."

"Yeah, call me later," Cash said shoving me.

Before Cash could close the door I turned around. "I don't know if you wanna hear all this, but you might be happy after I tell you it, anyway," I said.

"C'mon man, say what you gotta say..."

"Keya told Dawn that the baby might not be yours," I said and watched Cash jumping up and down, then started moon walking like Michael Jackson.

"Lord please let that baby be somebody else's for real, for real." Cash sang.

Billy Jean is not my lover

She's just a girl who thinks that I am the one

But the kid is not my own

Dawn got home from work without me getting her. It made me a little suspicious that she never called to find out why I didn't pick her up. She never missed an opportunity like that to call me out. Anyhow she was home with her parents and that was peaceful to my mind.

"Hey mommy, where's dad?" Dawn asked walking into the living room.

"Baby, sit down," her mother said in a grave tone.

"Why?" Dawn asked with apprehension.

"You're grown and should understand this. Dawn, your father and I have decided to get a divorce." Her mother said then went poker-faced. "Your father and I are still friends." Dawn heard her mother talking but the voice seemed to be coming from far away. After a minute, Dawn cleared her throat and was able to breathe again.

"Why? That means we all won't be living together?" Dawn asked in tears.

"Dawn, I know you are used to seeing us together, but your dad will come over as much as he's able to. I'm sure you can go over to his new place as much as you like." Her mother said in the same deadpan voice.

"How about I move over there with him? Do you even care, huh?"

Dawn began sobbing and ran to her room and slammed the door. At twenty-

three she always resided with both parents. Her friends considered her to be spoiled. She was happy to have both parents. Dawn had heard horror stories of friends who didn't. She didn't want to be like them. Her mother was about to knock on the door, but changed her mind at the last minute. She went downstairs, leaving Dawn to cool off. I rang the door bell rang. She wiped her teary eyes and answered the door.

"Hey Forster," she greeted.

"How're you, Mrs. Jones? I didn't pick her up from work, but..." Before I could finish I saw the tears rolling down her cheek. "What happened?"

"Come inside, Forster. It's just that...ah...well. I guess Dawn will eventually tell you, so I might as well. Dawn's father and I are getting a...ah...divorce," she said as flood of tears were released. I was startled and my heart fell to the floor. I felt as though my parents were giving me bad news.

"I'm sorry to hear that. This must be a very bad day for you. Where's Dawn?"

"In her room."

I gave Mrs. Jones a hug then ran upstairs to Dawn's room. Her door squeaked as I pushed it open.

"Get out!" She said without looking up.

"It's me," I said. Dawn recognized my voice and lifted her head off the pillow. "I'm sorry Forster," she said. I sat on her bed and held her.

"I know this hurt you bad, but I know they both still love you."

"Look at me I'm crying like a little girl," Dawn said. She tried smiling but her eyes were swollen.

"Hey it don't matter how old you are. You're blessed to have lived with both your parents this long and it hurts to see them split up. But you got me still," I said. "Your mom is hurting more than you. This man is all she knew. And I know she thought they'd be together until death they part. Maybe you need to show her some love too," I said and wiped her tears away.

"Forster you're a great friend and an excellent boyfriend. Thank you."

"I'm here because I love you too, sugar. Now what do you say we go get sump'n to eat at City Island. It looks like it's going to rain so let's try and beat it." I said. "But first go talk to your mom while I pack your overnight bag." I offered. Dawn shook her head jokingly but still went to talk to her mother.

While Dawn spoke with her mother, I got busy getting stuff from her drawer.

I saw some photos and decided to look at them. The first few photos were of Dawn and Keya dressed up like twins. The next shots showed Dawn and a young dude. There were shots of Keya and the same dude and maybe his friend. They were on a double date. I wasn't mad because these photos were taken before my time. I looked at the back of the picture and read the inscription. I was surprised when I read what was scrawled on the back.

'TOO LEGIT TO QUIT. ME, KEYA, HUNTER AND BOOBIE'

Boobie! My mind screamed while my eyes popped out the sockets from curiosity. I went to the next picture and focused on the young dude whose arms were wrapped around Dawn. It was the same Boobie I knew who had referred to himself as my big brother. The thought jolted me and I remembered when she gave Boobie that look back at the funeral parlor. When I had introduced them, they stared at each other for a long time. That would have gone over my head except now I had seen the photo. I was furious but couldn't cause a beef in her parents' house, especially now. I couldn't wait to get her alone. I replaced the pictures, except for the one with Dawn and Boobie all snuggled up.

I made my way downstairs with Dawn's bag and the picture. I saw Dawn and her mother still talking. If Dawn knew what was going through my mind, she would freak. I watched her talking to her mother and I could picture her with Boobie in various sexual positions. I was ready to take somebody's head off without hearing the story. I couldn't keep holding my anger in, so I bid adieu to Mrs. Jones. Then I waited uneasily for her daughter to come out. I needed someone to talk to and called Cash. When he answered I could hear music blasting in the background.

"Who's this?" Cash responded. I jumped right into the reason for the call.

"Did you know Boobie and Dawn use to go together?" I asked feeling the knots tighten in my stomach. The volume of the background music dropped.

"You mean since she's been seeing you?"

"Talk to me, man." I insisted.

"Yo sun, just say it and I'll smoke our fake-ass, big brotha."

His answer brought a nervous laughter out of me.

"Cash, I'm really heated. I saw some pictures of the two of them real comfy and all. It must have been the time we first started pitching rocks."

"Didn't you introduce the two of them?"

"Yeah and neither one of them said anything about knowing one another."

"That's messed up. I mean why didn't Dawn say something? If she had told you she used to fuck with him, would you still be mad?"

"No, but now I'm mad, because she didn't say nada, even after I introduced them. Remember when we first met them? Didn't we introduce her and Keya to Boobie?"

"Yeah, he could have that skeezer, Keya. I don't care."

"You's straight clown."

"Shit, if I was messing with that skeezer on the regular and found pictures of her and dude, I would call him and tell his dumb-ass to keep her," Cash said laughing. The conversation served to calm me down.

"So how should I bring this up to her?" I asked Cash, but was really questioning my love for Dawn.

"Do like I do. Bring her ass to your crib and sit her down. But before you ask her put that nina on the table."

"No fool. I just want to talk, not shoot her."

"That's exactly my point, homey. The gun will bring the truth out."

"You need help, Cash."

"Yeah, you a sucker for love, Forst. Good guys finish last."

"No Cash. That ain't me. I ain't built for that. She's gonna tell the truth. I just gotta know how to raise it."

"And if she doesn't?"

"Somebody will. Either Dawn or Boobie, one of them will. If I'm not satisfied then I'll dead the relationship."

"Yeah that's right. Lay that bitch out on her ass."

"No chump, I meant drop her, not keep her as my girl. You evil, sun. That's the reason I love black people and can't stand y'all niggas."

"Forst, what's that suppose to mean?"

"Niggas are ignorant people. No class. Black people are smart, classy, and have respect."

"What are you, the hip hop Martin Luther King?"

"I have a dream. Hopefully you'll support it."

"Support what?" Cash asked.

"Support me and the jump-off for teens," I said.

"You talking 'bout the youth center? You're still on that? Save that for Donahue. I told you I'd think about it."

"You was the one talking about I'm a young Martin. Well, he had a dream to make positive changes for all humanity. I want to make one positive change in the lives of teenagers. You feeling me, Cash?"

"Yep, and I heard all I need to from you," Cash said.

"If I need you I'll call."

"Yeah me and my little friend will be waiting."

"Ahight scar-face," I said ending the call. Not long after Dawn came out. She looked around then saw me and walked over to the car. I could no longer hold the doubts back. I was ready for her and as she got in the car, I threw the picture on her lap.

"Are we ready to go?" Dawn asked without acknowledging the photo.

"Dawn I'm going to ask you something just once," I said trying to control my anger but the look on my grill did not conceal what I felt.

"Okay, go ahead, Forster ask anything you want."

"Did you use to fuck with Boobie?" I asked and could tell that she was surprised by the question. Dawn remained cool.

"Did Boobie tell you something?" She asked without so much as glancing at the photo.

"No, but I found that picture in your dresser drawer," I said pointing at her lap.

"Why were you searching my drawers Forster?"

"First of all I wasn't searching. I'm secure person. I was getting you a pair of socks. I saw pictures and I just picked them up. I didn't think anything would be wrong with looking at pictures of my girl." I said and she glanced down at the picture without examining it. "Later for all that! Did you fuck with Boobie before?" I asked again. She hesitated which made me antsy. I glared at her nervously hoping for the best but expecting the worse.

"Are you sure you want the truth?" Dawn asked. For the first time I noticed she was giving me a pitiful look.

"Do I look like I'm clowning?" I asked getting angry.

"Alright, Boobie and I used to be together. I knew Lala is his wifey, but we started out as just friends. At first I'd see him and we talked about you and Cash. Then one thing led to another and he started taking me out," she said. I felt my blood boiling as if my head was about to explode. I seethed and bit my trembling lips. "So, you were in love with him?" I asked and really feared the answer.

"Not really," she responded.

I whistled a sigh of relief.

"What's not really?" I asked breathing easier.

"I really don't feel like going through the third degree with you, Forster." The pitiful expression reappeared on her face. She hugged me while looking closely at the photo.

"Listen Forster, I'm going to tell you about it."

"Nah, nah it's all good. I don't really wanna know all about you and him."

"Okay, but I want to keep it real. Listen to me very well, Forster. I will not repeat this again. He and I became really close. Boobie thinks he could buy everything. So for a minute, I played along with his game. I started using him for money. He would give me like six...up to eight hundred dollars a week for just being his friend. I knew he liked me so I let him take me out and he'd spend lavishly on me. Boobie thought his money would impress me. He thought he could buy me and change me into a gangsta princess. That's what he wanted. I wasn't for sale. The rest is pretty much history. I know how you men are. You'll probably confront him. So I'll tell you now. I aborted his child. That was the end of him and I. Shortly after that we made a pact that neither one of us would talk about what happened, especially to you. I knew how you felt about me, even though at the time we weren't a couple."

Dawn's explanation left me numb. It kept rewinding in my head like a useless jingle. I sat staring straight ahead trying to find loopholes for the anger I felt.

"Why didn't you say anything when I introduced you two?" I finally asked.

"Before you had introduced us, Boobie called my house. He was like 'you gonna fuck with my man, because I cut you off?' I told him you and I was bound to be together way before him. Then he started threatening me."

"Hold up, he did what?"

"It's nothing..."

"Nothing? Boobie's straight gangsta, he got a thug mentality. Baby, tell me please what kinda threats he made."

"What do you mean, thug mentality?"

"I'm saying if he tells you he gonna hurt you, he means it," I said.

"He was teling me that I should slap the shit out of you when I see you. I'm trifling and he was going to tell you everything. He wanted to mess up whatever you and I have. I knew deep down inside Boobie wanted to work things out with me. I just didn't want to be bothered anymore with him, that's all."

"I don't know how to feel right now," I said sounding more depressed than I intended. I knew my anger was boiling over. I had put her on a pedestal and she fell off.

"Forster, I wasn't with you. I hadn't seen you in all these years," Dawn said and tried to get closer to me. I pulled away.

"That's not the point. My man, who's like my big brother, was hitting you on a regular, girl. How am I supposed to feel Dawn?" I asked in resignation.

"He was before you Forster. I wouldn't take him back before. Now I'm having a relationship with you. We have a special chemistry, a totally different vibe."

"You were having unprotected sex. He shared everything; all your sex faces, the sounds you make, every inch of your sexy body. I'm having difficulty digesting it. Look, I know Boobie, he's real slick. Back then he used to always ask me on different occasions. 'Did I see you? Why I ain't messing with you?' I used to tell him that timing wasn't right. I would've loved to make you my girl. So I kept telling him I was going to make my move when I was ready to marry you. All that time he was hitting you." I spilled my guts and through the corner of my teary eyes I could see Dawn's tears.

"He wasn't sure of us. He kept asking me. 'Did you see Forster?' 'How's Forster?' Just to see if I was dealing with you. He would play mind-games. I thought nothing of it until now. For what this worth, Forster I've never felt this way for any other man. I shared moments with you that I never shared with anyone. Sexually, the things we've done, trust me. I haven't done with anyone else. I never went down on Boobie..."

"Okay, alright, you don't have to get graphic. For real, Dawn spare me the details." I said staring blankly. I need time to recover. It had been a low blow. "This happened before me, I understand. Stil, pretending not to know each other is some foul shit. I'm not going into that. Just don't try and play me while we're together. If you find your heart going another route, to different men. Let me know now because I don't

have time for games. I have too much on my plate for me to be worrying about anyone cheating on me. Am I clear?" I asked.

"Loud and clear, honey."

Dawn jumped over to my side of the car kissing me. I was not aware how much of a relief she felt until her tears began gushing.

"All right, since that's in the open I should tell you about your girl." I started without really knowing why. I watched as Dawn's eyes immediately widened with anticipation. "She's come onto me several times. Why? I don't know. Maybe because she knew you used to be with Boobie," I said.

"Kee never really knew I was messing with Boobie, not to any extent." Dawn said shaking her head. "I knew that bitch was shady. Every time a guy would try and talk to me, Kee always try to be in the mix. Several male friends have mentioned that Kee came on to them. I mean I don't know, but I'm not surprised. I'll let this one slide. But if that bitch say or try anything else with you, please let me know."

"Fo' sure, shortie. Now can we continue on with our day?"

"Long as everything is out our system. Then let's roll out."

We rode confidently to City Island. Our next problem was which of our favorite seafood restaurants we were feeling.

LOST IN LUV

Keya's pregnancy had reached full term. She declined a sonogram. Her mother and Dawn organized a baby shower. Pastel colors filled the house. Keya received lots of vital. Te'rena was six years old and in first grade. Friends and acquaintances made the shower a success. I was there with my sister, Tasha who moved back to our parents' home.

As expected, Cash skipped the affair. I had warned him that Keya was not trying to see him. The question of who the baby's father was lingered in the air like barbecue smoke at cookouts. It had the guests sniffing for information. Keya told Dawn the first prize would be decided between Cash and Smokey.

Smokey was doing five years on a ten-year bid Upstate. His incarceration had nothing to do with Mizo's murder. He was tried as a kingpin drug-dealer. Word on the street was that Mizo's crew had a bullet for anyone who snitched. Smokey couldn't keep his hands out of the illegal pot. His mother warned him to stick with the barbershop and he had planned to open another. Smokey wanted fast money and wound up taking a loss. Now he was facing the possibility of losing the barbershop and with his sisters away at college, his house was not being properly maintained. Keya dropped him a line every now and then but never mentioned anything about her pregnancy. He knew nothing of his chances to be her baby's father.

Dawn was acting as a midwife to Keya and would accompany her throughout the birthing process. Te'rena would stay home with her grandmother.

"Forster, I'm going to have to borrow your car today, okay?" Dawn requested.

I had spent quality time giving refresher driving lessons to Dawn. We were able to relight the flame that the Boobie situation had dampened. Now, she was an accomplished licensed driver who wanted to drive everywhere.

"Drop me off at work first. I'm going in late," I said.

"My mother and I are going shopping at the malls in Jersey. I took today off to chill with her." Dawn explained with a kiss.

"Whatever honey, drop me off at work. You don't even have to pick me up." I said. She picked her mother up first then she dropped me off in midtown Manhattan at the fancy hotel where I am the head chef. We kissed and Dawn and her mother were off through the Lincoln Tunnel.

"Mother I think I made the right choice, Forster is so loving and sweet." Dawn exclaimed.

"Ah...Dawn honey, your father and I've been meaning to talk about you moving in with Forster. I guess now is a good time for you to hear my side. It's okay if you want to be with Forster, but you know how your father and I are. We don't believe in sex before marriage. You don't live by that rule. As far as you just living with him, well honey, we're just not ready for that. I definitely taught you better. Not that I'm saying that there's something wrong with Forster. It's just that, honey. I raised you in the church."

"Mommy, don't I still attend church ma? I'm not sure if I'm ready to get married even if Forster does ask me."

"Maybe you should move back in with us until you are, you know?"

"Mommy, you and dad raised me well. And when judgment day comes, neither of you have to answer for me. I'll answer to God myself. I moved in with Forster, but I haven't lost my faith. I love you and dad, and respect your wishes. Nothing will change that. Don't think of it as me moving in with him, it's more like I enjoy being with him and we're best friends, that's why we spend a lot of time together. We enjoy each other's company."

"Dawn, we love you too. You'll forever be our baby. All I'm saying is just be very careful in all that you're doing. Now, I've said my piece. Let's enjoy the rest of our day shopping. And be sure to tell Forster, thanks for lending us the car."

"I will, mother," Dawn said. Gone was the exuberance of her tone. Her mother's word's left her deep in thoughts.

Back on the job, I was busy busting my chops preparing something special for a group of businessmen from New Orleans. The owner of the hotel was trying to impress and he was definitely stressing. I supervised, participated and made an impressive six course meal that kept the waiters bringing out the most exquisite dishes for all the guests. I glimpsed the owner's proud face nodding as all the guests ate heartily, much to his success.

He came in the kitchen, thanked me and asked me to show my face. I walked out to the thunderous applause of everyone in the restaurant. "Bravo!" They shouted. I felt important from the recognition.

I looked around at all the smiles from the customers and was surprised when I saw my mother, father and my sister looking on proudly. They were basking in the triumph of my moment. It was a moment I'll never forget for as long as I live. I couldn't have been happier. I rushed over to their table and greeted them. I got a friend of mine who was a waiter, to treat them well. I gave my mother and sister a kiss on their cheeks then hugged dad.

"May I take y'all order," the waiter politely asked. My mother ordered the lemon pepper chicken over buttered angel hair pasta. Tasha had pork chops with applesauce. My father ordered pot roast with mash potatoes sans gravy. He claimed to be watching his diet. They all laughed.

"The tab is on me," I said winking and pouring a glass of complementary wine for them. "Enjoy. And I'll have someone come over later to make sure everything is okay." I said then returned to the kitchen. After that, I took a ten-minute break and called Dawn. I couldn't wait to tell her about the great surprise I had just received. She answered laughing.

"Who has my baby cracking up?" I asked.

"My mom is so funny. How's work going, suga?" She asked.

"Guess what?"

"What?"

"My whole family's here." I announced unable to hide the happiness I was feeling.

"All of them? Your mother, dad and Tasha?"

"Yes babe, they surprised me. I just made ten freestyle dishes for some businessmen from New Orleans. I came out the kitchen, people were clapping and there was my family, all of them."

"It must have felt real good seeing them."

"What? It felt great seeing them all together. I just wanted to share that with one of the most important people in my life."

"Baby, that was sweet."

"Not as sweet as you being my wife," I said and heard Dawn giggling. "Seriously, will you marry me?"

"What?"

"I'm asking, if you'll marry me?" I repeated.

"Yes. Forster I...will," she answered. Dawn did not hear me and asked. "Forster?"

"Sorry, I was just praying you wouldn't say no."

"I will talk to you when I see you about what my mother and I talked about."

"Alright, let me go back to work too. I love you."

"Love you too, Forst."

Dawn was excited and screamed hysterically at her mother. "Mommy, Forster asked me to marry him." She kicked her feet going crazy. "And we were just talking about marriage, right mommy?"

"Well...ah, not exactly," Mrs. Jones stuttered. She was excited too.

"Mother, mother what am I gonna do?"

"Call daddy." Her mother replied and Dawn quickly dialed her father. Her mother took the phone to tell him herself. Dawn didn't care she was still thinking about Forster's proposal. Mr. Jones was home. Her mother told him to call Dawn's cell phone because she had some good news to share with him. Dawn and her mother proceeded to the mall laughing and talking about Dawn's future.

"Yo Cash, answer ya damn phone." I screamed on his answering machine.

"Yeah man, what you want?" Cash asked sounding as if he had just awoke.

"Oh, that's how you gonna talk to your boy?" I asked hardly able to conceal my excitement.

"C'mon, this ain't your girl, homey."

"Ahight, here goes. I asked Dawn to marry me." I waited for his reaction.

"So what she said?"

"Man, what you think? Hell she said yes, my man."

"Forst, you and Dawn doing y'all thing, huh?" Cash asked.

"We trying homey. I know we're both in our early twenties. But you know it feels right. Dawn's straight wifey material, you feel me?"

"Forst, member that time we met those two freaks in Vegas?" Cash asked.

"Yeah nigga and what?"

"I remembered that you wanted to marry them too."

"You stupid for even bringing that up. What happened there, is gonna stay there." I laughed.

"Yeah, that white chick was freaky on the real. But the black one was the bomb-diggie."

"Truthfully, neither one of them was wifey material. I need a woman with higher standards. You feel me?"

"I'm straight gangsta. Give me a sista, a bottle of sump'n and it's on. I don't need no independent-ass bitch. The ones who be talking all that yang, saying shit like you can't offer 'em nothing. I be too busy lying to these hos'. Uh, I don't care. I'll say anything to get up in them panties. After a minute, hos' be looking at the kid like I'm

bad news." Cash laughed.

"You's crazy fool," I said laughing. I knew Cash was being real.

"What about the time we ran a train on that shortie from BK?"

"Yo, you wildin', Cash. No, you didn't bring that tramp up. What was it she said? Wait, wait, I got it. 'I think both of you might be my baby daddy'," I said. Cash started laughing and I joined him.

"That trick was so drunk, she forgot we used rubbers. You did get up in that strapped, right Forst?"

"Yeah, Cash. Were you strapped and I ain't talking 'bout no gat?"

"I was. Shit, I stretched two rubbers over my dome, kid." We laughed at the memories. I was ready to bury them along with my past ways.

"We made good times out of the badness in our surroundings."

"You right, man. If it's your time to settle down then, I'm all for that. One of us got to be on the straight and narrow. I'm feeling all emotional and shit?"

"Don't tell me you a sucker for love now, Cash?"

"Nah, that's your role, Forst. But on the real though, my eyes are sad. You better not mention this to no one, not even your wifey!" Cash said with a chuckle.

"Your secret's safe with me." I chuckled. "On the real, Cash thanks for listening. You my brother from another mother."

"We've known each other for how many years? There's no way I won't hear you out. Even if I can't talk you outta doing it, love is love," Cash said.

"Not to cut you off or nothing, but what's up with Keya's baby? Do you think it's yours?"

"Now, here you go fucking up the moment. I don't know. When the little man comes then we'll ask him and we'll know, ahight?"

"You're sounding cool about this. Let me find out it's yours."

"Life is too short for me to worry 'bout a lil' man coming."

"I hear you. You need to at least talk to Keya."

"Okay, this is where the conversation ends," Cash said in a serious tone.

"Whatever man, later." The conversation ended with peace. I had gotten so excited, I felt like leaving work. Man, I was feeling good about having a fiancé and looking forward to marrying the person I love. I was giving her a beautiful ring. I dialed Tasha. I was surprised when my mother answered. "Hey mom, it's me. Is Tasha there?"

"What's wrong baby? You sound like you running or sump'n? I told everyone at the church that you're a real sharp cook and they all wanna…"

"Mommy, listen up, I asked Dawn to marry me." Before I could finish my mother shouted with joy to my father and other guests in her home.

"I need Tasha to help me pick out a ring before Dawn and her mother get back."

"Where are they now?"

"They're in a shopping mall in Jersey," I said quickly.

"Where are you?"

"Me? I'm about to leave work, mom." I answered.

"Why don't you come straight over here?"

Minutes later I was headed up to the Boogie Down. My thoughts raced as fast as my heartbeat. My palms had been dirty, now they were just wet. I was determined not to mess anything up. Would I be able to provide for her in this new life? whirled in my mind. I wiped sweat from my brow. The answer had to be: To the best of my ability. "Don't trip", I whispered to myself.

A case of nerves was getting the best of me. I wanted to scream and shout like I had won lotto. I felt like I had crossed over into paradise. I was aware of riding home in a yellow cab, kicking up city smog. Yet, the highway looked cleaner, the clouds whiter and the air smelled great.

I checked the cell thinking, things were getting to my head. We had not even set the wedding date. Slowly, I rolled to the cab music. It was classical and I didn't dig it, but didn't mind. Today, everything was fine. I sat back and conducted my invisible orchestra as the cabbie smiled and stepped on the gas. Wow, soon I'll be a married man. I have to stop acting the fool.

The flashing red light seized my attention. I saw the incoming call. I had been so caught-up, I didn't hear the ringing. It could be my future wife I thought and answered the call with a seductive greeting.

"Hello."

"Whut up with you," a male voice put me on notice.

"Who this?" I answered.

"It's me Boobie. Whut up punk?"

"Nothing much," I said and immediately the knots returned to my stomach.

123

My mind dipped back to the snapshots. I felt uneasy.

"I'm on the highway. I'll call you back," I said not wanting to speak.

I wanted to confront him face to face about the issue, not while I was in a taxi. His call had me boiling. I got my baby now. I shouldn't be bugging. I needed a drink to slow me down.

A few minutes later, I had the cab drop me at the liquor store. I paid the tab, went in and copped a pint of Henney. I walked to the corner store, downing the bottle on my trip there. I bought some Winter Fresh and a beer. Then I walked a couple of blocks, chewing, the great day at work, the proposal and Boobie's annoying phone call. Before I knew it, I was standing outside the door of my parents' house. I threw the rest of the beer away and unlocked the door with keys I had since junior high. I entered confidently and was greeted open-armed by dad.

"I'm proud of you my son." He embraced me while pumping my hand.

"That means a lot dad, thanks," I said my voice cracking.

"My little brother ain't little no more." Tasha kissed and hugged me until mother took over. She was wearing a big smile with tears welling in her eyes.

"Come here my baby boy, I'm glad you chose Dawn. You two have enough time to plan and fulfill all your dreams. I am truly proud of both of you. And you know momma is going to be decked out at the wedding, right?" She said cupping my emotional face with both her hands. "Okay, close your eyes," she demanded. I did as requested. I could hear footsteps. Then I heard my mother's voice. "Open your eyes." I did and saw a red velvet ring box in mother's hands.

"Mommy...ah... what's this?" I asked nervous and feeling new sweat building.

"Go ahead and open it Forster." She answered. I opened it delicately as if it was made of glass. My eyes lit up immediately when I saw a marquise diamond ring with twin rocks on each side.

"Now that's a four carat rock!" Dad shouted. I was dumbfounded. I heard everyone shouting congratulations and then listened as my mother spoke.

"This is for the hard times I've given this family. And it is also for you and Dawn to share the great moments of this family future." I was moved to tears.

"I'm so... Mom, I can't believe...I didn't know you were planning all this."

"I gave your mother that ring before you or your sister was even thought of. I knew that I had a woman who would be by my side through thick and thin. Even though time to time she'd whip my butt." My father's candor had everyone laughing.

"That's not funny. We aren't living in the past," mother said in mock defense.

"I know baby. But we can laugh at those things now," father said. Tasha and I continued laughing.

"Mommy, you and Daddy deserve much more. I love all of you. Now see what y'all did to this thug?" I was joking.

"Listen, why don't you bring Dawn over here later so we could congratulate her too," father suggested.

"I surely will. Hate to leave so soon. But I have to go home and prepare a romantic setting." I said with a wink then hugged everyone. After reassuring all that I'd return with my fiancé, I was out. "Dad lemme hold your car," I said.

"On this occasion, my car, my house, anything you want is yours." He threw me the keys without the usual lecture and didn't even ask to smell my breath.

"Thanks dad." My dad was happy. Before I got in the car, I heard my name.

"Hey Forster."

I turned and saw Te'rena and Keya standing on the other side of the street. A big smile crossed my face. I ran over to where they stood and picked up Te'rena and kissed her on the cheek.

"Hi Te'rena. Hey Keya, what's good?" I greeted.

"Nothing much, just trying to walk this baby down. I am well overdue. And Te'rena drives me crazy from sun up to sun down," she laughed.

"I heard that."

"Where's Dawn? I called her cell and her voice mail came right on," Keya said.

"Dawn and her mom went to some mall in Jersey and you can't get no signal inside." I responded. "By the way, I proposed to your girl today." I said trying to keep an even keel. This proved impossible with a smile spreading wide as a mile.

"Stop playing. Are you serious?" She asked. Her face glowed.

"Yes I am and she said yes." I said getting louder. "Can you keep a secret?"

"Yeah, hell yeah, of course I can. What is it?"

"Look at this." I said and opened the ring box.

"Oh this ring looks expensive."

Keya shouted almost grabbing the box from my hand. "Damn how's DJ gonna

keep this ring on her finger?"

"My mom just gave it to me. Dawn doesn't know I have it. I have a great idea," I said looking at my watch. "It is three-fifty. What are you doing around six pm?"

"Nothing. Why?"

"Meet me in the park at six sharp. I have a good idea," I said and kissed Te'rena goodbye.

Walking away, I was on the phone and asked Dawn how everything was going at the mall. I was surprised to learn that they were already on their way back to the city.

"Dawn I want to give you a lil' sump'n, sump'n," I said.

I overheard Dawn telling her mother that I had a surprise. Time was of the essence. I got off the phone and stopped briefly at the florist. I bought several dozens of my favorite colored roses and had a couple dozen delivered to her office on different days of the week. Next stop was the liquor store. Then I made it home with the quickness. I checked to make sure everything was neat. I pulled out couple bottles of Moet and strawberries. I placed a bouquet here and there and in the bedroom, pink, red and white rose petals littered the floor and the bed. After setting up my favorite romantic songs from Anita Baker to Rome, I ordered her favorite Italian food, shrimp with freshly made tomato sauce, mozzarella cheese and linguini noodles.

I took a quick shower, dressed and while sipping a beer, the food was delivered. I paid, set the food neatly on the dinner table then called Cash to let him know what time to meet me at the Magenta Courts. I knew Cash was on CP time so I told him five pm sharp. That meant Cash would arrive at six pm. My mind relaxed as everything seemed to be going according to plan. I drove slowly thinking about all bases and met Dawn in front of her mother's house. They both hugged me.

"I wish you two the best of all the best," Mrs. Jones said. Dawn beamed.

"Sorry I've got to steal my fiancé away so soon. It's just I have so much planned for her right now."

"No explanation necessary, young man. Please, by all means take her. We had a great time at the mall," Mrs. Jones said laughing.

"Mommy thanks. I had a great time too," Dawn said and gave her mother a kiss. "But don't think you're gonna get rid of me that easy." Dawn playfully cautioned. I held her hand and escorted her to the car.

"Isn't this your father's car?" She asked.

"Yep," I answered and opened the door for her. Inside, I gave her a long kiss.

"Where did all of this come from?" Dawn asked when I released her.

"I wanted this since the first time I was with you. I told you that."

"You did. So what is up with...?" Dawn asked and I sealed her lips with another kiss.

"Patience," I said checking the time. We were running a little behind schedule, but that was good because I was with the main attraction. Five minutes after six we arrived. The sun hadn't completely gone down so it would still be romantic. I rushed from the car and opened the door for Dawn.

"Why are we going to the Courts?" She asked. I smiled because she really seemed concerned.

"You'll see. Just walk with me, honey." I held her hand tightly. This had to be love. I walked confidently into Magenta and saw Keya on one end of a bench. The scowl on Cash's grill registered he was not having a great time. He sat on the other end. "You two get y'all asses over here, now." I huffed as I stood in the middle. I glanced both ways to see that both immediately made their way to meet Dawn and I at center court. "Everyone already knows that I proposed to Dawn today. You're our closest friends. Cash, you're like my brother and Keya, although you and Dawn had y'all differences I know that you're rooting for each other. I'm about to share a moment in my life that I probably wouldn't share with anyone else other than Mrs. Forster Brown to be."

Cash nodded and had a slight crooked smile on his face. I knew the sight of Keya turned his stomach. Cash kept his cool. He damn sure wasn't about to spoil it for his boy. Keya was genuinely happy for us. On the low, I caught her throwing short glimpses in Cash's direction. He was decked out fly in dark Gucci suit with matching gators. She was bold in a red tight dress and smiled at everyone easily. Keya never let Cash know how she really felt.

"All right let's go," she clapped and yelled.

"Here it goes. In front of my friends, my first family, I propose to you Dawn Jones." I said kneeling on one knee. Keya was so overcome, she began to cry. Cash watched like an eagle. Dawn's tears came rolling down. "Dawn, will you take me to be your future husband?" I asked. Dawn nodded her head and paused.

"Yes," she said smiling and crying at the same time.

Dawn was rubbing her hands together when I pulled out the diamond ring. I could see her smile radiating from the glimmer of the huge rock. Cash's eyes widened.

"Wow!" Dawn beamed as I placed the ring on her finger. She couldn't believe it was a perfect fit. She kissed me so hard I thought her teeth would cut into my bottom lip. We had a hug fest and even Cash and Keya joined.

"Before we all leave, I have something for my future husband." Dawn announced then turned to me. "Forster I appreciate you picking me to spend the rest of your life with you. I want to give you this gift. I want you to accept this bracelet as a token of my love and acceptance to your proposal. This is from my heart and to assure you this ring you put on my finger is a circle of life for us," Dawn said kissing me again.

The gift was a custom designed diamond bracelet that fit my wrist perfectly. The design was one of branches twisted in a white gold frame and laced with diamonds. Dawn sure had good taste and it didn't hurt that she had a fat bank account.

"Let's celebrate," Cash suggested as he hugged me.

"For now, this is where it has to end my friend. I have to shoot over to my parents' house then take my princess home," I said then grabbing Dawn around her waist.

"I'm glad to see we're all back here again at Magenta," Dawn said.

"Yeah I'm glad too," Cash said looking at Keya. She tried to play it off but she was blushing.

"Y'all remember when we first met and the Jamaicans had that shoot out?" I asked.

"Yeah you two bitched up," Cash said laughing and gazed at Keya to confirm his story.

"Now it's like that?" Dawn asked looking at Keya and Cash.

"You two are crazy. That's exactly what this is all about," I said jumping in the conversation.

"I miss those days. Some nights the breeze is just right and you can sit on the stoop all night long. That's when I remember I used to sit in the park, wearing my boyfriend's jacket," Dawn said while in my arms.

"I remember that. We used to have our face painted on our leather jackets." I added.

"And you two were always playing the kissing game." Dawn interrupted referring to Cash and Keya.

"I miss those days. Especially before I had my daughter not that I'm not appreciative of her. But y'all know what I mean," Keya said reflectively.

"Speaking of your daughter what's up with this baby?" I asked. Dawn and I turned to Cash.

"What the hell are you two looking at?" He asked.

"I mean are you going to step up to the plate if the baby's yours or what?" I asked.

"Forst, you don't have to put me on the spot, ahight?" Cash replied.

"Why not? She's here and so are we," Dawn said.

"Y'all can go ahead with all of that. I'm chillin'. Plus Keya have a mouth of her own and she knows where I rest when her baby is out," Cash said nonchalantly.

"Thanks but I don't need no one to speak for me," Keya replied.

"Well let's make a toast. We can all drink except for you Keya." Cash laughed, removed the backpack from his back and pulled out a bottle of Moet with four plastic champagne glasses.

"Ah shit..." Dawn said.

"Gangsta style. Feel me?" Cash smiled with the bottle in his hand.

"Why don't I get a glass?" Keya asked.

"Oh, my bad, Kee. Here's your apple juice," Cash said smiling and handing Keya a small bottle of apple juice.

"Oh, good looking out." She smiled digging what Cash did.

"Put them up," Cash interrupted the small talk amongst us when he raised his glass.

"All the best to our friendship and y'alls' future. To Keya and her babies, much, much success. Forst, you my man one hundred grand, together we'll always stand. Here's to the dime piece and most dedicated woman I've met so far. I don't have to tell you, but I'll say it; you're a lucky man. And last but not least here's to the most important place that keeps us together: The good ol' Boogie Down."

We all laughed, smiled and continued drinking, keeping watch for the police. We finished the bottle of champagne out in the park. Keya didn't toast but she smiled at everything Cash said. I was committed to my queen. Cash put the empty Moet bottle in

his backpack along with the plastic champagne glasses. The four of us reminisced while sitting on the bench. Cash sat next to Keya and I sat next to my fiancé.

"So baby I guess this means I should bring all my things to your crib huh?" Dawn asked.

"You mean you should bring all your stuff to our crib."

I smiled, held her hand and felt genuine happiness coursing through my blood.

"We haven't discussed our living arrangements. What about splitting the bills?"

"You don't have to worry about that right now. Just save your chips till we reach that bridge, aight?" I said and kissed her.

"Alright lovers it's curtain time. Are we ready to go?" Keya asked.

Cash looked at Dawn and me. We nodded. Then the four of us hugged and headed to the cars.

"Are we taking Keya home?" Dawn asked. There was a pregnant pause.

"Nah, I'll take her," Cash said. That brought a smile to Keya's lips.

"Call me later, DJ. We gotta a lot to talk about, girl," Keya said. Then hugged Dawn and me.

"Holla atcha boy," Cash said, gave me a pound and we hugged.

I jetted over to Dawn's parents and got my car, then hurried to see my parents for a hot minute. Dawn drove my car and I returned my father's. We went inside so my family could see their future daughter-in-law. Dawn was almost out on her feet from all the bubbly. She wasn't a drinker and the few glasses made her a woozy. Dawn playfully rubbed my crotch while I attempted to open the door to my parents' home.

"Save that for home. You're really gonna get every bit of it."

Dawn had a pretentious smile on her face. Tasha met us giggling at the door.

"Mommy, here they are," she announced and hugged Dawn.

"Bring her back here." My parents shouted from the back of the house. I led the way to the living room. Dawn followed while chatting with Tasha.

"Hi beautiful," Dad said hugging and kissing Dawn. Her pretty smile was glimmering.

"Come on over here and sit Dawn." Mother requested and gave Dawn a hug.

"How're you feeling about all of this, Dawn?" She asked the moment Dawn sat.

"I am so overwhelmed. I love your son, Mrs. Brown. He's been wonderful to me," Dawn said looking up at me. I winked, she smiled and blushed.

"I raised him right." Mother said with a smile.

"Planned a date yet?" Dad asked. Again Dawn looked at me.

"Baby, don't look at me. They asked you the question," I said.

"I'm hoping this time next year." Dawn replied nodding.

"Give us enough time to help plan a big wedding," Tasha said.

"I'm gonna need all the help in the world. And besides I don't have a sister, so I'm looking forward to us coming closer," Dawn said.

"Mom, dad I hate to rush off with y'all future daughter-n-law, but we both have to get up in the morning. Don't worry I'll bring her back again," I said jokingly. Tasha hit me playfully on the arm.

"Don't worry Dawn I'll be stealing you away from him soon." Tasha joked.

"I'd like that, Tasha." Dawn smiled.

We left my parents and headed home. Dawn had one more surprise coming. I had straightened up and her favorite food was already there. When she saw the rose petals and strawberries she swooned in my arms. Running around had sapped our energy. We ate a small portion of our food and dessert was up to Dawn.

I laid her down, opened a bottle of whipped cream and turned her body parts into a face. Her thirty-six C size breasts were covered with whipped cream. Her belly button was also filled up. Her sweet vagina had whipped cream on it too. I dimmed the lights and placed a silk scarf around her eyes and bound her hands above her head onto the headboard of the cherry wood bed frame. Dawn was all giggles. I always surprised her with different sexual fantasies. I began licking, sucking and massaging her soft brown skin. I was fully erect. My bulging hardness strained against my underpants. The whipped cream slowly vanished. Her nipples were firm and one by one, I nibbled on them until her juices flowed and I heard her softly moaning.

"Ahh...Oh yeah, Forster. Ooh yeah my future husband. Ooh yeah you do it well."

I held myself back from actually penetrating her. She squirmed like a snake in a sack. Slowly, I made my way down to her cookies. Dawn moaned. Her hands guided my lips to her erogenous zone.

Without any warning I spread her legs then sucked and licked her clit. She tossed her head side to side. She was helpless to the onslaught of my tongue probing between her legs. Dawn screamed for release.

"This is what you like?"

"Yeah baby, you're doing it so right. Oooh God! Don't stop. Keep it there. Keep it right there, Forster. Oh, gosh. My, you're my baby, yeah, yeah. Oooh you know that's my spot, baby."

"When daddy's finished with his dessert are you going to suck on this chocolate bar?" I asked. Dawn moaned but could not answer intelligibly. Her body shuddered while she climaxed.

"Yes, yes daddy. Please put it in me. Then take it out and come in my mouth." Dawn whispered throatily.

I loosened her bondage. Dawn reacted like there was a fire inside her. Shyness, classy ways, of the educated young black female, went out the window. I knew she'd be hungry and she attacked me ravenously. I loved that about her. Dawn had opened up more and more sexually with me. Her mouth sucked and her teeth nibbled and her tongue licked me to ecstasy. I became so hard I thought I'd explode in her mouth. Then I grabbed her, roughly turned her to face me and pounded her cookies. She screamed so loudly I thought she'd wake up the neighbors. I kissed and fondled her breasts until she climaxed. Then I rolled her over and gave it to her doggy-style. After the explosion, I wore the biggest smile. I was the man, I thought as I felt an earth shattering orgasm building inside me.

"Aaahhgggadd!" I screamed as I honored my future wife's request of skeeting all over her pretty round shaped ass, her hair and face. I was on my knees as she turned and sucked me dry. "Oh, oh, oh, yeah sugar," I said and fell exhausted next to her.

We were spent and fell asleep spooning, my left hand in her right hand.

The house phone rang at approximately eight fifteen am. I didn't even bother to get it. Dawn had already left for work. She never played when it came to her job. A few minutes after I heard the phone, I got up to use the bathroom with a morning hard-on.

"Damn, at least a sista could hit a brother off again before she ran off to work," I said while taking a piss.

I stood in front of the full-length mirror admiring myself then brushed my teeth. While going through my daily cleaning routine, I thought of job security. Since I was going to get married I had to make sure that I had a solid foundation in the restaurant business. I had to remain extra clean. I quickly got dressed, drank some orange juice and proceeded to the bedroom where I sat retrieving messages. The first message was my boss informing me of a presentation next month in Philadelphia. I smiled about that and decided to save the message. The machine continued on.

"I'm at Einstein Hospital with Kee. It's going down for real. Please get here quickly."

I immediately called and told Dawn then headed straight to the hospital. At the hospital I ran into Mrs. Jordan and a few friends of Keya. Cash stood nervously and alone in a corner. I chuckled as I made my way over.

"I need a camera. Nothing ever had you this shook." I laughed.

"Now is not the time to be messing with me. I didn't know what we did wrong."

"Man, what are you talking about?"

"We was having sex and I think her water broke, or sump'n."

"Cheer up, my man." I responded jokingly. Everyone milled around in the waiting area while Keya went in the delivery room. "Yo dog who's in there with Keya?"

"Nobody, Forst."

"So get your ass up and go in there with her. Whether that's your baby or not, you should be in there with that girl. You was bumping her and made that baby's head come out. The least you can do is support her a little," I said offering encouragement.

"You right dog. You coming with me?"

"Hell no, negro. I don't want to see all that and besides Dawn will flip"

"Ahight, I'm going in. Be back with good news," Cash said opening the door and disappearing inside.

Delivery rooms are busy terrifying places, bustling with doctors and nurses. Impatient mothers straddled with pain, waiting for relief. When Cash walked in, he saw the doctor, assistants and nurses around Keya. Her legs were wide open with the aid of two metal stirrups. She was sweaty and looked exhausted. Everyone turned around when he entered. Keya was shocked. Tears were rolling down her face and she was bawling loudly.

"Oh please God, help me. Cash, help me. Oh God, it hurts soo bad."

"Are you the father of this baby?" An assistant asked.

"Yes I am," Cash answered.

Cash was instructed to put on the green hospital pants and shirt along with the hat and mask. He came to Keya's side and wiped her forehead and watched as she was instructed to push the baby out. Cash whispered in her ear to help her get the pain off her mind.

"We're almost there," the doctor reassured them. Her contractions were coming much faster. The doctor gave the thumbs up as Keya cried louder. "Keep pushing, the baby is coming." The doctor called his nurse over and spoke quietly to her. She hurried away then he addressed Keya and Cash. "We're having minor complications and I'll have to perform an episiotomy," the doctor said. "The circumference of the baby's..." he started. He saw the look of confusion on our faces and the doctor broke it down in layman's term. "The baby's head is too large and there seems to be problems... I'm going to have to operate," he said.

"Do it, damn it. The longer you stand there explaining is the agh..." Keya interrupted.

"Come on Kee you can do it. Push harder baby so our son can come out," Cash said. Keya glared at him and let her rage go.

"I hate you so much right now, Cash baby, huh?"

Keya screamed while the doctor cut her to help the baby's head exit the cervix. The local anesthesia helped. Keya wanted her baby out and the ordeal to be over.

"Oh doctor, doctor tell me how much longer...agh..ah... I have to do this? I can't do it no more." She cried.

"Stay with it, Kee. You doing good, baby girl," Cash said.

"I can't... I can't do this..." Keya screamed blowing air like a train.

"Here it comes." The nurse announced. The doctor moved into receiving position.

"Keya, keep breathing. I need you to help me by giving one last, good push. Ah that's good. Here comes the baby," the doctor shouted excitedly.

Keya pushed while Cash anxiously looked down at the baby's head coming out. His scowl stayed on his grill when he saw the shoulders. "It's a boy," the doctor yelled out. Sweat rolled off Cash's excited face. Tears were evident on his face. The baby had a bluish color to it with globs of body waste on him.

Yuck, Cash thought, holding back from saying it out loud. The doctor and assistant rushed the baby over to the infant bed where they clean him up. A brief moment of silence swept the room Keya and Cash stared in the direction of the baby.

"My little man is a soldier. He ain't even crying." Cash noted while holding Keya's hand. Two other doctors burst into the room and without any hesitation they rushed over to the baby. Keya and Cash became suspicious on what the hell was going on. "Hello. What is going on? The parents are right here." Cash interrupted.

The doctor assisting Keya walked back to Keya and Cash while the other doctors and assistants worked on the baby. "Keya I'm so sorry. We tried everything possible to save him. At first it seemed as if it would be a routine delivery but was already stillborn. I'm so sorry," the doctor said taking off his mask.

With tears, Keya looked up at Cash. She wasn't sure what the doctor had said. Cash leaned over her and held her tight.

"What happened, Cash? What is he trying to say? Doc is you saying my baby is dead? Tell me it's not true. Tell me that ain't what just came outta this doctor's mouth, Cash? Tell me my fucking baby ain't dead! Please, oh please someone tell me my baby is alive. Why me, Lord? Why me? No-o-o-o..." Keya yelled out uncontrollably. Cash couldn't help but cry along with her. Besides his mother passing away this was the saddest moment in his life. "What did I do so wrong?" Keya kept repeating. "Please, please." Keya desperately pleaded. "Why...? Cash, please make 'em to do something they're wasting time." She wept.

Cash was speechless. He tried hard to make believe that this was really not happening. The doctor brought the baby over to Keya and Cash. Cash was sobbing so bad tears clung to his hospital robe. Keya was lying down helpless. The baby looked just like Cash. His features were strong for a newborn. There was no resemblance of Keya on his little face. The baby boy did not have color, his skin was ashy. Keya cried so hard she didn't realize the doctor had sutured her vagina.

"We'll need blood for a HIV testing. Let's get samples stat."

The nurses got busy and Keya was speechless and exhausted. All the hard times and situations she had faced could not compare to this. Keya and Cash were not prepared for this. The doctors and all assistants left the room so Keya and Cash could be alone with the baby boy. Cash had flashes of many images in his head. He asked God

for forgiveness in everything he did. If this was paying him back for all the cruel things he did in his past, he was sorry. Whether the baby looked like him or not, was the last thing on Cash's mind. This baby was his. The befuddled, shaken parents looked at their stillborn son for the last time.

"He is so soft," Cash said holding his hand. "Can I hold him please?" Cash asked. A weeping sound came out of Cash mouth as he clinched the baby to his chest. "Y-o-u a-r-e s-o-o- p-e-r-f-e-c-t l-i-t-t-l-e m-a-n," Cash said stuttering to the stillborn. "Daddy loves you soo much. I know you are in a better place because you didn't even have a chance to make your own decisions. I love you, I will always love and remember you shortie," he cried. Cash kissed his head and handed him back to Keya. He really didn't want to give his son back to his mother. Cash also knew how hard it was on Keya.

The doctors returned with a priest after informing Mrs. Jordan and other family members of Keya's progress. Everyone was in tears including myself. I accompanied Mrs. Jordan inside the delivery room. We joined Keya and Cash in the delivery room. There were no dry eyes in sight. Keya asked her mother what went wrong. Her mother just held her. She told Keya the baby didn't suffer and that's what really mattered. Keya was yelling and carrying on once the baby was taken away. Cash and her mother were there by her side trying to calm her down. Everyone present stayed around for hours. I called Dawn and gave her the details. She rushed right over.

When Dawn got to the hospital, she cried so much while hugging Keya that she complained of a headache something terrible. I drove her and Mrs. Jordan home along with some of the members of Keya's family and friends. Cash stayed with Keya. She would have to stay in the hospital overnight for observation. Mrs. Jordan explained to her granddaughter that her little brother is in heaven now. Though Te'rena heard, she still wanted to see her mommy and little brother. It was a tough test for four friends to overcome.

Later Cash would ask: "Did the baby stop moving at some point ? Why didn't Keya check that out?" He never did ask Keya because she was out of it and had suffered enough.

BETTER OFF UNKNOWN...

My cell phone rang. I checked the caller id but didn't recognize the number. I answered it anyway.

"Who this?"

"Yo, whut up kid?"

On hearing Boobie's voice I grimaced.

"Whut up with yourself?" I asked.

"I ain't heard from you and Cash in a minute. What y'all can't holla at a brother?" He asked.

"First of all, Cash's not fucking with you. Secondly, everyone is chilling. My fiancée and my peeps, everyone's all good. Speaking of my future wife, I've been meaning to get a few things off my chest with you."

"My numbers still the same, Forst. Come holla at me, whenever." Boobie's response drained with sarcasm. It pissed me off but I decided to be cool.

"Yeah I should do that. But I don't appreciate you not telling me you dealt with my future wife."

"Man, back then, you and Dawn wasn't together. It wasn't my fault you was taking your sweet time with the pussy."

"Don't get disrespectful, dogs," I said rudely and could hear Boobie chuckling before speaking.

"Check it, you been bent out of shape all this time over the p-u-s-s-y, Forster?"

"Nah, Boobie. I know she'll always be mine. That wasn't it at all. I just recognized real game and niggas with shame."

"What's that suppose to mean? Don't get college-cute with me, Forst. I made you two little dudes and I could smash y'all too."

"You threatening me? I think you should choose your words very carefully right now because you might be high, but you can fall."

"Yo Forster, do you wanna make this a war, you punk-ass, bitch?" Boobie asked then hung up.

I was so pissed I wanted to run up in his crib right then. I had to play my cards right. I couldn't let it escalate because Cash would become involved. I'd let Cash know when I was ready. My phone rang again and I assumed it was that fool calling back.

"Yo nigga, name the place and time man and I'll see you whenever," I said picking up.

"I don't want no beef with you, homey," Cash laughed.

"That wasn't meant for you, Cash."

"So who the hell was it directed to, Forst?"

"Nah, nah some dude must have had the wrong number and tried to get loose with the mouth on me." I lied.

"My cell is always on. Call me if a nigga is ready for his suicide." Cash's tone shifted from clowning to seriousness.

"What's going on?"

"Guess who called me with a bullshit message?"

"I don't feel like playing the guessing game. Just tell me."

"Stacey. She left me mad messages talking about she's prego and about to go in with our baby."

"Word Cash? You think it's yours?"

"Yeah, I know it's my baby but I just don't appreciate her telling me now. I mean she don't even know what I just went through with Keya. I ain't ready for another let down."

"You won't get another let down. I know it's going on a year since y'all lost the baby. But nothing's gonna happen to your baby this time." I assured him.

"True dat. Forst, some of the players from the old school still down with that Hoops Dream. What time are you going? No telling who might be there. Peeps we haven't seen in a minute." Cash replied.

"Whenever you're making that move, swing by the crib and scoop me."

Finally, Cash called Keya to see how things were going. Keya had been working at the Sterns Department store in Yonkers where she was a manager. Her outgoing message was immediately heard.

"Check it ma, we got to talk. I'm gonna be at Magenta. There's an anniversary reunion tonight. I had forgotten all about it. Forster and I are meeting up to go. Dawn ain't going cause she's working. So, if you gonna roll call me on my cell. Peace," Cash said ending the call.

After she lost her son, Keya's frivolous behavior simmered. Cash had been seeing her on the low, low. I reached Cash's crib to find him waiting outside. I pulled up, jumped out the ride and gave Cash a pound. He was with three other dudes from Connecticut. One had a luxury van and suggested we ride.

Cash and I left our cars in front of his building. Jokes were cracking and bottles popping as we all hopped off the Bronx River Parkway to Gunhill Road. The sound of Nice and Smooth blasted. The driver was whistling at the chicks with the tightest shirts and shortest skirts. Cash and I were laid back in the cut. The other dudes from Connecticut were spitting their game at the girls.

"These city girls, they ahight. I dig their style."

"You can have them." Cash yelled from the back seat and we all laughed.

The ride was going down. There was a thirteen-inch television in the van along with a bed. It was pimped out. The ride to the Bronx wasn't long. We cruised by the Rucker and checked out a Pro-Am basketball game in progress. The crowd was going nuts, the game was exciting and there were girls all over. We chilled for a minute slinging game then we headed to the real uptown, Magenta park.

"Yeah dogs, I used to be out here whenever we get a chance. Come watch the

Goat, Pee Wee and all them from the golden era of b-balling."

"Now its players like Hot Sauce, Dribbling Machine and Skip-to-my-Lou running things."

I looked around at the basketball courts and realized that the shine of the old playground had been restored. The whole scene reminded me of the times we hung here. All the smiles on the young ones reminded me of the times when Dawn, Keya, Cash and me stomped here. It was the dance contest, I smiled at the memory.

"Cash and I were always in here. Even after the games, we'd chill out here at nights. This was where we met our girls as well. Now she's my fiancée," I bragged.

Everyone gave me a congratulatory dap. The place was nearly jam-packed. Most of the old timers wore different shades of orange and blue. The new jacks represented too. Cash and I made our way through the throngs of crowd to the deejay booth. We knew him for a long time and kicked it with him for a minute.

"That's my joint right there," Cash hollered when the deejay spun KRS1 and Boogie Down Productions', *You Must Learn.* The deejay busted loose with Whodini's, *Friends.*

The dudes were mixing with honeys from the Bronx. I excused myself and made my way toward a girl I used to kick it with from way back. At first I wasn't sure but I recognized her coke-bottle frame with that plump butt and her small waistline leading up to buttercup size breast. Her girlfriend signaled for her to look my way. She did and to her surprise, here was her first love staring in her face.

"Hey Kitty," I said. She looked beautiful when she smiled. Kitty let out a loud shriek and hugged me.

"Oh my God, it's Forster. What's up? You're looking good." She said hugging me and rubbing her hands all over my butt. I smelled her cheap perfume.

"I'm chilling. Cash is here playing rock star."

"You're still handsome, how many kids do you have?" She smiled and winked.

"No children as yet, girl. I am engaged, though. I think you know her? Member when you thought I was talking to this girl named Dawn when we used to kick it?"

"Yeah, I couldn't stand that show-off girl. I mean she didn't do anything, but you always be chatting her up."

"I feel you now. I was going on and on about her. Truthfully we weren't messing with each other like that back then. We decided to stay friends."

"I'm happy for the both of you. I don't think anyone else was meant for you," Kitty said smiling. "You take care," she said rudely pushing me away. She still got it, I thought staring at her fine ass. I was distracted by raucous. I spotted Cash with the C-crew dancing to Rob Base song, *It Takes Two*. The next song up was *OPP*, some in the crowd sang along while others sang against the song. I got in the midst and joined the guys singing:

"*...I'm down with OPP...*"

"*You won't know me...*"

A crew of girls responded. Despite the noise, I heard a cell phone going off. My phone was ringing off the hook.

"Hi honey bun," I answered.

"Ahh..." they shouted. I laughed.

"Hi sweetie, how's everything going in the park?" Dawn asked.

"Huh what did you say?"

"I said how is it going?"

"Yo everyone is here. It's really crazy. If you were I'd be in heaven. You should come through."

"Sweetie I am still very busy. I'll be home before you and I'll start dinner, alright?"

"I ran into Kitty. Remember her?"

"I couldn't stand the way she was treating you."

"It's funny you should say that she was just saying she couldn't stand me talking about you all the time." We laughed.

"I'm just checking on my baby boy. Holla if you need me," Dawn said with a kiss.

"Hmm...I surely will," I said returning the kiss. I was tucking away the phone, when I felt a tap on my shoulder. Before I could turn to see who it was, I felt the sucker-punch to my face.

"Oh shit! The party is off the hook. Now I gotta go fuck up someone."

One of the guys from Connecticut shouted. Cash was alerted and was making his way over to us.

My dukes were up and I was in stance to defend myself. Without hesitation, I

stepped up in position and let my fists go. Left, right, left, I was swinging and we were thumping. Blows were being exchanged like crazy. Cash had my back, joining me in beating down any other chumps who dared to jump. Hordes of people were pushed around as others ran for cover fearing gunshots. Luckily these dudes did not pull out. The chaos was busting loose attracting some and scaring others.

Despite their fright some stayed and watched, Cash pound out some guy. The fight escalated going from the bleachers to the basketball court. The dudes from Connecticut began to rumble when one of the troublemakers tried to sneak Cash. Ten years later and still a function in the park couldn't end without a fight.

The deejay, emcee and others ran over to us after they heard Cash and I were involved in the brawl. I had dude on the hardtop stomping his guts. Cash clocked two dudes in the face before his hand moved to his waist, looking for his steel. Momentarily, I froze. I was surprised that the dude I was beating on was Boobie. With his hat pulled low over his eyes, he could have been anybody. Boobie and me were tight. I couldn't throw another blow. He was on the ground, an older brother to me. My hesitation led Boobie to plant a kick in my groin. I went berserk stomping on that piece of shit.

The fight was eventually broken up when Cash started letting off shots at two of Boobie's crew. One suffered a gunshot to the leg, barely missing the other. He looked over at me and I saw his shirt crimson red, from blood. I looked behind me and discovered that the punk who had shot him was Boobie. Cash pushed me away from Boobie and another shot went off hitting Boobie. He fell and Cash walked over to where he struggled to move.

"Think you gonna live sucka ass, big brotha?" Cash asked in a matter fact tone.

He walked next to Boobie with the gun down.

"I guess, you hit me, but I'm a be good," Boobie answered.

I was moving along with them and breathed a sigh of relief thinking the skirmish was over when Cash smiled.

"I don't think so," he said pumped another two rounds into Boobie's face.

All there was left were ass and elbows. The crowd frantically ran like there was no tomorrow. They were stampeding, knocking one another over, boyfriends running and leaving their dates. He walked over and blasted Boobie from close range. Then nonchalantly dealt with the snitches.

"No one seen nothing, right? I'll come looking for ya snitching asses!" Cash yelled at a scared girl. She urinated and cowered when Cash waved the steel.

The Connecticut set was out when irons started to clap. I was frozen to the spot on the court and Cash had to pull me in order for me to move. I tried but I was too shocked by what I'd just seen.

"Yo, hurry the fuck up, man!" Cash shouted while running to the van. "If these jack rabbits left us, all be on my mother's grave. I'm going to Connecticut looking for they ass." Surprisingly, the van was still there. The driver shouted at us to hurry up. We ran faster and the door closed after Cash jumped inside. Then the van peeled off. "Yo, is everyone alright?" Cash asked.

"Yeah man, we good. Y'all alright?" The driver asked.

"I got nicked, but we good." Cash answered. I nodded still shaken from the episode.

Cash wasn't bleeding badly. The bullet grazed his shoulder.

"Why didn't you ask me that back then, instead of just shooting?" I asked.

"I shoot now and talk later. You know my steel-low. Ain't no dudes gonna run up on you or me and be wilding like that. I'm so glad I brought my gat," Cash said and kissing the Ruger. The guys in the van started laughing.

"Nigga you's crazy," the driver said. It was all part of the memories we took from hanging out in the parks in da Boogie Down. We used to be ducking and running out now we were the cause for the party breaking up.

"Why did you...Oh man." I was angry and saddened by Boobie's demise.

"You need to be thanking me instead of yelling at a nigga," Cash said looking at me. I did not respond. "I'm waiting for an answer. What the hell happen between y'all?"

"Just take me to my car, man." I replied. Cash looked at the driver and said, "You heard the man."

Once we reached Cash's place I gave everyone dap and got in my car and jetted. I did not care if anyone understood, especially Cash. He had known Boobie since we were kids. I didn't want to think about my best friend shooting my so-called brother in the head at close range. Unlike Cash and I everyone else in the van was from out of town. I rode around the Boogie Down feeling sick then pulled over on the side of the Bronx River and called Earl. I had contemplated moving far away after the wedding. Now moving loomed larger.

THINGS FALL APART

Cash and the driver hopped town to lay low for a while. The driver knew a spot in Bridgeport that was perfect. I could've gone but didn't want to live like a villain. Dawn was worried about my safety. She figured that whoever was riding with Boobie could identify Cash. If they knew Cash, they damn sure knew me. Cash wasn't around, so they would want to get the closest one to him. We sat on pins and needles in our glass world thinking of the retaliatory consequences for Cash's actions. Only time would determine the havoc that would be wreaked.

"Sugar, are you going back to work ever?" Dawn asked and I shook my head.

"Nah, I'm taking off this week."

"Do you want me to stay home with you?"

The question alarmed me. I stared at her face searching for the right answer. Dawn offered to stay home from work? My mind snapped.

"Nah, it's all good. Go to work. I'll be ahight."

Dawn kissed me softly on the lips and rushed off to work. I turned on the television. It happened on the weekend but it seemed like minutes ago. The fight replayed like a broken record over and over in my head. The whole scenario had me so tight that all I could do was hold my head down. Tears came.

I didn't care if he had snuffed me. We would've kept thumping until the best man won. Then be mad at each other for a minute. Eventually that too would've blew

by. We had gotten emotional over something that should've been kept in the past. I couldn't understand why something so simple became so complicated. There was nothing I could do. The feeling of helplessness was a bitter pill to swallow, it caused me to vomit. I cleaned up the bloody mess as memories haunted. I wandered around the place thinking about coming up, hitting hard times and turning to Boobie. He looked out while sharing his stories. Now I'm remembering gunshots and his life leaking away. Bad news.

Dawn showed strength but deep down inside I knew she was not only disappointed but sad. She tried to hide the remorse she felt, but I understood. Boobie was someone she had a relationship with. Days went by and I decided to call Cash. I blocked my number. A female answered.

"Put Cash on."

"Who dis?"

"This Forst."

"What's good son?" Cash asked.

"I feel real fucked up about what happened," I said.

"You know I ain't the apologetic-type." Cash started and cleared his throat. He continued. "But I'm a say that to you my nigga. I know that ain't gonna bring him back, but you have to stop and think. His ass brought it to us side-ways. He grimy and I ain't the one. When dramas pop on my peeps, what!" There was a pause. Cash must be catching his breath.

"You there, dogs?"

"Yeah, I'm still here. I wanna apologize. You mean more to me than anyone... Wait, wait except for some good pussy." Cash was laughing. I needed the relief and hearing Cash's voice offered me that. I couldn't help but to join him in laughter. "Nah, you know I'm joking. No female worth our friendship. Seriously, who's collecting our money from those little pitchers?"

"Cash, I really don't know. I mean why don't you get one of your mans' up there drive you down here. Don't let them know you coming, just roll up."

"Yeah, that's a good idea. I'm about to move up here in New Haven or sump'n."

"Word? What about Harlem it's one of a kind, kid?"

"I'm a leave that to Stace. She claims she needs a place to stay because she's gonna be taking a managerial position in some midtown hotel. It'll be cool for the baby and her."

"I hear that. What about that center for the teens?"

"Fo sure. They need it out here too. But the location is up to you. Holla if you need me. I have no problems flying down there with highway patrol chasing. You know I'm running up on the scene blazing. I is a natural born ready to kill muthafuckas."

"Be careful. You's crazy. I feel you. Hate you or love you, you my brotha. Peace." I really didn't like that Cash wanted to live way out there in Connecticut. We had been close for years. Maybe that would be the best thing for him.

"Te'rena watch what you're fucking doing!" Keya screamed at her daughter for dropping the bowl of cereal. Te'rena was looking at television and walking to the dinner table. "Now clean all that shit up!" Keya shouted at the frightened Te'rena. Tears rolled down her angelic face as she wiped up the milk and cereal with paper towel. Her grandmother came in the living room and flipped on Keya.

"She isn't one of your little friends on the streets. Stop cursing at her like that! And speaking of the streets, she's not the reason why your results came back positive."

Keya stood in shock when her mother gave her the news. She was too busy to remember the test from the hospital. Keya never read the letter, she thought it had to do with her stillborn son.

"You fucking nosey ass, how dare you read my letters? That's none of your damn business," Keya responded glaring at her mother.

"You write to that jailbird and let him know you're damaged goods. My grandchild didn't do you no harm. It's the life you chose that harmed you. So treat her like a decent human being. She's not an animal."

"Don't think you could raise my daughter because JB took Kenya down south with him. You let your daughter go. My baby sister didn't even get to grow up with me. So don't think you are going to fit Te'rena in her shoes. She's my daughter and I'll raise

her the way I know how."

"I said my piece, okay? And there won't be no more yelling in this house, period." Her mother then helped Te'rena pick up the cereal and fixed her another bowl. The house phone rang. Keya didn't budge. Her mother answered. The call was for Keya.

"Tell him too, he may have to get a check-up."

Her mother threw the cordless phone on the sofa next to Keya.

"Hello," Keya said.

"Hey mama. What's good?" Cash said.

"Hey, Cash." Keya said and her face lit up. "How're you feeling, Cash?"

"I'm maintaining, ma. What's good with you?"

"Oh, a little stressed. I just yelled at Te'rena. I didn't mean to, but..." Keya's voice trailed as her eyes filled with tears.

"Don't be yelling at her. Grab her and give her a kiss for me. Hug her and tell her you sorry. Don't be bothering my little sweetie. Matter of fact yo, do that shit while I'm on the phone. Call her over right now and apologize to my sweetie." Cash demanded and Keya giggled, but called Te'rena over. Her daughter walked slowly with her head hanging low.

"Look at me, baby. Mommy's very sorry, okay?" Keya apologized kissing her daughter's forehead. Te'rena's frown turned to a dimpled cheek smile. "Te'rena, Cash is on the phone." Keya said and handed the phone to Te'rena. Her face lit up just like her mommy's.

"Hi Cashmere," she said with a soft, innocent voice.

"Hi sweetie-pie how's everything? Are you still playing with the toys I bought you?"

"Yes. I still play with them. And I'm going in grandma's room to watch cartoons."

"You be good to mommy and I'll see you soon, okay?"

"Okay Cashmere, see you soon." Te'rena said and passed the phone to Keya. Cash could hear her telling her about what Cash told her.

"Hello," Keya said sounding better.

"Yeah shortie, what's been on your mind? I hope me." Cash said laughing.

"Yeah, you better laugh. I have my ups and downs you know how that go. I miss my son. I want him back."

"I feel you. You know I go through it every night, Kee."

"Hard rock as you is. Get out! You do?"

"Hell yeah, I do. I take my little man's face, fingers, stomach, legs, and every part of his body. I placed them in my memory bank."

"That's what you suppose to do, Cash. Keep good memory of all your loved ones."

"See, I'm kind a different, Kee."

"Why are you different?"

"You know? 'Member my moms?" Cash asked in a whisper. People around him never heard the full story. He never talked about it. On the low he still visited with his second mom, Miss Carroll and adopted brother, Gabriel. "So what's up with homey in jail?"

"Who that? Smokey?"

"Stop playing, you know who I'm dealing with?"

"I wrote him and told him everything that happened, Cash. And the fool asked me to marry him."

"Word? He did that?"

"He asked me to marry him and I told him I'd think about it." Keya laughed.

"Why did you tell him you think about it?"

"Because my memory bank recalls he always treated me good," Keya said knowing Cash would get upset.

"I wish you would go up there and try something with that nigga. I know he up North but I'll have a nigga run up on him with a shank," Cash said angrily.

"Why would you want to do that?" Keya asked smiling.

"Whatever, bitch!" Cash replied then hung up.

Keya was still laughing when she put the cordless phone on the base to recharge. She returned to watching television still laughing at what Cash had just said. Keya thought a lot about Smokey's proposal. She would be family and move into his house. The possibilities streamed through her mind with the television on. The ringing of the phone snapped her thoughts.

"Hello," Keya answered assuming it was Cash calling her back.

"Is this Nakeya Jordan?"

"Yes, this is she."

"You have a collect call from Emanuel Jockton at the Bedford Correctional Facility will you accept the charges?" An operator explained.

"Yes, sure," Keya replied excitedly. There was a delay then the call was through.

"Hey what's going on baby? I didn't think you'd be home." Smokey's voice was warm.

"I'm doing okay. But I'm not about to go outside unless its job related..."

"I hear that. Did you get my last letter...?"

"Yes..."

After Keya hung up from Smokey, she called Dawn.

"Russell and Friedman, Ms. Jones speaking how may I help you?"

"DJ, it's me, Kee, are you busy?"

"I got a few minutes, Kee. What's going on?"

"I told you Smokey asked me to marry him, right?"

"Hmm, hmm..."

"Why he told me to do a three way and then told his mother to give me five hundred beans, girl."

"Say word?"

"Word to my mother. I wanna ask a favor?"

"Go ahead, ask away."

"Could you drive me somewhere when you're free?"

"Sure, yeah, I'll drive you. Where?"

"Yonkers, I got the address and all. I got you for the gas."

"Don't play with me, Kee. You ain't gotta hook me up with nothing. You know I'll do anything for you."

"DJ, for real, that's my bad."

"Listen, tomorrow after work is good for me. I don't have to work late. Call Smokey's mother and make sure tomorrow is good for her. Then call me back because I got an intern here and I have to show him the ropes right now. Call me back with the details. Okay Kee?"

"Will do. Thanks a lot DJ." Keya answered. The line went dead and Dawn continued training the new intern.

Keya picked up the envelope with Smokey's mother's number on it and dialed it.

"Hello," she answered.

"Hi, it's me Keya. I just want to know, if tomorrow is good for us to meet?"

"My son told me he wants to marry you. I'm accepting his decision, but don't think for one minute that all his money will be spent on you and your child while he's away. He's not going to want you for anything when he comes home. And his old lifestyle will be in his past. I'll make sure of that. If you are planning on marrying him, I hope it's for the right reasons. You can guarantee that I'll be by my son's side every step of the way." Mrs. Jockton got right to the point and ran it down to Keya. Her heart pounded in her chest and Keya was left speechless. "Now tomorrow evening will be fine for me. Let me get your home number just in case anything changes." Keya mumbled the number and the conversation ended.

Keya didn't know how to feel or what to think. She knew she'd better think about whether she wanted to be Smokey's wife while he was locked down. Keya had told Dawn and shared with Cash that she was thinking of doing it. Keya's mother had no idea of her plan to marry Smokey while he was locked up. Keya knew she had to tell her mother before she made any other marital plans.

Dawn had her hands full training the new intern. He was prompt and took excellent notes. She gave the intern work left over from the other day. Yesterday she decided to clear her desk before the end of the day. He completed her task quickly. The telephone rang.

"Russell and Friedman's Ms. Jones speaking," she answered.

"Hi sweets, how is your day going?" I asked.

"Just fine now, honey. I just sent the intern home. He is really focused. Unlike most interns we've gotten before."

"Hon, I'm calling because the two shorties Cash and I had working for us got knocked."

"Forst, I told you..." Dawn complained and I cut her off.

"I went to meet them earlier to get my dough. I jetted back to work and hours later, peoples called saying the cops just bagged them."

"Do you think they'll tell the cops anything about you?"

"I'm not gonna think that. I just feel bad for them. I can't even help with a lawyer."

"Baby, the court will provide them legal representation. I work at a law firm, right?"

"Yeah, but them court-appointed lawyers ain't no good."

"It's better than having no rep. Let's go out later to eat and discuss it, okay?"

"I would love to. You drove today?"

"No, I didn't. Pick me up?"

"What time, my love?"

"You know what time I get off. Be on time." The call ended. I dialed Cash. He was still out in Connecticut. His man answered.

"This Forster, put Cash on."

"What up money-grip?" Cash answered.

"D's knocked our pitchers."

"Aw, fuck, Forst!"

"I got the cheddar this morning before they were picked up. I think someone from the block snitched on them."

"You got the cheddar, that's good. I feel for the little homeys and all, but they'll learn from this and get another profession," Cash said while laughing along with people in the background.

"Cash, that shit ain't funny, man. I'm a go and try to see if they need anything."

"Man, tell the little homeys its part of the game and do not drop that soap," Cash said entertaining his friends in the background. I wanted to chuckle right along with them. It was part of the hazard of the job. Still, Cash was not right. Something should be done to help them out. "Those little homeys are under-age so they won't be there long. Anyway I have to holla at you later because this shit is funny as hell and I don't want to blow my high while you're on the phone hating," Cash said and hung up.

I left the head-cook in charge of the kitchen and rushed off to buy Dawn some roses. She loved the red and white long stem ones.

"Mommy, can you come here for a minute please?" Keya said to her mother. Te'rena and her grandmother came playfully running into the living room.

"Have you calmed down now?" Mrs. Jordan asked.

"Yes mother. I told you I was sorry earlier. Te'rena I need you to watch TV in grandma's room while we talk, 'kay?" Keya asked. Te'rena put her pitiful look on hesitated then hugged her grandma and did the same with her mother and ran out the room. "I need your undivided attention, mother." Keya demanded. Her mother sat down on the sofa. Keya stood up and got straight to the point. "Ma, you know Smokey right?" Her mother nodded. "You also know he is locked up right?" Her mother nodded again in agreement. "I think you know that if Smokey was out here he and I would be together. Anyways to make a long story short, he asked me to marry him and I haven't given him a response yet." Keya added quickly.

"Well, are you going to accept?" Her mother shouted. "Do you have dementia? The only thing you should do is tell him the truth."

"Ma..."

With tears clouding her eyes, Keya sat down and began to write Smokey.

CHANGES...

Cash had become a father. Having a daughter made him as soft as marshmallows when she was around. Cash was even contemplating on moving back into his old crib, just to be around his daughter, little Sydney. Stacey, his daughter's mother, didn't have to call Cash for anything. He was always there, on time, even spending nights. There was nothing sexually going on between him and Stacey. She didn't want to go back to the old ways and having sex would put them right back to arguing over stupid stuff. Now they were working on real friendship terms.

He left Stacey's apartment around mid afternoon before she had a chance to check the mailbox. Stacey speed dialed Cash's cell phone and told him he had mail. Cash brushed it off stating he only received bills in his mailbox. Stacey told him that it was not a bill or junk mail but a letter from his father, Casmere. Cash paused on the phone for a brief moment. He then demanded that Stacey rip it to pieces. He also mouthed-off about his father but Stacey didn't pay him any mind.

"Yeah, okay I'll throw it away Cash," Stacey said and as soon as she hung up, Stacey opened the letter and read it.

By the time she was finished, tears were rolling down Stacey's cheeks. She looked over at her seven month-old-daughter, Sydney and smiled. Even though she had never met him, Sydney had a grandfather who loved her. Stacey read the letter one more time. Cash had never gone into the details of his mother's death. Stacey never

bothered asking because he was touchy about it. Now she understood Cash a little better. She was proud of giving birth to a daughter who carried his mother's name.

Cash had cut contacts with the drug dealers, the young guys were no longer slinging for him. His daughter's name was constantly on his lips and seemed to be all he cared for. Cash would often call and tell Stacey to whisper 'Daddy loves you,' in his daughter's ear. Stacey loved the way the bond between him and Sydney had grown tighter. His attitude toward living was changing because of Sydney.

He proudly told everyone that he loved the expression on his little girl's face when she saw him. She had her daddy's face especially the smile. He loved herthe moment since she was born. Sidney followed her daddy everywhere. Stacey's friend from upstate went into the delivery room with her. Cash didn't want to do it again, he felt like he was bad luck. Cash had lost his mother and his son. He did not want to experience the loss of someone again.

Stacey wrote a response to Cash's father's letter. She didn't know the whole story about what really happened to Cash's mother. She understood Cash's animosity toward his father, but she didn't want to deprive her daughter of a grandfather. Sydney was sound asleep as Stacey went in her room to get a wallet size picture of her and Sydney. She finished writing and included the photo in the envelope. Stacey wanted to be finished with the letter and have it mailed before Cash visited. She read the letter before sealing the envelope.

Back at work, Dawn was promoted. Her coworkers threw her a lunchtime celebration. I had to do a presentation for a hotel manager and couldn't make her promotion celebration. Lately, I'd been extremely busy generating business for the hotel. I was also trying to branch out and become a restaurant owner. Dawn was not keen on me spending more time away from her. She understood that business sometimes took precedence over everything else. I came home many nights feeling extremely tired. Dawn's patience was running thin. The fact that I was doing this for the greater good was no longer comforting.

"Dawn put down that phone unless it's Forster."

Dawn hurriedly gave directions to the client regarding his case. Then she hung up the phone.

"Let's party," her boss shouted. Dawn was happy. Co-workers chipped in for the party's expenses. She always wore a smile and everyone thought that she was a sweetheart. "Dawn, how does it feel to have your own office?" Her boss asked.

"I'm speechless. But it feels good," she said thinking of the beautiful view it offered.

"Attention everyone, Dawn you've been with me for many years. You came on the staff straight out of school. And your work ethics made me a better and a more patient person. When I get stressed you help me out, when I am down you pull me through. You're like the daughter I never had and a hell of a business partner," her boss said.

Dawn smiled when she saw glasses filled with champagne floating around and was presented with one. Wow, they're treating me like I'm a partner, she thought. Then her boss spoke: "To your future, to our relationship and to this firm, here, here." The other staff members followed suit raising their glasses in recognition. Food was plentiful. Too bad, Keya couldn't make it because she was at Mrs. Jockton's house.

Early in the morning, Keya caught a van in the Bronx and took the long ride straight to the correctional facility. When she saw the road signs, Keya became nervous and excited. She didn't know what to expect when she entered the prison. She checked to see if she had her documents and singles for the vending machines. Smokey had warned her.

Women with babies and other family members were visiting. This was a surprise to Keya. There were women who came faithfully with one another to visit their man or husband. Keya hardly saw any men but there were two bathrooms, one for men and the other women. She got tired of waiting on the long line for the women's bathroom. Keya decided to use the men's bathroom. There were no stalls just a toilet, sink and a counter. It suited Keya just fine.

Other women started going to the men's bathroom after Keya went in. Some women were on the bus looking busted until they reached the facility and put make-up on their faces. Keya overheard two females talking about their lovers in jail. One female said she visited every two weeks and he expected her to bring him a package and take care of his kids.

"I didn't put him in here," the first female said giving the other female a pound. Keya was amazed to see so many women, nice looking ones too. She heard the correction officer shouting:

"If you are not on the list of the inmate you came to see, you'll not be allowed to see them. Please come to the front desk if you have any questions. For those who don't, form a line on my right."

Keya felt the butterflies multiplying in her stomach. She was in the middle of the line, because she was putting her personal belongings in her locker. Keya took her sweet time she figured she would be admitted. Keya looked ahead and saw a woman and her child removing their shoes. The COs' then handed each female a receipt after they checked off the inmate the woman came to visit. The line moved quickly enough. Finally Keya approached the CO and took off her shoes then went through the metal detector. The light on the metal detector flashed red and the sound went off.

"Step back Miss and come through again," the CO suggested. Keya did exactly what he said still the buzzer sounded again. She began to panic.

"Sir, I have taken everything out of my pockets." Keya put her arms up so the female officer could search her. Then she was informed that she had to go in the bathroom and remove her bra. She could put her shirt back on while the CO searched her bra. Keya's eyebrows went up.

"You have to search my bra?" She asked.

"Yes ma'am," the female CO responded.

"That's some nasty shit. I don't want all y'all hands on something that has to go back on my body," Keya replied.

"Well, ma'am we must take proper precautions," the female CO responded. Keya huffed while listening to the women.

"If she don't want to, why don't she get off the line?" One woman said. Keya stormed into the bathroom and took off the bra. She put her arms through the sleeves of her shirt, but didn't button it. Keya wore a screw-face when she exited the bathroom. The female correction officer went inside the bathroom with gloves on and searched Keya's bra. She felt violated after the search had ended. She stormed through the gate only to come to a stop waiting for them to open the other gate. A loud noise startled her as the gate slammed behind her and in front of her. She was given the okay to continue.

KEISHA SEIGNIOUS

Her mind was clouded with thoughts of never coming back. She was happy she never had to do hard time. Keya sat and waited for her number to be called. She held the yellow slip of paper the CO handed to her and looked at it reading the number over and over. Finally she heard him shouting the number thirty-one. She walked checking the aisle numbers. She saw on the first table number twenty-nine. A few tables down, Smokey should be waiting. The visiting area was crowded with visitors and officers. Smokey stood up and Keya finally felt joy. She grinned from ear to ear as she hurried to him. Smokey had a big smile on his mug. He got up and hugged Keya tightly. He was well-groomed and pulled out a chair for her.

Before sitting, she said: "I see you keep yourself well groomed in here, huh?" Her observation brought laughter from Smokey. He finally sat down and greeted another inmate who had taken a seat at the next table from Smokey and Keya. The CO's were watching like hawks. Smokey held Keya's hands and stared lovingly in her eyes.

"You look beautiful as ever." He said and Keya blushed and smiled nervously. "Don't be shy now. Talk to me, baby. What's going on?" Smokey asked. Keya continued to smile at him while her eyes searched her surroundings.

"This is some place. Can you believe I had to take off my bra to get in here?"

"You must have had on a wire bra."

"Well excuse me, Mister-know-it-all," Keya said with a smile.

"I asked you to come here for a reason. I want to know if you're ready to do this bid with me?" He asked. Keya hesitated before answering.

"Well, it doesn't sound so promising since you put it like that," she said.

"Nah ma, it's not like you locked down too. I mean all I ask is; you stand by me. I asked you to marry me and I thought you were ready," he said and kissed her left hand. "I know you better than a lot of these cats out there. I'm willing to trust you with everything, including my baby. And you know I'm feeling you. I was ready to move you and your daughter in when I was out. So you know a brother ain't trying to just hit and quit like most of the cats round here. Again Miss Lady, are you ready?" Smokey asked with his head tilted, smiling and hoping she'd say yes.

"Wow Smokey, that's the best offer I've ever had." Keya's eyes watered.

"Come on ma, don't do that. Please?" He softly asked while caressing her face.

"I am glad you chose me and I'm willing to wait," Keya said.

159

"Oh fo' sho, ma. You know how I do? I want you and Te'rena to stay at my crib and maintain it." Smokey started to speak but Keya interrupted him.

"How am I going to maintain your house?"

"Baby, I have all the information you need to maintain my barber shop. But I'm not passing all of these things over to just my girl. Follow me?"

"How's your house going to be maintained as far as the plumbing and all that? And I don't know the first thing about a damn barber shop."

"You don't have to worry. My mortgage is paid up. Any maintenance necessary, the payments come straight out of my mother's account. Which is my account but you know how that goes. I'm willing to lay out my demands. You have some, right?"

"I guess so."

"You guess? Ma, you ain't the guessing type. You's a-get-the-job-done-down-girl. Can I trust you with my baby?" He asked and Keya nodded. Smokey pulled his body half way over the table to give her a kiss. She was feeling all tingly inside. "I'm not mad at the fact that you didn't know who your son's father was. I was a little disappointed, because you should be using protection." he said gripping her hands. "I expect before we get married, which won't be long now, I wanna know: Do you use any protection against the virus? Once you say I do it's a wrap for you with any dudes. My peoples are all over. Not that I'm going to have you watched but I'll know. Again ma, I may be asking a lot from you right now. That's why I want you to think about it carefully. I won't mind if you say no or that you need more time. Time is all I have right now. So be real with me." Smokey said with sincerity in his voice. Keya was stunned by his revelations.

"I am ready for what you're asking, but I'm not sure about taking on the responsibility of your house and barbershop. I don't know the first thing about either. I have my daughter and I'll have to get her transferred to another school. All that might be too much."

"Baby, it's not about adding up all I asked, it's about just doing what's right in your heart. Kee, I don't want to put pressure on you. The ball is in your court."

"Smokey, I love you and it took you getting locked up for me to realize that. You pretty much helped me get off the streets," Keya said with tears in her eyes.

"Tell me what is in that pretty little head of yours?"

"I'm a daddy's girl. I miss my father," Keya said and held her head down. Smokey reached over and lifted her head up.

"That's a lot on one person, especially a woman. Fathers play a major role in the lives of children. I understand how you feel, the majority of my friends have one parent in the household and I'm sure you know it's not usually the fathers who stay."

"Everyone does not think like you Smokey. You see I only remember the good times my dad and I had. I remember how I felt around him."

"So what happened to him?"

"To my knowledge, he just stop coming around. That's what my mother told me." Keya's tone saddened.

"Did you or your mother tried to find him?"

"How would I know where to look?"

"Ma, there are a lot of ways to locate a person. Talk to your mother about it and if she's not interested ask Dawn. She works at a law firm, right?"

"I'll ask Dawn first before my mother. I figured if my father wanted to see me he would find me."

"Not necessarily, and I say that because you don't know what went down between him and your moms. You are older and have a child. I think its time you hunt him down for answers. Feel me?" Smokey asked with a smile on his face. Keya smiled back at him and squeezed his hand tighter. "So how is little Miss Te'rena and your mother doing?"

"They're good. Both of them are getting on my last nerves. Mom spoils Te'rena like crazy and it gets me sick."

"That's what grandma's are for. My grandmother spoiled us to no return before she passed away." Smokey said with a smile.

"My grandmother was too good for her grand kids. My mother is my father, grandmother, grandfather and brother all in one. We had our differences but we always overcame them. I love my mother. We don't always see eye to eye but I'm learning to appreciate her more. She helps me so much with my daughter that it's not funny. I'm getting back to reality now," Keya said.

"Listen, I don't know 'bout you but I'm starving. Let's go get something to eat from the machines." Smokey suggested. He escorted Keya to the vending machine. The line was pretty long but they waited.

"What do you want to eat?" Keya asked.

"I want burgers, pizza, chips whatever," Smokey said.

"Here is the money," Keya said handing Smokey fifteen dollars in singles.

"No ma, I can't handle the money, you have to," he responded quickly. The correction officers' eyes were glued to the inmates and their visitors whether they were on line or just sitting down. Keya's eyes were red from crying but she was now more comfortable with her surroundings. "I miss your sweet juices on my face." Smokey whispered in her ear. Keya blushed.

She leaned closer to him and said: "Now why you trying to make me wet while we're on this line?"

"You're supposed to feel that way, it's me."

"True, true but you know that goes without question."

"Give me your hand," Smokey whispered in her ear. Keya didn't hesitate she put her hand in his. Smokey placed her hand on his crotch. Keya just smiled and gave it a little squeeze to show how much she missed it. Smokey was a freak and didn't care how many people could see. Keya managed to steal touches here and there until they reached the vending machines. Smokey's big bulge was making an impression.

They made their way back to the table after micro waving the food. While talking and eating, he reached across the table, touched her face and kissed her.

"Am I going to see you next week?" Smokey asked with a serious expression.

"Am I allowed back here next week?" Keya playfully asked.

"I'm inviting you right?" He asked.

"I don't know, I'll let you know. Because they told us that the person we came to visit, the last name has to be for the date. Other than that we won't be allowed to see the person." She explained.

"Say word? I wasn't sure about that I just thought long as we put our guests on the calling and mailing list it would be good enough."

"Let me ask the CO coming this way. Yo CO, excuse me. Can you come here for a minute, please," Smokey said to a female CO. "My wife said y'all going by last names. Does this mean I won't get visit next week?" Smokey asked.

"You can get a visit two weekends from this date. Check the new list it will be brought out soon," the officer responded.

"You heard her yourself, ma. Now, will I?" He asked.

"Fo sho," Keya responded. She reached over and kissed him full on the lips.

Smokey slipped his tongue and they stayed that way for a couple minutes.

"I see you opened up more to me than before. I feel genuine interest," Smokey said.

"It's all real, baby. I want you to be in my life for a very long time Smokey. My loyalty will never change as long as you keep me and my child happy," Keya said getting serious.

"I hear that shit. I only want to keep y'all happy. And ma, I know you know by now how I roll. I just need a woman the opposite of me. And I found her." Smokey said and kissed Keya's hand. "My mom gave me her opinion. Listen don't worry about her. I am her only son and she is a strong black woman. We have a tight bond and I never talked about marrying any woman before so my mother feels she may lose me. She knows how dedicated I am and she taught me that. My mother did a damn good job on me. She whipped my behind every time I did wrong. She put me through school. I mean you name it my moms did it for me and my sisters. She focused..." Smokey laughed. "Am I boring you?"

"No way. I'm feeling your mother and I understand how she feels. I think about Te'rena and her first little boyfriend." Keya confessed. Smokey raised his hand and interrupted.

"What boyfriend? She ain't having no boyfriend as long as I'm around," he said in jest and Keya laughed.

"Listen up. I think they're signaling for the visit to be over. I really appreciate you taking the time to visit me. Kee, give me a shot and if I mess up, then you have all rights to move on to the next man. I know you probably heard all this yang before, but you should know from what I've shown you, I'm bout it, baby," he said.

Keya smiled back at him while the CO's called each table to exit while the inmates sat at the table.

"The time flew by. I don't want to leave," Keya said while wiping the tears streaming down her cheeks, all the while smiling.

"Don't do this please," Smokey begged as his eyes filled with tears too. They stood and hugged. He held her tight and caressed her back with masculine strokes. Keya hugged him with her head under his chin since she was way shorter than him. They kissed and Smokey sucked her neck until there was a bruise. The sensation left her weak in the knees. There was no protesting from Keya. "Write me tonight, alright?"

Smokey requested. Their table number was called. "I will talk to my mom about getting you some more money. I don't want you working right now. Focus on Te'rena, aight?"

"Ahight..." Keya nodded slowly like a toddler whose favorite toy was about to be taken away. Her tears came rapidly down her face.

"Don't worry shortie, I'm okay and you are always on my mind alright?" Keya just kept moving her head up and down. When Smokey said he loved her, she said, "Me too."

Keya sat in the van feeling like Cinderella, daydreaming about what just happened. Smokey's offer sounded too good to be true. The tears continued to roll down her face. She paid no attention to the conversations on the ride back. Keya slipped her headphones over her head and found comfort in the music she had recorded from the Quiet Storm. There were new songs by Toni Terry, and the old school acts like, Ready For The World, and Anita Baker. The ride home seemed shorter. Thoughts of Smokey stayed on her mind.

Dawn called Keya's house to find out if she wanted to go to the jam at the park tonight. A talent show featuring various singers and dancers was planned. She was told that Keya was not back from visiting Smokey. Mrs. Jordan promised to give Keya the message. I was still at work when Dawn called.

"Hi baby," she said seductively.

"Hi sweetheart," I greeted.

"Listen, I know you don't want to go to Magenta, but Keya and I are going to go later on. So I'll be home a little late, alright?"

"I have to work late anyway. I'll bring in dinner, that way you can just go home and change," I suggested.

"Cool, thanks honey. I love you," she said.

"Be careful and I love you too," I said.

Dawn hung up and finished the last of her day's work. It was busy at the restaurant. Cash called several times and left a message making me wonder how he was doing. I decided to call him on my break. The cell phone rang twice before he picked up.

"Who this?" Cash answered gruffly.

"It's ya boy. What's good?"

"I know you was busy and all, but guess what?"

"What?"

"My father wrote me a letter, kid."

"Did you read it or threw it in the trash."

"Nah I didn't read it." Cash replied.

"You threw that shit in the trash?"

"Nah man, I should ball the shit up and toss it."

"Why?" I asked getting hyped.

"Man I'm scared to hear what he's gonna say. I would've been a better person if my mother was here. I know my life isn't what she had in mind for me. It still hurts. I'm gonna be the best dad possible for my daughter. She's a part of my moms and me."

"Yeah, there's a better reason to read your father's letter and tell him how you feel. You haven't seen or talked him since...ah eighty-six or so. Read the kite and tell me what you think after. I mean if you feel like your father isn't worth you sending him a kite then don't."

"Ahight Forst, good looking out, I needed to hear that. I'll hit you back after I read the letter," Cash said. Then we ended the call.

Cash called Stacey to see how his daughter was doing.

"Stace, how's my little girl?" Cash asked.

"How do you think she's doing?" Stacey asked.

"What has your drawers up in a bunch?"

"Real funny," Stacey laughed and Cash joined her.

"Sydney is napping. Seriously Cash, I want to talk to you about your father's letter."

"Well save all that. I'm on my way to read it." Stacey's face lit up.

"Did you eat?" She asked surprised that he came to his senses.

"Why what you're cooking?"

"What would you like?"

"You on a platter, if that's possible." Cash laughed.

"Boy please, it's been almost a year now since we did that. I don't need you." Stacey laughed.

"Ha, ha, ha, just cook me something to eat. I'll be there in a few," Cash said ending the call.

Stacey immediately called her girlfriend. "Girl, my baby daddy is coming over

and I want to jump his bones."

"I don't see why not? That's guaranteed penis."

"So agree that I hit him off?"

"You gonna do it anyway..."

"C'mon, Renee you know I haven't had sex with anyone since Cash. I've been eating like crazy thinking that's going to keep my mind off sex.

"Where's Syd?"

"She just woke up laughing at me. She probably know her mommy is backed up." Stacey laughed. Renee shared the laughter.

"Girl you're soo crazy. All I could say is grab your condoms and do the do with your baby daddy." Renee said.

"I have some good ones that tickle."

"You're soo bad, Stacey. Call me again. I'm about to get it on." The call ended on that note.

Stacey set about to prepare Cash's favorite meal. She also made a gallon of iced tea in jug and placed it in the freezer. Whenever Cash visited, he always wanted to drink iced cold tea. She wanted the best for her daughter and if that meant accepting Cash's thugging, she would do whatever it took.

Cash cleaned up and got ready to leave his man's Connecticut townhouse. He had hit his man with three hundred dollars a month. Cash told him he'd be back tomorrow. Daps were shared then Cash was on his way to Harlem. Cash called Miss Carroll to let her know that he was going to Stacey's to read the letter his father had sent. He hummed to some H-Town, Jodeci, and Boys II Men as he drove. Miss Carroll assured him that she would be up late just in case he needed her. Cash was relieved he was realizing how many friends and family members he had. Miss Carroll was a blessing to him because she always responded to him like his mother. My parents always welcomed him with open arms in their home.

Stacey was someone Cash knew he could talk to and not be judged. Cash suddenly realized that all this time his mother existed through his closest friends and his daughter. Cash was pushing eighty on the high ninety-five, southbound. So intrigued by what the letter may say, that he floored the pedal. Cash pressed number three on his cell phone and automatically dialed Keya's house number.

"Hello," Te'rena answered.

"Hello Te'rena. How are you? This Cash."

"Hi Cash. I'm doing fine. Me and my grandma's making a cake."

"A cake? Wow that's nice. Can I get a slice?"

"You sure could. Grandma, Cash sez he wants a slice."

"Te-Te, give mommy the phone." Mrs. Jordan was heard saying.

"Hold on okay, Cash?" Te'rena ran upstairs to her mother. "Mommy, mommy Cash is on the phone." Keya was out of breath when she got on the phone.

"Hello," she said.

"What's up shortie?" Cash answered.

"I'm rushing to get dressed."

"Where are you going?"

"I vividly remembered leaving my man in prison today." Keya replied sarcastically.

"Real cute, Kee. You sticking out with dude?"

"Yes, he's been looking out for me and my daughter. I would be a fool to let him slip by. Anyways, Dawn and I are hanging."

"What's popping there?"

"They're having a talent show. Every year they have one."

"Yeah, I hear that. It's too hot for me to show my face in Magenta. I may have to blam someone up in there. I keeps it real gangsta.."

"All that shoot 'em up stuff, is that suppose to be funny, Cash?"

"You know what I'm saying so don't trip. I'm really calling about my father sending me a letter and now I'm going to read it."

"That's good Cash."

"Yeah, I hear you."

"I mean at least you can get closer to him if you want to. I can't. My dad is a deadbeat. And you know, on my way from seeing Smokey I realized that I shouldn't even search for his tired ass. He should be searching for me."

"But you know our circumstances are different, my father...I mean you know what I'm saying," Cash said.

"No, I don't know, so say it." Keya demanded.

"Why should I say it when you know what went down?" There was a pause before he continued. "Kee, I didn't call you to hear all this flapping of lips. I'm nervous. I don't know if it was intended or not, but my father murk madukes. I'm missing her," Cash said then remained silent for a few seconds.

"I feel your pain, Cash. Trust me, I do. You need to hear him out. Maybe get closure on that part of your life. Listen to ya girl and hit me on the hip when you finished reading the letter, aight?"

"Okay, shortie." When the phone call ended, Cash checked the road sign and found that he was about half hour away from Harlem.

Keya immediately called Dawn to tell her about the conversation with Cash.

"Hey Kee, what's up? Are you ready girl or what?" Dawn asked without waiting for an answer to the first question.

"I was born ready, DJ. But that's not why I called. Guess what Cash just told me?"

"What girl? Later for the guessing game, spit it."

"Well, gosh are we impatient today. His father sent him a letter after all these years of being locked up."

"Say what?"

"Yes girl. He just hung up with me. Cash is on his way to read the letter. He was saying that at first he wasn't going to and I told him at least he could get some closure on his situation."

"You know that's right, Kee. That was really good advice. Cash can use positive things more than the negativity he's surrounded with."

"Thank you, Miss Paralegal."

"Girl, leave my profession out of this. I'll be at your house on the dot, in twenty minutes. You better be ready," Dawn said then they hung up.

Cash reached the apartment building. He was hoping a lot of people would not be hanging out front. He really did not want the attention or be seen by any of Boobie's peoples. Cash pulled his Kangol over his eyes, rushed into the building and quickly opened the downstairs door. He had kept the keys to his old crib. Cash startled Stacey when he turned his key in the door. He heard her jump up from where she was breastfeeding Sydney. Stacey was old school like that.

"Hi boo," she said before even seeing his face.

"Hey, where's my daughter?"

"Come around the corner before you start asking for her. Where the hell is she going to be other than right here with me? Cash you're getting on my nerves about this little girl." Stacey said with a hint of jealousy in her voice.

"Shut up and give me a kiss, dammit." Cash demanded. Stacey did not hesitate. She puckered up and he kissed his daughter on her forehead.

"What about me?" Stacey asked.

As soon as Sydney saw her daddy she removed her mother's breast from her mouth and reached out to him. Stacey kept on trying to feed her.

"Oh, every time daddy comes up in here you want to jump away from me, huh stinky butt?"

"Tell mommy to leave daddy's little girl alone."

"You and your daughter can go somewhere and leave me alone." Stacey joked.

"Is the food ready Stace?"

"I know you're not trying to play yourself?" Stacey said looking at him with a mean grill.

"Woman, calm you ass. I'm just playing," Cash said.

"Don't try and put me in no category with your hos'."

"Meow! Be easy wild child. What's all that about? I'm only playing. And don't

you be calling my female friends hos'." Cash responded.

"Whatever! Your food is in the microwave."

"What, you really cooked?"

"Open the microwave and look," Stacey replied with attitude.

"Hmm, I haven't had this chicken thing in a minute. Good looking out, Stace," he said and gave Stacey a kiss.

"The iced tea is in the freezer." She said with a smile. Cash did the running man. Stacey burped Sydney. Cash set the timer, poured a tall glass of iced tea and went to wash his hands. When he returned he picked up Sydney.

"How's daddy's baby-girl doing?"

He saw the twinkle in his daughter's eyes. She smiled while he playfully held his daughter above his head. Cash made farting sounds on her tummy. He pretended he was going to bite her and that made her laugh hysterically. Stacey stood in the background enjoying the way Cash played with his daughter. She felt conflicted that Sydney got all his attention.

"Cash, Sydney needs to be changed," Stacey interrupted.

"Let mommy change you bootie and daddy will get you after he eats. Okay mama?" Stacey brought Sydney in the bedroom to clean while Cash ate. "So where's this famous letter?" He asked with a mouthful of food.

"I'll get it. Wait a minute." Stacey said. He turned the television to ESPN and stuffed his face. Cash drank most of the iced tea he had poured. Stacey finished changing Sydney and put her in the playpen with the musical toys her godfather, Forster had purchased for her. Stacey walked by Cash and took the iced tea out of the freezer. She placed it on her coffee table where he sat eating. Stacey knew he drank a lot when he ate. She went in her drawer and took out both letters. She handed him the letter his father wrote and the one she had written in response.

"He wrote two letters?" Cash asked.

"No, I responded to his letter and I wasn't going to let you read it, but now that you're willing to give him a chance, I figure I'll let you read both of them."

"Oh really?"

Cash asked Stacey for a second helping of her delicious chicken. She took his plate and headed toward the kitchen without question. Cash slowly removed the letter from the envelope. He took a deep breath, carefully unfolded it and started reading.

Stacey set his plate in front of him then went to check on Sydney, playing with the stuffed animals and doing baby talk.

Cash was deep into the letter his father wrote. His eyes were watery and he lifted his head so tears would not stain the page. Cash continued reading. He was touched by his father mentioning a lot of the good things his mother had done. Cash could no longer control the tears from streaming down his face. He turned to see where Stacey was because he didn't want her to see him crying. Stacey had left him to privately read the letter.

He began to beat himself up mentally, thinking how much he'd suffered because he didn't really give his father a chance. Cash thought if his father spoke so highly of his mother, why didn't he give her the respect? His mind was a whirl with all sorts of thoughts as he read on. He saw where his father spoke of Sydney. Tears came by the time he reached the mentioned diamond earrings. Cash cried even harder. He pictured his mother's face when she used to smile at him. She had a glow about her every time she smiled and spoke softly to him before he went to bed.

Cash pictured his mother holding Sydney. So many thoughts and visions ran across his mind while reading this letter. He even reminisced on his father hugging and talking to him at night. The years went by. Cash had never given a thought to how good his father had been to him regardless of the situation. Cash suddenly realized how much he missed his father. He finished reading the letter and wiped his eyes with his shirt. Before he knew it he was reading his father's letter over again. Stacey eased her way right next to him on the sofa with Sydney in her lap. She put her arm around his lower back, while Sydney leaned over urging her daddy to pick her up.

"Babe, don't cry we're here for you," Stacey said. Cash picked up his daughter and began to sing:

"They say a man ain't supposed to cry..."

"Did you read both letters?" Stacey asked.

"Nah, I can't read it right now, but give me a few minutes." He responded without looking at her. Stacey leaned on him while he held their daughter. "Hold Sydney and let me read your response to Casmere." Cash said calling his father by his first name. Stacey took Sydney while he opened her letter. Cash didn't waste time. He was surprised to know how well Stacey expressed herself to a man she never met. "This is good. I probably wouldn't have condoned it, but I'm glad you wrote it," he said smiling.

"I am going to send it out tomorrow. Do you want me to mail yours out with it?"

"I didn't say I was writing him back," Cash said. Before Stacey could get another word in, his cell phone rang. He glanced at the number before answering.

"What's up Forst?" Cash asked.

"Nothing's up. Did you read your father's letter or what?"

"I just read it and it touched me. I ain't gonna front. After my mother passed away I didn't give him a chance to explain himself and shut him out of my life. Miss Carroll tried to keep me updated but I just brushed her."

"Are you going to visit him?"

"I didn't say all of that. Now you're pushing it. I'll write him tonight and I'll be sure to keep you posted, ahight?"

"You do that. Oh, did I tell you they're having a talent show at the park tonight?"

"Yeah, Keya told me that she and your wifey were going. Are you?"

"Nah, you know I don't fuck with Magenta without my dog."

"That's realest shit you ever said, Forst, my nigga."

"Hit me on the hip after your baby is asleep cuz I know how you are with Sydney. Tell her that her godfather loves her."

"Ahight..."

"I'm gonna call Dawn and see what's what. I know she went to pick up Keya and you know Keya is slow. Let me go, so remember write your father, ahight?"

"No doubt money," Cash said jokingly.

They enjoyed the laugh before hanging up. My phone rang. Dawn had beaten me to the punch.

"Hey baby, I was just about to call you."

"Oh really now. Baby we found parking and it is crazy off the hook out here. I saw this girl that Keya and I went to school with. I think she has her kids with her, she's nuts."

"Honey, you be careful and have fun. I'll be in the house waiting for you to come home."

"Kisses to you," she said and hung up.

Keya and Dawn headed into the park. The deejay, Kut Master C and Red Alert from back in the days was spinning. The crowd was throwing down Bronx style.

"Say yeeeaahh..."

Dawn ran into her old friends and Keya kept running into all her old tricks. One of them told her she was looking real good and if she still accepted money for sex, he wanted to be the first on her list for round two. Keya told him that was her past and she was about to get married. The poor slob's mouth fell to the asphalt.

"Someone's gonna wife you?"

"What kind a wise-ass crack is that supposed to be?" Keya asked. Before either of them could respond Dawn dragged Keya away.

"If you listen to petty peoples you will want to stoop to their level. You moved on, so later for him," Dawn said dancing her way through the crowd all the while holding Keya by the arm.

Fellows were pulling on Keya as she made her way through the crowd. The emcee announced the start of the show and everyone sat on the benches in the bleachers. Special judges were Busta, the entertainer and Just-ICE, the rapper.

The contest was like Showtime at the Apollo, sans the Sandman. If the audience liked the act, they would cheer loud. Booing was louder. The first group consisted of four young girls from Queens. The guys booed the young girls even though they sounded good. Most of the guys were asking to see more skins. The next act was solo. She was young, around twelve years old and from Harlem. Her name was Coco and she did a Whitney Houston's number, rapped to the beat and ripped it. She threw a freestyle dance in the middle. She was definitely fierce, confident and bold. The crowd went crazy especially when she started hitting those notes like Whitney. The girl had moves to go along with her act. The crowd cheered so loud, she was automatically a finalist. Dawn knew the judges so she and Keya sat on the lower benches. Most of the crowd had to sit further up top. Dawn and Keya felt good to be in Magenta again. The next contestant came up and he sang a Keith Sweat song. Before he could get to the chorus, the crowd shouted:

"You're begging just like him."

Then the boo-birds came out in full force. The young man was escorted off the stage. There were two entrances and at the entrance on the left there were rowdy guys. When the contestant left the stage some of the guys in the crowd threw objects at him. One of the judges went over there to calm the bullies down. It looked like the

rep of the park would be advanced. Then one of the judges came back over where Dawn and Keya were sitting and explained that the guys were throwing bottles at the kid who had left the stage. The incident would probably have a damaging effect on his stage performance but the show did not end abruptly, which had been the tradition.

"That kid deserved a prize from us. I mean he did participate in the contest." The Judge announced.

The show went on uninterrupted through outbursts from the crowd. Keya didn't know why but she struck up a conversation with a girl that sat next to her. They were talking about kids and day care. When the contest was over, the judges ruled that the four girls from the Q-Boro and Coco from Harlem were the winners. They received great prizes, a Sony stereo set, gift certificates to clothing stores and another chance to perform again, this time on the Harlem summer stage.

The talent show was over and everyone was mingling, dancing to the funky beats of old and new school. The crowd was reveling then it happened. A fight broke out and people were running everywhere.

"Aw shit, the party was off the easy until some idiot pulled out a gun." Keya said amidst the chaos.

"This wouldn't be Magenta, would it?" Dawn noted.

They remained calm and kept their eyes peeled in the direction of the fight. A crowd had gathered around the combatants making it difficult to see who was fighting. Loud explosions were heard as gunplay was introduced. People scattered in all directions. Dawn and Keya were standing on the side close to the judges. Bullets were flying everywhere. The judges and deejay made a dash toward their cars. Dawn and Keya did likewise. Keya fell over someone's boot and Dawn turned to pick her up, suddenly Dawn stumbled. They kept running holding hands until they were out the park. Keya felt Dawn slowing down.

"What's wrong DJ?"

"I don't know why but my leg feels mad numb." Dawn looked at her lower left leg and she saw a hole in her pants and a few drips of blood. Keya immediately lifted up Dawn's pants leg and saw blood.

"DJ, I think you've been shot!" Keya screamed. She couldn't believe her eyes.

"I was?" Dawn asked.

"Oh, oh my great God, DJ you're bleeding!" Keya screamed as tears rolled down her face.

"Don't cry Keya, I'm okay," Dawn said.

Keya took out her phone, immediately called 911 and gave the operator the location. Keya took off her sweater from around her shoulders and wrapped it around Dawn's leg. Dawn leaned on a car and Keya knelt to tie the sweater around the wound.

"Oh shit you could bleed to death. Where the damn ambulance at?"

"Kee, calm down. I am alright. It doesn't hurt I'm not bleeding hard."

Dawn examined her leg while Keya sobbed uncontrollably. Dawn held her trying to console her. Then she called me while they waited.

"Hi my sweetie," I answered.

"Baby don't get all upset just listen to me carefully," Dawn said seriously.

"Tell me what happened?"

"I was shot." She said as nonchalant as possible. I flipped.

"Where'd you get shot? What you mean? Come on Dawn don't play with me now." I was worried and scared.

"The bullet hit my leg."

"Who did it? Was it Boobie's peeps?"

"No, no it was an accident. I don't know them."

"Is Keya with you?"

"Yes she's here with me."

"I'm on my way."

I jumped into my sneakers and grabbed my car keys. I called Dawn's cell phone.

"Baby, please talk to me till I get close to you, ahight?"

"Okay baby."

"Tell me what happened?" I asked.

Before Dawn could get into the details, I heard sirens. The ambulance had arrived. Dawn asked the paramedics which hospital they were taking her to. The female paramedic told her Bronx Lebanon Hospital. Dawn repeated that to me. I hung up after telling her I would meet them there. The male paramedic brought out the stretcher. She told them she could walk to the ambulance. Keya was shook.

The paramedics helped Dawn and Keya in the ambulance and questioned them

regarding the shooting. Dawn was very cooperative and the paramedic complimented her on being brave while cleaning and bandaging her leg. He explained that there would be a follow up by the police another medical procedures and x-rays. Dawn remained positive.

I jetted to the hospital almost hitting a car and a pedestrian. Dawn entered the emergency room and the doctors removed the temporary bandages. They examined the wound, all the time asking if it was hurting. She responded that it felt numb and that it wasn't hurting but was uncomfortable. Keya called Mrs. Jones who informed Dawn's father and they were both on their way to the hospital.

Dawn was relaxed kidding around with the doctors. They treated her well giving her goodies and food while she waited for her results. It was about that time that I came bursting in the emergency room. Dawn could tell that I'd been crying.

"Dawn, Dawn are you okay? You know who did it?"

"Baby no, I don't know who did it and I am okay. Nothing hurts. I am waiting for the results of my x-rays. Okay?" She responded.

I was so happy, I began kissing her cheeks and caressing her back. Keya stood nearby crying. Dawn called her over. I put my arm around Keya and told her my baby was strong so she didn't have to worry. Dawn gave Keya a hug to calm her.

"She's gonna be alright," I said.

We were busy consoling one another when Mr. and Mrs. Jones hurriedly walked in.

"Mommy, please don't cry," Dawn begged as her eyes began to fill up in tears from seeing her mother cry. Her father was worried. The deep lines of wrinkle on his forehead made that obvious. They greeted Dawn with hugs and kisses then they hugged Keya and me.

"What happened?" Her father asked.

"Mommy daddy I'm okay. I'm not in any pain. We're just waiting for the x-ray results to come back. I can go home today."

The doctor came over to where we were and gave the results.

"Fortunately the bullet didn't hit any arteries. You're okay to go home," he said.

"Thank you Jesus," her mother exclaimed. Keya breathed a sigh of relief. "I am taking my daughter home with me Forster. You are welcome to come," Mrs. Jones said. Dawn was discharged from the hospital with prescriptions to fill to prevent any infection and an appointment for follow-up tests. She went home with her parents and Keya slept all the way home as I drove in silence. I called Cash and as expected his reaction was to ride, shoot up somebody's corner or crib.

"Look Cash, we don't know who was clapping at who. Let it rest for now, ahight?"

"Forster man, you need to leave all that to me. Someone will squeal if I squeeze a few necks."

"Cash, I'm telling you there's no need for anyone's wig to get push back."

"Leave that to me. I'm ready to push a few back right now. That shit is fucked up."

"You know sometimes that's how things go down in the park. The important thing is my honey didn't lose her life in the park," I said.

"True, true. Yo Forster, take care of your wifey, man."

"Ahight my brother, I'm getting ready to do that right now."

"Ask her if she ain't seen the shooter."

"Forget about it for now, Cash. I'll holla."

"Peace, Forst. Holla when you hear sump'n. I'm strapped and ready."

"Peace Cash..."

I dropped Keya off, went home and got Dawn some clothes and her favorite snacks. I took a pair of my best pajamas. I was not leaving the side of my injured fiancée. We stayed in the living room. Dawn had a sofa bed and I slept on the air mattress. I nearly caught a leg-cramp from stepping on the pump trying to fill the bed to its full size. I was most grateful to Mrs. Jones for letting me stay over. I knew she did it only because we were engaged. I really didn't care where I slept as long as I could be of service to my honey.

We were all settling down when Cash called my cell phone to speak with Dawn. While they were on the phone, I busied myself in the kitchen preparing homemade ice

cream. It included brownies that Mrs. Jones had made earlier, strawberries, chocolate ice cream with peanuts and whip cream. Dawn asked for a snack and I made her one of her favorites. She had no idea of the treat I had in store for her.

Cash was running up my minutes reassuring my honey that he would find out who shot her. My sweetheart was such a peaceful person. She kept telling Cash to forget about it.

"Leave it all in God's hand. That's where it belongs, Cash."

"Yeah, that's good and well but I want to get at them gangsta style."

"God will take care of everything in His style," she said as I came back with the trays and dessert.

I gave her a signal to end the conversation and her soft brown eyes widened with surprise when she saw the snack. Dawn quickly shoved the phone at me.

"Take care Dawn." I heard Cash saying as I put the phone to my ear.

"Yeah we'll do that. You do the same, Cash," I said.

"Ahight, peace," he said and hung up.

I cozied up to Dawn, ate and watched The Honeymooners. After some time things got warm and I wanted to do more than cuddle. I didn't because it was important to show respect. It made Dawn happy that her father was back in the home. I spoon-fed her the dessert and she loved it. Her smile stretched from ear to ear. Her beauty had me trapped. It was too much, I thought as I cleaned up the spillage from her exposed cleavage. I decided to talk about the incident instead.

"Were you scared sugar?"

"No, because I didn't know I was shot. I didn't feel anything, I was numb," she replied.

"Man that's crazy."

"Talk about crazy? Kee was all bent out of shape," Dawn said.

"I'm not gonna front, honey. My heart fell to the floor when you called me. For some reason the calmness in your voice made me a little sane." I said and gave her another spoon of ice cream. I kissed her lips tasting the ice cream. Dawn smiled.

"Forst, I'm so lucky to have you in my life."

"No, no I'm the lucky one."

"You're genuine sweetness."

Dawn's smile was sexy on her. I wanted her badly. It wasn't going to happen.

I changed the subject.

"Tomorrow I'll fill your prescription so you can take the pills. I don't want my baby to get any infections," I said and fed Dawn another spoonful of delicious ice cream.

I clowned a little showing her how she had to walk. She was unable to put pressure on her left leg, so her butt stuck out as she tried to move around. I called it her Howard the Duck walk. Dawn waved her hand pretending she was paying me no mind. Her parents found it entertaining and joined in the fun. Being shot had one positive effect on Dawn's family situation. Her father's presence in the home kept her excited and hopeful that her parents would be back together.

We were knocked out asleep the morning after. Her parents came down the stairs to see how we were doing. Tears filled her mother's eyes as she watched Dawn sleeping peacefully. Her father put his arm around his wife to comfort her.

"I thought being that we have one child and she's a girl that we won't have to worry too much about her. She was on the right track and out of all these years Dawn been safe. Just when I let my fears ease, this happens."

Her mother's tears rolled down her face. I called my boss and told him that I needed a few days off. He was hesitant but understood after I explained Dawn's condition.

Some of her co-workers and boss called and were already planning visits for the afternoon. The smell of turkey bacon and French toast greeted my hungry face. I stretched and saw Dawn asleep on the sofa bed.

"Well good morning sleepy-head, you slept well," Mrs. Jones said.

"Good morning ma. Yes it was good, thanks," I said and went off to the bathroom.

Mr. Jones grabbed a cup of coffee before heading to work. Dawn slept like a baby while her mother prepared the morning feast consisting of turkey bacon; eggs with cheese, French toast, and corn beef hash, all Dawn's favorites. Her mother loved to cook for Dawn and I was beginning to feel unwanted. She spent a lot of time with me and we were always eating together. Now that she was home, her mother relished the opportunity.

It was eleven-fifteen when her mother woke her. I had already eaten and gone to the pharmacy.

"Ma, where's daddy?" She asked while stretching.

"He went to work. He'll call you later."

Dawn limped to the bathroom. Her mother laughed when she saw Dawn walking.

"You and Forster are gonna have to stop messing with me," she said with mock seriousness.

"Sweetie your butt is sticking out every time you swing that left leg around," her mother added. "The doctor said you can walk like that for at least two days before you have to put pressure on your leg. We're going to work on that in a day or two, so you better not get used to walking like that."

"Yes mother." Her mother prepared a plate for Dawn, when the doorbell interrupted her. She put down the plate and headed towards the door.

"Hi come on in. What a surprise." It was Cash and his daughter. "Give me this precious little baby." Mrs. Jones requested. "Make yourself at home," she added.

"I surely will by washing my hands and having breakfast with y'all," Cash said.

"Go right ahead, Cash there's plenty, and please help DJ with her plate. She's in the bathroom."

Dawn brushed her teeth and stared into the mirror. She really couldn't believe she'd gotten shot. This is a guy thing, she thought. Dawn sat on the edge of the bathtub and slowly pulled back the bandage so she could look at her wound. "Uh, this looks nasty," she said out loud. She quickly covered it. Someone was downstairs visiting. She made her way to the living room and the aroma from the food made her limp a little faster. When she turned the corner she was surprised to see Cash. He immediately put his plate down and rushed over. They embraced each other while Cash whispered in her ear.

"I swear to you on my mother's grave I'll find him."

He kissed her on her cheek. Before pulling apart, Dawn told him not to worry because it hadn't been intentional. Cash wasn't about to let her know that he would still search for the shooter.

"Hi beautiful," Dawn said to Sydney, who was playing and laughing.

"Eat your food DJ then you can hold the baby," Mrs. Jones said.

Dawn didn't argue. She sat and Cash brought her a plate with a tall glass of orange juice. Then he joined her. They laughed and talked about old times. The doorbell rang again. Cash insisted on answering it this time.

"Hello, is Dawn in?" A middle-aged woman asked. Cash opened the door so Dawn and her mother could see who it was. The expression on Dawn's face said everything was cool. It was her boss with a few balloons and a gift. "How's my favorite employee?" She asked, leaned over and gave Dawn a hug. The phone rang as they greeted and chatted. Dawn gave Cash the okay with a wave of her hand and he answered the call. It was a Detective asking for Dawn. Cash brought the phone over and she excused herself.

"Ms. Jones speaking," she answered.

"Hello Ms. Jones, this is the Detective that was questioning you yesterday and I wanted to make sure you are doing okay?"

"I'm doing fine. I have my wonderful family looking after me," she said looking at her mother and Cash.

"I am calling because you told us you didn't see the shooter. I was wondering, if after getting some rest you remembered anything else about the incident?"

"No sir. But if I did, trust me I would've told you guys everything."

All the while Cash was shaking his head no and pointing to himself as to say he would deal with the guys not the police. Dawn held the phone and laughed a little at Cash's gestures.

"I will let you get back to doing what you were doing. But remember if there is anything someone might tell you or whatever, even if you don't think it's important, it may help us solve this. Give me a call. Take it easy on that leg, alright?" The detective cautioned. "You still have my card, correct?"

"Yes, I do and I'll call if I hear anything. Bye."

Cash happily placed the phone on its charger. By now, Sydney had eaten and Mrs. Jones changed her. Cash was child-free for the moment. I rang the bell and was surprised when Cash opened the door.

"My man, what's popping?" I greeted Cash.

"Nothing but breakfast," Cash said rubbing his belly.

"Thanks for coming through dog," I said.

"You know, Dawn's fam. There's no way I wouldn't have come," Cash said.

I greeted Dawn's boss then gave Dawn and her mother a kiss on their cheeks.

Then the five of us, including Sydney talked. Dawn, her mother and boss discussed her condition while Cash and I was shooting the breeze.

Ten minutes later the phone rang. Dawn, her boss and mother were still in a deep discussion. None of them glanced in the direction of the telephone. Cash was the closest to the phone and did the honors like he was Mr. Belvedere.

"Hello," Cash answered.

"May I speak with Dawn please," a familiar voice requested.

"Hey ma," Cash replied.

"Who's this?" Keya asked.

"It's ya baby's father," Cash responded.

"Why in the hell will you say something like that?" Keya asked.

"I'm not?" He asked.

"You know what Cash?" Keya paused before saying: "Never mind just put Dawn on the phone," she demanded. Cash turned to Dawn and she asked who was on the line.

"It's your girl. Her drawers up in a bunch?" Cash laughed loudly so Keya could hear him. I joined in.

"Hey Kee."

"DJ, why is that ignorant..?"

"He came to see me unlike you."

"I just came back from seeing my fiancée."

"Your what?"

"You know? I told you that Smokey asked me to marry him."

"Yep, but you didn't say you told him yes."

"Well I'm telling you now," Keya said sounding annoyed.

"Okay..."

"You think you're the only female that a guy could ask to marry?"

"First of all I don't know why you have an attitude problem."

"I don't have an attitude problem. But if something special happens to DJ, it's not suppose to happen to anyone else."

"Why would you think something like that?"

"You don't have to say anything when good things happen to you because you feel it won't happen for others."

"I don't give a damn. Marry who you want. If you accepted his proposal then more power to you both. I'm living my life the way I want to and you should do the same. I only gave you advice as a friend."

"How're you gonna call that giving me advice? I've been your best friend and over the years all you do is belittle me every chance you've gotten."

"You are so full of shit Keya and you know it. I was there when you had your daughter. I was there when you were selling yourself and the whole nine."

"See this is exactly what I'm talking about, DJ. Everyone is there at your house and you throwing my business out there like that."

"Throwing your business out there? Everyone knows what you've done and what you're probably doing now. That has nothing to do with me. Maybe you should look in the mirror and ask yourself why you put yourself out there."

Mrs. Jones and Dawn's boss stopped their conversation to listen to Dawn's. I tried to remove the phone from Dawn's grip, but she wouldn't let me. Cash shook his head because he knew Keya was jealous of Dawn. And that's what this feud was about.

"You're always talking wild shit and can't back it up," Keya said.

"Cuse me ho' the last time you fought my battles was when we were younger. Don't get cute or let my injury fool you, Kee."

"Whatcha saying, DJ? You don't bring no fear over here, bitch!"

"Kee, I'm not trying to scare anyone but I'm gonna leave you on this note. You know where I am, so if you want to see me over some petty shit, then come see me. If not lose my number, tramp!" Dawn said angrily and hung up immediately. As soon as the call ended, everyone rushed to find out what was wrong.

"All I said was that I didn't know she was going to marry Smokey while he's incarcerated. Then Kee went into 'I don't want to see anyone else happy and I feel no one else can be happy or something like that'."

"Don't stress it because she'll need you before you need her," I said.

"That's real," Cash said clearing his throat and adding two cents.

"You two have been friends too long. I know firsthand that you've done nothing but help that girl. So don't let her get to you just as long as your love is genuine," Mrs. Jones said.

"How long has she been acting like that towards you?" Dawn's boss asked.

"Truthfully it could have been our entire friendship for all I know," Dawn

said.

Her tone was low. She loved Keya like a sister and did not want the relationship to end. I sat next to her and held her hand as she tried to recover from the phone drama.

"Baby, you know Keya is moody and she doesn't know how to separate the bad feelings from good ones. She'll come around don't you worry," I said.

"Later for her she's a hater and you don't need no chick like that in your corner anyway," Cash said. Everyone nodded in agreement. "Listen, we all came here to cheer you up and for real, that's what's up," Cash said.

Sydney slept through the loud discussion. Dawn's boss bid her goodbye and Cash walked her to her car. Mrs. Jones continued to talk about Keya's behavior.

The mood was the same in Mrs. Jordan's home. It was the place where Keya and her daughter were for the moment.

"Why were you yelling on top of your voice, Keya?" Keya's mother asked coming from out her kitchen.

"DJ was getting on my nerves," Keya responded.

"Why?"

"When I was pregnant with Te'rena she was like; 'you shouldn't keep her.' She was trying to get pregnant by her boyfriend and because she didn't, she didn't want to see me get mine. Now that Forster asked her to marry him she feels I can't get proposed to."

"I don't think she meant it to be taken that way."

"Ma, you're not around DJ. Trust me, she don't want no one else to shine when she is. I told her Smokey asked me to run his barbershop and she was like he's stupid for asking me that. She on a hating mission instead of being happy for me. She works for someone and even though it's a good job, but I'd rather work for myself. I don't see me being ahead of her financially, but I'm about to make moves and it seems she don't like it. Trust me ma, I've known the girl for years and I'm tired of her hating ways."

"How's Smokey doing?" Her mother asked after seeing Keya becoming angrier. This flipped a switch and put a smile on Keya's face.

"Ma, he's so well groomed. I mean he looked good when he was home and even in prison he still looks fine and in good spirits. Smokey wants me, ma. I mean, I hesitated because he's in prison. He doesn't have a long time to go. Smokey could easily wait till he gets home to marry me. I guess he doesn't want anyone else to bag me."

"You and this slang, try talking some English around here," her mother said smiling.

"Ma you know I'm gangsta princess so don't front," Keya said walking away with a mean bop. Her mother laughed.

"When are you picking up my granddaughter?" Mrs. Jordan asked.

"I asked Smokey's mother to get Te'rena and she asked Te'rena if she wants to come home. When I spoke to your grandchild she said tell nana I see her tomorrow," Keya said with a giggle. "Seems like you've been replaced," Keya said jokingly.

"The hell I am. You know I don't play with my baby so don't get Smokey's mother slapped."

"Ooh ma, now I see why I'm so gangsta. You've been fronting on the low, like you this goody, goody," Keya said with one of her eyebrows up in the air. "Ma, by you saying what you just said, I know you was wilding." Mrs. Jordan laughed and went in the living room. "Nah, don't run off now, mommy tell me the truth. Were you gangsta when you were younger?" Her mother was still laughing. "Come on ma, tell me. It'll be our little secret. I promise I won't tell anyone." Keya reassured her mother.

"Alright, alright, I was a bully and ran with a girl and boy posse back in my days." Her mother confessed. Keya jumped up and down.

"I knew it, I knew it," she said excitedly.

"I didn't say I was an angel now, Keya. I even sold a little weed." Her mother added.

"Ma, you could've been arrested. So, so that's where I get the hustling part from?"

"Your father was the opposite of me. Not one soul could see what the two of us had in common. But it was love."

"Not to change any subjects but I thought my sister was coming up for the summer, ma?"

"I am waiting for her stupid father to get back to me. Did you know that Kenya might be staying for good?" Her mother asked.

"That's good because Te'rena could get to know her auntie and Kenya can spend some weekends with me at Smokey's house," Keya said with a wink.

"So you are really going to marry him while he's incarcerated?"

"Ma, Smokey is the man for me, just based on what he's done for me and Te'rena. I don't want this opportunity passing me by. I gotta live for today, tomorrow is not a given."

"Kee, if he loves you now and wants to marry you then he should have the same feelings three years from now."

"Ma, I'm not arguing that. I want to do it now. Smokey isn't pressuring me. It's up to me. I'm thinking about my daughter's future too, you know," Keya said.

"Well I can only stand behind you if you've decided what's best for you and your daughter."

"Thanks ma, that means a lot to me, especially coming from you," Keya said. She thought for a moment before adding: "Mommy, I know you retired from your job, but can you please help me with the barber shop, until I get the hang of it? I don't want Smokey's friends to help me because I don't know if I can trust them."

"Sure I'll help. I'm also good with keeping the books up to date."

"I'll give Smokey the good news when I visit him next weekend. Tomorrow I'm gonna have the keys to his house. Maybe you can meet his mom then."

"That's all right by me."

"Why couldn't you have said that, years ago?" Keya asked with a laugh.

"No cause your little butt wanted to be grown so I couldn't just agree with whatever you wanted to do," her mother said and went into her bedroom.

Keya sat in the living room thinking about the phone call she had with Dawn. She knew Dawn did not mean any harm but it hurt her feelings to know that her friend didn't want her to shine. Keya was lost in her thoughts and she fell asleep on the sofa with the television on.

She dreamt of Smokey and her wedding. He wore a white tuxedo and Keya had on all white too. Her veil was white her dress was short in the front and long in the back. The dress was laced with white pearls and her hair was pinned up with white beads. Te'rena wore a pink flower girl dress and their son had on a white suit. He wasn't walking yet. Mrs. Jordan sat in the front row holding little Smokey while the ceremony took place. It went quickly until a woman wearing all black interrupted them. That woman busted the door open and screamed.

"I'm here to stop this wedding because the bride is a prostitute and has the virus."

The entire seventy five guests had their mouths wide open. Just as Keya turned to see who this woman was, Smokey's mother begged him not to marry her. The woman in black had a hat covering her face. When Keya began to walk toward the mysterious woman she lifted her hat.

"DJ, you jealous bitch!" Keya yelled attacking Dawn.

The bell began to toll. It was loud. Keya awoke and wiped the saliva drool from her cheek. Keya realized it was the phone but didn't see it. "Damn, where is it?" She cursed. Keya slowed down, took a breath and listened to where the ringing came from. Finally, she spotted it on the floor near the sofa. She dived for it and answered right away.

"Hello," she answered out of breath. It was the same operator with the message of a call from the correctional facility. Keya accepted the charges.

"Hey sweetie," a man's voice greeted her after a few seconds.

"Hi Smokey I was just dreaming about you."

"Was it good?"

"In a way" Keya giggled.

"What you mean in a way?" Smokey asked.

"Well we were getting married in a church when Dawn busted into the church and declared me a super-ho."

"Why would you dream something like that?"

"Dawn and I argued. Maybe that's why she was in my dream."

"That is so high school and the two of you just need to cut it out. There aren't many females who've been friends as long as you two have been."

"I know but it's not me."

"Anyway, y'all be aight. How's my sweetie doing?"

"I'm good now thanks to you and I've been thinking really hard about

everything you've asked me."

"Is that right?"

"Yup, and my mom is cool with whatever decision I make. That's why I don't see why Dawn can't feel the same way."

"Baby you have to do what makes you happy. Believe me, she's doing the same."

"You're absolutely right and I am going to do just that."

"Baby once you run my business like I tell you, you'll have so many haters they won't be able to stand the sight of you. Are you going to move in our house now or what?"

"I am. I'll meet with your mother tomorrow."

"Speaking of my mom, have you spoken with her today?"

"Earlier, Te'rena is still with her."

"Oh yeah?" Smokey asked. Keya sensed his excitement through the line. "That's real nice of her. I'll call her tomorrow and thank her for watching our daughter."

"You don't want me to do a three way with your mom?"

"Nah, I can't have my mother in all our conversations and plus this is different. You're my fiancée now and about to be woman of my house."

He couldn't see the smile on Keya's face but she was cheesing from ear to ear.

"I am excited about us getting married. I made up my mind regardless of how it makes certain people feel. I only have one life and I choose to be happy. Smokey you make me happy and you've always shown my daughter and me mad love."

"You won't regret your decision."

"You don't know how I feel about you asking me the question. If it's up to my friends and mother, I'll never marry anyone."

"Why would you say that?"

"They're peeps but they don't really know me. You see I'll do whatever it is I have to do for Te'rena and me. I just refused to go back into stripping and all that. But like those girls, I had to hustle on the side. Smokey I'm glad you didn't judge me. You know me better than a lot of my closest friends and I'm thankful for you taking time out to get into my head and not just my underwear, that's love."

"Ma, listen you don't need friends who's gonna be hating once you become an entrepreneur. You're gonna be making more money then they will ever see. I have big plans for us. I want to know all your ideas and dreams."

"I want you Smokey as badly as you want me."

"This phone call is about to come to an end. I gotta go do laundry," Keya said.

"Getting off the phone is getting harder for me."

"Don't even start me because my eyes are watery already."

"Give me a kiss and I'll talk to you soon."

Keya blew him a kiss and Smokey returned it as the phone call ended. Keya had a big smile on her face as she walked to the receiver and she placed the cordless phone on it. Her mother was in the kitchen preparing lunch and saw Keya's smile.

"I see someone is making you happy, huh? Told him the truth about your health yet?" She asked.

"Ma, I told you how I feel about Smokey and I dont wanna hurt him," Keya said.

"I am happy for the two of you, but my decision stays the same."

"Ma, life is soo short. I want to be happy and enjoy the rest of it. Smokey has become a big part of both Te'rena and my lives. I don't want anything to change that."

"He desrves the truth. Don't let me have to open my mouth. I will."

""Ma you can't be selfish, let him have his happiness too," Keya said and walked away.

WEIGHING ALL OPTIONS

Dawn made her last doctor's visit for the gunshot wound in her leg. I accompanied her. Mrs. Jones was under the weather. The doctor took an x-ray for the last time to make sure there were no additional injuries. He examined her leg.

"Your x-rays are back," the doctor said while holding it up to the light. We both curiously observed. "As you can see everything is fine and you're healing very well. If anything occurs, give me a call." The doctor recommended. Dawn thanked him with a handshake. I did the same and we exited.

"Baby, you've been very brave," I said giving her a kiss.

"If the doctor panics then I'll panic." She smiled.

"Really?"

"Really, I am always calm in scary situations because if I was to panic I will make my condition worse."

We walked happily to my car. Her limp was not as noticeable as before. We went to my job and I picked up my paycheck and then we went shopping for food. Neither of us spent much time in the apartment. Since the incident, we both had been staying at her parents The cell phone rang.

"Babe, answer that for me."

"Hello," she said in a sweet sounding tone.

"What up? Is this Dawn?" The person questioned.

"Yeah, who's this?" Dawn asked.

"It's Cash, where my boy at?"

"Right here," she handed me the phone.

"Yo Cash, what's up, money?" I greeted.

"I just wanted to know, if you'll come with me to visit my pops?"

"Hell yeah, I'll go. I'm just glad that the two of you are mature enough to settle this. I'll holla at you later, aight?"

"Aight, good-looking," Cash said ending the call.

"What was that all about?" Dawn asked.

"He wants me to go with him to visit his father in jail."

"Are you going?"

"Yep, cause my boy needs me."

"Why are you going to a jail to see someone else's father?"

"That someone else is my best friend. I'm sure he would do the same for me." I said then glanced briefly at Dawn.

"Why you looking at me like that?"

"Why would you fix your mouth to ask something like that? You know how long I've been down with Cash. This is very important to him. His father accidentally pushed his mother out the window or whatever. All these years went by and Cash didn't want any parts of his father. Now, you wanna question my support for my man?" I asked and continued when Dawn didn't respond. "I am surprised at you. I mean, now I see where Keya's coming from."

It was then that Dawn gave me her coldest stare yet.

"How dare you try and use that against me. I always have you and Kee's backs. I try looking out for y'alls best interest and I get kicked in the ass."

"How are you getting kicked, when you're putting us down?"

"Forster, how dare you say that? I'm not putting anyone down because I'm not perfect. I was just trying to give y'all some advice, but betcha from now on Dawn Jones ain't gonna have shit to say about nothing." She folded her arms and stared straight ahead.

"Dawn, maybe you think you know it all. Trust me you have no idea."

"Exactly what's that suppose to mean?"

"Listen I'm turned off right now and I don't feel like shopping. I'm dropping you off at your mother's."

"And where do you think you're going?" Dawn asked but I was too angry to respond intelligently to her.

I turned up the volume on the radio. We were in midtown getting ready to go across the Lincoln Tunnel when the argument had occurred. It was our first major falling-out. I turned around and headed back uptown to drop her off as promised. The car ride was silent all the way to her mother's. I was steaming at first but then relented and asked if she wanted something to eat before we reached her mother's. She shook her head no. I tried to kiss her but she slammed the car door in my face.

I left it at that and peeled off from her block. I had no idea where I was going. I kept driving, wandering and thinking. Somehow I wound up at Magenta. It was the middle of summer and the place should be rocking. I expected a basketball tournament, or a regular jam. Something should be happening every day in the summer.

I pulled up on the block. Crowds of people were out in white Tees and blue jeans. White uptowns and white fitted, the dress of the day. A celebration was in progress, music was pumping and mad people were out frolicking. The streets around Magenta were crowded. I double-parked and stood around kicking it with a few of the fellas.

"What's good?" I asked sharing pounds and hugs with all.

"We just checking out the scenery," one of them said.

"I feel you," I said smiling and nodding in agreement. There were plenty chickens running loose. They were out there showing skins and asses. Sexy, scantily dressed girls out and about. I looked but couldn't touch. It felt like Dawn was right there, on my shoulders.

"Yo Forster, what's this I heard, you're engaged to your childhood sweetheart?" One of the guys saw me peeping at asses and asked.

"Yeah, yeah that's my boo for life." I answered.

Everyone's attention turned to me.

"I was going to ask my baby moms to be my wife, but she be tripping. Always want to know my every move."

"I feel you dog, but I don't have that problem. Let me put it this way I never gave my girl a reason to be that way toward me," I said.

"You know what dog? You right. I did give my baby moms mad reasons," he

said.

"Show her you ain't about that no more. Then you both can take it from there," I said.

"Hmm, you know what? I'm glad I ran into you because no other dude I be chilling with would be trying to give that type of advice. I mean I am my own man but you know how us fellas be?" He said laughing. I joined in the laughter.

"You have to do what you gotta do to be happy. Most dudes out here don't even care for themselves. How they gonna care for somebody else?" I asked.

"I always thought you were a cool dude and I like the way you just kicked it to me. I appreciate that homey." The second guy said giving me another pound on the strength of my honesty.

"It ain't nothing man, anytime. But remember do what you have to for you and yours," I said and gave him another pound getting back into my car.

I wanted to get into the mix of the party. I didn't want another parking ticket, so I parked a block away. I was in a mood to hang and I made my way through the crowd. I'd stop to give pound and kick game. At one point I ran into an old girlfriend from junior high. She gave me a big hug. I gave her ass a squeeze.

"Look at you gorgeous," she said.

"Look at you. You haven't changed a bit," I said.

"So what's new with you?"

"I'm engaged to Dawn. I don't know if you remember her but we use to always chill back in the days."

"Dawn? She used to fuck with Boobie, right?" I froze for a moment remembering that my former close friend and enemy was dead.

"Ah, that...that..."

"What's wrong?" She asked.

"I just got choked up for a minute..."

"I'm sorry. You didn't know she was messing with him?"

"No it's not that, at all. Boobie and I use to be real close until..." I started then I felt the words cutting off my breath. I paused.

"What Forst?" She was staring in my eyes but actually she wanted to see my insides. I hid it well.

"Boobie got killed almost a year now."

I answered not wanting to think about his death. Even after all this time his death still affected me. She covered her mouth with her hand. Her tears came quickly.

"I didn't know. I was away at college in South Carolina. I haven't been out here for about two years because my grades were bad. My mom and dad said they weren't sending for me unless I pick up my grades." Tears continued to roll.

"I'm sorry." I said kissing her cheek.

"No, it's not your fault. But what happened to him?" I heard her ask and again I paused. I did not want to drudge up the incident. I was trying desperately to forget it.

"He...ah...got shot." I slowly answered. By this time tears were rolling down her face. I tried to put my arms around her but her body stiffened.

"I know y'all were close because he used to tell me about you two. Boobie was like my big brother even though my parents didn't approve of my relationship with a drug dealer. Boobie would take time out and write me and send me things. We would joke on what if my parents found out about it. Will my father bring all the stuff to his block and dump it on the streets."

She laughed despite the tears. I felt bad because I knew who had ended his life. It brought that sickening feeling back to my stomach. As if by reflex my eyes started watering. I was happy when she waved at someone else and decided to end the conversation on a good note.

"Forster, I hope for your sake and your fiancée that you're still not in that game. It is real out here," she said.

"I been dead all that. I am about to be a married man. Trust me my priorities are straighter now." I chuckled. We hugged again and parted ways. I continued through the sea of blue and white, crowds of people everywhere. I wandered around looking for friends, associates and customers who I had not seen in a long time.

Someone tapped me on the shoulder. I turned quickly to see Cash grinning in front of me.

"What're you doing up in this piece?"

"Chilling, why?" Cash said glancing around on the girls passing us by.

"You know you shouldn't be here."

"What's my muthafucking name?"

"Yo, I don't have my gat on me, so don't start shit."

"Dogs don't worry. I got my wolves with me and they'll hold me down if anything jumps off."

He could tell I was annoyed. From the look on my face, Cash knew I was ready to fly his head.

"I'm out, man," I announced.

"Why you leaving, dogs?" Cash asked grabbing my arm.

"Holla at me when you're ready to see ya pops," I said and gave Cash a pound.

Before he could say goodbye, I was storming my way through the crowd and back to my car. Cash had to be out of his mind showing up at Magenta after the Boobie shooting incident. What if someone saw him? I thought Cash was going to lay low for a minute. I didn't want to deal with Cash. I thought about driving to get Dawn. I couldn't even play my music. I drove in silence thinking of my fiancée. Finally, I took a deep breath and called her from my cell. I told her to meet me outside her mother's house. She was shocked to hear my voice and thought I'd stay away longer to calm down after the argument we had.

Dawn told her mother she was going home. I was on my way to get her. Dawn and her mother put her clothes in two bags. She placed them by the door and grabbed another bag that I had left there for her.

"Alright mommy, that's it. I don't have to take every little thing with me, unless of course you're really kicking me to the curb."

"You know you're my only baby. Why would I want to do that?"

"You can't anyway because I won't let you and neither will daddy."

"Is everything going to be alright between you two?"

"Yeah, Forster just needs to calm down a little."

"But honey, you've got to watch your mouth. Sometimes your words can hurt people feelings. Be a little cautious when speaking your mind," her mother said and gave her a hug.

I saw them and got out the car. Dawn ran to the door to greet me. I gave her a kiss and we embraced.

"I thought you wanted me to come outside?"

"How're you gonna carry all these bags. I'm not letting you carry no bags," I said and gave her mother a hug. "Mrs. Jones, thanks for being such a nice host."

"You're more than welcome, Forster," Mrs. Jones replied. Dawn and I headed home immediately after.

"I haven't been home for a few weeks. Did you keep it clean?" She asked. I stared at the road and laughed. "Forst, you didn't clean up?"

"Baby, I've been busy at work. I'm running back and forth from here to your mom's. Please, I'll clean up, okay?"

"I'm glad you came to get me," Dawn said holding my hand and leaning her head close to me. "I'm sorry for what I said. I just don't like the jail thing and I know you'll do anything for Cash. Just forgive me please and I promise I'll try and be open-minded from now on," Dawn said with the sweetest smile on her face. I smiled and nodded.

"You'll have your chance to make it up later in bed."

"Is that a threat?" She laughed.

"Bust who I saw in the park a minute ago?" I asked changing the subject.

"Who?"

"Cash."

"What? Why was he there?"

"I don't know. But I do know his head is very hard. You know what they say about a hard head?"

"It makes a soft behind." We both laughed.

"That's your friend," Dawn said.

"I told this fool he shouldn't be there but he told me his wolves were with him. I mean if Boobie soldiers find him, it's on."

"And what, you're going to run to his rescue too?" Dawn asked with sarcasm.

"We aren't going to get back into that. He's my boy and you know that. But let's not think negatively right now, ahight?"

"Ahight, ahight I am ready to go back to work tomorrow."

"When we get settled in the crib, I'll pick out all your outfits for the rest of this week and get them ready. How does that sound?"

"Sounds good to me. Can I get breakfast too?"

"You sure can. What would you like, my queen?"

"I would like home fries, eggs well done with one slice of cheese and beef

sausages."

"How about I take you to breakfast tomorrow?"

We giggled like school children. Dawn knew I wouldn't be up to cooking all that food. We made our way up to their apartment carrying the bags. I opened the door and Dawn entered. She walked in and dropped the bag she had been toting.

"You're such a big liar." She laughed.

"What?" I countered.

"I thought you said the house was messy?"

"I figure I'll surprise you."

"Give me a kiss, liar." I locked the door behind me then landed a big juicy one on her soft lips. "It's been a while, huh?" She asked catching her breath.

"Yeah, well you know we couldn't really get our freak on at your mom's."

"As soon as I come out of the bath, I'm gonna teach you not to lie." Dawn said and walked sexily into the bedroom. I was more excited than a kid in a candy store. I placed the bags against the wall.

She went into the bedroom, undressed and jumped into something sexier. She was in a good mood undressing when she saw the lights flashing on the answering machine. Dawn didn't hesitate to listen to all the messages. The first one was her boss, wishing her well. The second was from my mother, and the third message caught her full attention. It was Keya.

"I know you are at your mother's house but I had to leave you this message. I want you to know that I miss our friendship the way it used to be. I mean, before my daughter was born, before you had sex you know I've been doing the do before you. Anyway maybe I was out of line, but that doesn't mean you shouldn't see other people's point of view. I love you like a sister but I'm grown and I'm gonna make plenty more decisions that you or my mother probably won't approve of. Regardless I will never judge neither one of you and that's something I don't get in return. Dag, DJ you have the longest answering machine. That's why I like it. Anyway I know this might be cheesy over the phone, but I would like for you to be my bridesmaid on my wedding day with Smokey. Pick up your jaw and answer me later. See ya." Keya said ending the message.

She sat on the bed when she first heard Keya's voice on her machine. Her tears came by the end of the long message. She knew deep down inside Keya was a good person and had been through a lot.

"What now, baby?" I asked jumping into the room with no underwear on startling her.

"Boy you crazy, jumping in here like that? You know my nerves are bad."

"What's wrong?" I asked fearing the worst.

"Keya left me a nice message and something I don't want to go into right now. As a matter of fact you can listen to it tomorrow. Now get out my way and let me start my bathwater."

"Baby, you're a little too late. I did already." I said and gave her a big wet kiss. She went into the bathroom and I called Cash to make sure he was alright. His voicemail came on. I hung up the phone and dialed Stacey's house because I figured Cash might be with his daughter.

"Hello," Cash answered.

"What up with you, dogs?" I asked.

"Same shit, what up with you?" Cash repeated.

"I figure your ass will be there with Sydney. How's my goddaughter doing?"

"She's sleeping in my arms. Stacey been taking our pictures all damn day."

"Ain't nothing wrong with that."

"I was like you when my boo started that picture taking bit. After awhile it wasn't that bad and I felt good that she captured those moments."

"Ah Forst, now you sound all mushy. Don't tell me, you're really a sucker for love, man." Cash jokingly responded.

"That's why she's my fiancée."

"Whatever, man."

"Nah, on some real shit I'm calling to see when you're going to see your pops."

"I feel I need to go by myself. I don't know, it's different if someone else is there with me on a visit for six hours. I might not vent like I wanna. You feel me?"

"I'm feeling you dog. I'm not mad at that. I am very proud of you. Your daughter really helped change your mind and heart. I'm glad she's in this world."

"So am I." Cash responded and gave Sydney a kiss on her head.

"I'm a go see pops this weekend. And I'm not gonna front, Forst, I'm mad nervous. I hear a lot of dudes talk about not having their pops around and most of them feel if their fathers was around they probably turned out better."

"I hear you, Cash."

"Forst, I have to see my father and I need to keep my head clear of negative thoughts because I'll wind up snatching that man out his chair." Cash laughed.

"And I know he knows your temper. I don't think he'll be trying to upset you anyway."

Sydney was lying in her daddy's lap fast asleep as he spoke on the phone. Stacey saw her daughter and moved to relieve Cash.

"Cash let me put her in the bed," Stacey suggested.

"She ahight. You just finish cooking my food." Cash shouted in a playful manner while hitting Stacey on her butt. Stacey loved cooking and Cash enjoyed it. "Where's wifey?" Cash asked.

"In the shower. Keya called and left a message."

"What she saying?" Cash asked.

"I don't know. Dawn claimed it wasn't bad. You know I don't get into women, she-say biz," I said and Cash laughed.

"You crazy," Cash said still laughing.

"Let me go man, I just wanted to holla and see if you wanted me to still go with you."

"Okay," Cash said and hung up.

I tiptoed into the bathroom to see what Dawn was doing. The bubbles floated high, her bathtub pillow was underneath her head and her eyes were closed. I stood in the bathroom doorway admiringly staring at her.

"You are even beautiful with your eyes closed," I said.

Her eyelids fluttered as she looked up at me.

"Hey you," she said. I sat down on the floor next to the tub.

"I can't wait till you are my bride." I kissed her wet hand. She smiled.

"We are lucky to have one another. Do you know that?"

"I know."

"No seriously, we're young and we both make good money and we have a beautiful relationship. We have no children, so we can travel and enjoy life. We're not abusive to one another. We don't argue and fight. I mean, we have our disagreements here and there but other than that it's really smooth sailing. I'm appreciative for just having you in my life as my friend."

She kissed my hand. I was moved and smiled from ear to ear.

The telephone rang at Keya's but no one answered. The machine picked up. Smokey dialed his mother. The operator came on the same way she did at Keya's. His mother picked up.

"Hey ma," Smokey said.

"Hi baby," she replied. And without Smokey asking her anything she yelled for Keya. Smokey was relieved because he was about to ask his mother if she had heard from Keya. Smokey smiled when Keya laughed in the background. When she picked up the call she was a little out of breath.

"Hi sweetie pie," she said.

"You had my heart pumping mad fast for a minute there," Smokey said.

"Why?" Keya asked worriedly.

"Nah, it ain't nothing bad. I had called your house and when no one answered I assumed I wasn't going to speak to you today."

"I've been bringing my mother over to your mom's house so they can get to know each other better. Being that they will both take on an in-law soon," she replied.

"Wow you're touching my heart on the real."

"Isn't that the truth?"

"You have to pick a date, missy."

"Why I gotta pick the date?"

"Cause isn't that what females love to do?"

"But I want you to have a say too."

"I just want to give you the money to get whatever it is that's going to make your day perfect. Besides you can wait three to four years until I come home. It's really up to you."

"I don't want to wait for nothing because time isn't on our side. We aren't promised tomorrow so I want to live for today. You make me happy and I want to spend the rest of my life with the man who captured my heart."

"Okay ma, let me say this and I'm not getting off the subject. My man is going to call you so you can open the shop, alright?"

"Sure you know I'm down. Besides I need to start staying in my future home."

"I told you to already. But I love you and will talk to you soon. Before you put my mother on can you get one of your friends to take your picture in sexy lingerie for me?"

"No digga. I love you too." Keya responded and handed the phone to her future mother-in-law.

"Yeah Baby."

"Ma, Keya is going to open back up the shop for me. Please help her out. I know you know my business like I do and I need you on this. Love you and my time is up but I'll call you this week. Love you mom."

She heard the dial tone. Smokey's mother went back and talked to Keya's mother while Keya and her daughter put a puzzle together.

"Are you guys staying the night?" Mrs. Jockton asked. Keya looked at her mother and nodded her head.

"Ma, you're tired you have to get up in the morning."

"Te'rena has clothes here and I could drive you all back to the Bronx after dropping her off to school." Mrs. Jockton suggested and Mrs. Jordan agreed.

Later they sat looking at pictures of young Smokey with his sisters. Keya pondered what her mother would say if she opened her big mouth. With fear in her heart, she put Te'rena to sleep. She sat and wrote Smokey a letter.

When she was finished, Keya folded it and put it under her pillow. Both Mrs. Jockton and Mrs. Jordan camped out in the living room. Keya cried herself to sleep as both Mrs. Jockton and her mother stayed up for hours shooting the breeze.

CASH'S VISIT

Cash had been in jail plenty of times but never to visit anyone then leave. He was amazed to see how visitors were treated while trying to see their loved ones. Even though Cash heard complaints from his loved ones but experiencing it first-hand was vexing. A CO spoke over the loud speaker.

"Store all jewelries, change, keys or any metal objects you have in your pockets into the lockers. Once you insert a quarter the key to the locker will be yours for the duration of the visit. That's the only object allowed inside along with your money. If you want to leave any money for inmates, do so now before entering. By the time you're finished with your visit, the cashier will be closed. At this time we are asking for family and friends who have loved ones with the last name that starts with A through L to form a line, right here. Have your State Driver's ID ready. If you are not on the visitation list by inmates then you will not be allowed to see anyone. After initials A through L, then we'll be taking last names starting with M through R."

Cash saw that visitors were bum rushing the lockers like it was the end of the world and that was the only place they had to hide. He heard a woman and man yelling at the CO's.

"Why didn't anyone notify us that there are certain days for inmates who last name starts with S? Y'all on some bullshit! I took off from work and now I have to

wait eight hours to go back to the city because y'all not informing us correctly." The middle-aged woman argued. Her gentlemen friend was trying to calm her. Another CO spoke on the loudspeaker.

"We've just made those changes and all inmates have been informed."

He turned off the microphone as the same woman shouted at him.

"Bullshit," she yelled. "Y'all make me fucking sick. You treat us like criminals when we haven't done shit. I'm outta here." She grabbed her jacket. The gentleman with her escorted her out. Cash watched them go outside while he prepared to see his father. He placed his cell phone in the locker and emptied his pockets. He then took off his do-rag that matched his outfit and headed for the line. For the first time in a long time Cash wore a button up with some baggie jeans and his white kicks. A woman was in front of Cash with her little daughter. Her daughter looked the same age as Cash's daughter. He waved hello at the little girl and she smiled. Her mother saw her smiling and looked Cash up and down in a friendly way.

"She reminds me of my daughter, and it makes me miss her right now," he said. "Do you see your daughter often?" The woman asked.

"Do I? I change my life around because of her. I moved in with her and her mother because I wanted to wake up and see my baby."

"That's good, because you hear a lot of men diss their children," she said.

"I don't know how brothers can do that? I may be thuggish but not as much as I was before my daughter was born."

"That's real good and God will bless you for taking care of her. You see this beautiful little girl I have?" She asked. "I was faithful to him but I still asked him if he wanted a blood test. And I never heard from him again even after I offered to pay for the test. She looks just like him too."

"Ma, don't stress him. Just keep doing the mommy thing, you'll be ahight." He put a smile on her face. Then the line started moving. Five people were entering a small space at a time. A huge metal door opened and the people stepped in then it shut. They gave the CO's the inmate's last name and CO informed the visitors the number on the table the inmates were at. It was easy to spot the inmate you were visiting. Cash's heart raced when the big metal door opened.

"Next five," the CO yelled.

Cash was the first and four others followed. All five persons gave their loved ones last name and the CO opened the second gate. The number to Cash's father was twenty-one. Cash felt his knees buckling as he walked to where his father waited. He was nervous. He couldn't identify his father immediately because the visiting area was packed with visitors hugging loved ones. When everyone settled down Cash was close to the number twenty-one. He saw a well groomed man resembling himself. As Cash approached twenty-one he saw himself at age forty-something. On seeing Cash his father rose to his feet. Cash silently shook his father's hand and sat down at the table. There were tears in his father's eyes.

"You look just like I did when I was your age. Man that's scary." His father said. Cash wore a smirk on his face. "I can't express how much this means to me. You are like my king and I look up to you," his father said. Cash was caught off-guard by his father's response. He couldn't even open his mouth. "Son, I want to get straight to the point. I've been in here for years and not a day goes by I don't cry. I lost the two most important people in my life. If I'm out of line right now or, if there's a subject you don't want me to touch then just say the word."

"I'm here to hear what you have to say," Cash said without looking directly at his father.

"Alright, here goes: Your mother was my first love and ..." He paused as tears fell down his face uncontrollably. "I never cheated on her." He said with his head down. Then he looked Cash straight in his eyes. "I love you like I love myself. I loved your mother like she was God. I had a drinking problem, a gambling problem and she was trying to help me be straight. I was like a crack-head tied to a chair and the drug dealer spread crack all over the floor in front of me. Now don't you think the crack-head will eat that rope off to get to the drugs? Well, your mother was that rope and the love I had for her was stopping me, at least slowing me down. The other thing that was really making me drink was this situation I had to deal with by myself. Not even the love of my life knew my secret. My parents didn't, my best friend didn't. I mean your godfather and I was tighter than tight. He was my best friend for real, not like these now a days nigga. You follow me?"

"Yeah, go on." The whole time his father kicked the tale Cash was nodding his head.

"Anyway my main man didn't know what this burden was on my back. If I had gotten professional help for my situation, I don't know, maybe my temper and drinking

could have been resolved." His father said reading Cash's reaction. He needed to talk some more and did. "But son there's no excuse for me taking it out on your mother. She only wanted the best for all of us. Especially you..." A few more tears flowed and Big Cas wiped his eyes before he continued. Cash's eyes began to get teary as he watched his father and thought of his dearly departed mother. He heard her voice urging him to listen to his father and work it out.

He was surprised to see this side of his father. Cash had only witnessed the hardcore. It moved him to tears to watch his father cry. Slowly the realization hit him; the man sitting in front of him was doing life for a crime that he hadn't mean to do. His mother falling out the window was purely accidental. Cash was caught up and didn't hear his father.

"Damn!" Cash hissed.

"Son, son it's all good." His father started and turned his head so Cash wouldn't see his tears falling. After several minutes he finally said. "Why don't you go over to the food machine and get us something to drink?"

Cash didn't hesitate or respond he just got up and headed to the machine. There was a line for the soda machine. Cash was glad he needed the time out of his father's face. He didn't want his tears loose. Furthermore, he had thought he would probably get mad at his father and beat on him until correction officers had to drag him off. Instead Cash cleared his mind and prepared himself to hear his father. There were many thoughts and questions running through Cash's head. He blocked out all the noise in the facility. Cash glanced over at his father. He was still wiping his eyes. A CO had walked over to him but Cash couldn't hear what they were talking about. The line was getting shorter. Cash was so caught up in his mental anguish that he didn't realize the line was moving, until a dude yelled at him.

"Yo money, move it or lose it!"

Cash turned around and the guy saw the screw he wore on his face. The visitor became shook and almost ran off the line. Cash started to go after him. He wanted to choke the loud-mouth for yelling and trying to embarrass him on line. Cash checked himself. The visitor breathed easy and was having a lucky day. Cash calmly proceeded to the machines.

He bought two bottles of water and two chicken sandwiches with barbecue potato chips. As Cash headed back to his father, he walked by the dude who had a staring match with him. He showed Cash there was no beef by turning his head and keeping eyes down. Not a peep came from his lips.

Cash sat down and offered his father a bottle of water, the chicken sandwich and chips. His father wore a smile.

"What?" Cash asked.

"Just that you eat the same things I eat. I thought people eat chips with sandwiches like turkey and cheese. You know?"

"Nah, every time I eat anything that includes bread I have to have barbecue chips," Cash said.

"Tell me do you eat spaghetti with ketchup?"

Cash stared, shocked by what his father had just asked. He gripped the table to prevent falling out his seat.

"That's where I get that weird eating shit from? You...?" Cash asked laughing. His father joined him in the laughter. "My friends always be gigging on me cuz I be eating crazy combinations. I like ketchup on my pizza and ketchup on my white rice." Cash laughed.

"You are really just like me. Your mother used to say that. 'That boy of yours is just like you'. She knew how much you meant to me. You are all I have left son, and I just wanted you to hear me out before you completely shut me out of your life. I am still part of you and your mother. She will always live on through us," Big Cas said and lifted his sleeve of his muscular left arm.

Cash saw his mother's face tattooed on his father's arm. His father did the same for his right arm. Cash saw his own face tattooed on his father's arm. The man wore his family's memories on his biceps. Tears rolled and Cash held his head down. His father cried again. "Cash you see I still wear my wedding band because in my mind I'll always be married to your mother. Her face is on my left arm because that's where my heart is. And you are on my right because you'll always be my right hand man." His father said and the tears poured from his eyes. Cash felt helpless. He moved his chair closer to his father and hugged him. His father wept some more after receiving affection from his son. His son silently cried next to him. They hugged each other and in that moment there was forgiveness as all their emotions poured out. The C.O. came and interrupted their private moment.

"Sir, you need to move your chair back to the other side."

Cash and his father gave him the look of death.

"I'm following my orders," he said and walked away when Cash moved his chair back to its original spot.

"Man, you are my son," his father said laughing. Cash shared the laughter. "Okay, now I'm all cried out. You speak now. Tell me about the adult you that I've missed out on." His father suggested. Cash shook his head like a shy boy. His father nodded his head yes.

"Aw c'mon, tell me. You can tell me anything Cashmere. I won't ever be the one to hurt you. I'm here in your corner, Cash."

"That's real," Cash responded thinking of what to say. "I felt my life would've turned out better if my mother was still alive. I was mad at the world. I mean I felt my mother was ah...cheated out of life. She didn't get a chance to watch me grow up. I was furious at my boys that had their mother in their life. I didn't want to hear what their mother bought them or how she treated them because my mother wasn't here to do those things for me." Cash paused. His father was all ears and Cash continued. "Fighting was the escape. I set out to demolish cats who wanted to bring it. Whether it be with knives, guns or shooting a fair one. I had so much more on my back then they had. No one could stop me. My enemies chose their weapons I did too and I'm better at anything." Cash paused. His father nodded quietly urging him to continue. He did. "I only have one best friend. His name's Forster. He's been do-or-die down with me from jump. On top of that he also had problems in his home. So we'd relate to one another on some levels. He's mad different than me. I like that. He's calm, cool and collected. Me on the other hand, I'll shoot first and ask questions last. But since the birth of my daughter, I think I changed a lot of my ways." Cash glanced around. Everyone seemed into the different conversations.

"Go on, son. Don't stop. I'm learning a lot right now."

"I don't know if you heard but I...ah lost a son. This girl I knew from back in the days, got pregnant. The baby died...it's been a while now but it feels like it was yesterday. That was hard, it still stay's on my mind. And that make me love and appreciate my daughter even more. And I know mom would've loved her too. She's a good baby and she looks like my mother too."

"She does?" His father interrupted. "Well this is a visit worth waiting for all these years. Time flew by mad-fast and I want to thank you for coming to hear your old man."

"Where you get old man from? You mad down to earth and you look mad young."

"I got to give all these looks and knowledge up to God. Without him I don't know how I could cope with my problems all these years. And you should try God too, he'll show you the right way to life decisions. Just start with a little prayer," his father suggested.

"Nah, I'll leave that to you, old man." Cash said and both of them laughed out loud.

"Oh, now I'm old because I'm talking about God? I ask God all the time to watch over you. So there." His father said with a smile on his face. Then he stood up and hugged Cash as tightly as he could. I love you son and don't be a stranger either. Give my granddaughter a hug for me and stay positive for her." His father said as their visit ended.

"I love you too dad. I'm glad I came to hear your side."

"I'm glad you did, son. I am your father and I am always on your side."

Cash felt happy to see his father. He couldn't wait to tell Stacey and me.

"Yo Big Cas, that's your seed?" An inmate asked.

"Yeah that's a mini-me." Big Cas responded with a laugh.

Cash turned to the inmate and nodded, acknowledging him. He was glad his father had been seated at table number twenty-one. They had a few extra minutes to chat.

"Dad I want you to meet my daughter's mother. If that's alright with you I'll bring her up?"

"Son, I'd love to meet her."

"And if it's alright with you I'd like to propose to her when we get up here."

"That's all good, my son. Listen, they calling our number, Cash. Write me sometimes."

"Fo sho." Cash joined the line to exit the visiting room. The bus ride back to the city took no time. What his father had said remained in his head. He felt a big relief lifted off his heart. He called me as soon as the bus pulled off the facility.

"It's about time fool. What's good?"

"Nigga, I told you I was going to see my pops."

"Oh, my bad, I forgot. I've been busy with Dawn and all. She went back to work and I'm making sure she's comfortable. You know?"

"Fo, sure that's wifey for real. I can't be mad at that, Forst."

"How was the visit?"

"Man, it didn't go the way I thought it would."

"What you mean by that?"

"I was going on some rah, rah money-better-not-even-mention-my-mom type a shit."

"You stupid, how you gonna say that about your pops?"

"This some serious sh..." Cash said and I joined in his laughter.

"You mad funny. Your pops better not had said nothing slick, huh?"

"Yo Forst, man you breaking up, man. I can't hear you. I'll holla when I get better reception. One."

The bus swerved through the suburbs. When it hit the city limits. Cash dialed again.

"Cash, you could hear me?"

"Yeah, you good. I was saying I loved him. I didn't want to leave, but I wanted to at the same time. Man, I was in lockup."

"I feel you."

"Forst, he touched my thug heart. On da real to real my brother."

"No shit..."

"Yo man, we need to stop cursing too."

"Listen to this nigga. If I knew it was going to scare you straight, I would've sent your ass to visit prison a long time ago."

"While I was there, guess what I thought about from back in the days? I mean junior high school days?"

"Wait, wait let me guess. Yeah, yeah when the school took us to the jail cell like we suppose to be scared or some shit, right? I'm not gonna front. I was a little shook back then." I confessed and Cash laughed so hard all the people on the bus turned to look at him.

"Man, you stupid. You weren't really scared?"

"Hell yeah, why you think I kept making jokes, cuz I almost pissed on myself when they let us stand in the jail cell." We laughed until our stomach ached.

"You chicken."

"You my dogs for real, Cash. I'm glad you called me after sharing that moment with your pops." I said.

"Don't get soft on me now. I cried enough with pops. I didn't tell him but I cried thinking about my baby girl. I want to see her grow up cause in case I have to pull my gat on these young boys and put heat in their pants."

"Look at you? How you gonna say you want to see her grow up and then you turn around and want to pull out your gun?"

"I'm talking about not wilding in the streets anymore. That don't have nothing to do with my baby. On some real shit that will be the only reason I go to my closet."

"What's in your closet?" I asked.

"You know that's where I keep all them things."

"What happened to the one in your car and the two around your waist?" I asked. Cash laughed before responding.

"You stupid for real," Cash said with a chuckle. "That's me for real son."

"No that's Clint Eastwood. Like I said before, if I'd known jail would change your crazy ass around I would have been suggested you go. But I want to go on the next visit so I could tell your father about the new you," I said laughing.

"I'll make all the changes for my daughter, man. I just want to see her grow and plus I want another baby too. At first I was like, nah I wanna be selfish with my baby girl. Then I thought my mom didn't get a chance to give me a sister or brother and I really don't know what it's like having a sibling. You know? By blood."

"You better had said a blood sibling, because I was just about to interrupt your ass? I am your blood and you know that."

"No doubt, you know I know what it is between us. You be playing dumb right now. You know exactly what I'm getting at, so don't front," Cash said.

"I feel you too. I mean even though my sister been down south. I did miss her. Now that she is back, I really been trying to get closer to her. She's my only sister and I want her to know I got her back no matter what."

"I feel you on that, so that's why before I lay this on Stacey you know about another baby and all I'm gonna need you to take me to get a girly ring."

"A girly what? Like a name ring?" I asked trying to be funny.

"Forst, stop playing, you know what ring I'm talking about. Talking about that

engagement rock, man. Do I have to say it out loud?"

"Let me find out, my nigga is finally trying to wake up and smell the coffee. That's what's up. I am more than ready to take you where I buy my jewelry."

"Why do you think I'm asking you? See you good with all the girly stuff, I'm not. I'll throw a little three or four G's on the bed and tell her to go pick out her own joint."

"Are you stupid or what? Don't you ever do something dumb like that. A woman would leave you and your money right on the bed. That's crazy. Be patient I'll take you."

"I'm gonna hit you later. I'm going to see the two loves of my life."

"Yeah, hit me up later and don't forget. One more thing man congratulations on finally growing up."

"I just need to thank G-O-D for taking real good care of me since I was born."

"That's what's up."

"Yeah nigga, you heard me right. I'm gonna praise him in my own way."

"I ain't mad at you. Dawn and I are about to start attending her parents' church. Ain't nothing wrong praising the Man above. I just never heard you mentioned God."

"God spared me through all these years and He didn't have to. I am grateful to Him, trust me."

"I hear that. Hit me up later," I said and we hung up the phone.

Dawn was very excited about being back at work. Her desk was stacked with get-well cards and flowers. Her boss was more excited than the rest of the law firm because she was a hard worker. Dawn thanked all her co-workers and boss. They even paid for her lunch. She had work on her desk which her boss only trusted her to do. She was satisfied with the way everyone showed they cared. Dawn called her father to let him know that she reached work with no problems. She called her mother and talked to her for a while before starting work. She called me and then her phone rang. She thought it was me again.

"Russell and Friedman, Ms. Jones speaking how may I help you?" She answered smiling.

"Hello, I'm glad to see you're back at work," Keya said.

"Hey Kee."

"DJ, I know it's been a long time, but I felt I should break the ice because I'm getting married soon and I know you and Forster will be there for me. But I need my best friend now. So much is happening and so fast. I don't mean because I'm marrying Smokey. I know what I am doing as far as him and I go, but as far as the Barber Shop and his house and other bills, I am confused. It's all taking a toll on me and I don't want to bother him about it. Smokey is already upset that he's in there, you know?" Keya sounded worried.

"Yeah honey, I know. I know that is rough on you, Kee. I mean you also have to take care of Te'rena. I'm here for you. I could help you out on the weekends if you want. And maybe Forster and I could spend some nights with you in your big new home."

"Would you, DJ?" Keya asked excitedly.

"Kee, you know we had differences before but nothing was as serious as it was now and I feel we came along way to let minor things stop us from being around one another. I have my own opinion and you have yours. That doesn't mean we are suppose to like one another opinions, but we have to respect what one another is saying and understand where the both of us is coming from. I love you like a sister and you know that, so why won't we put the past behind us and move on. We're about to become married women."

"I know and I'm really looking forward to being Smokey's wife. The feeling is electrifying from my stomach to my heart. I've never been so happy, as far a man being in my life. Smokey understands me and he loves me. I know he does and who am I to judge anyone. Smokey could easily have judged me through my past and from what people have told him, but because he knew me he didn't fall into their trap. But let me holla at any of those guys and they would jump right in the bed with me and Smokey knows that. Some of those guys felt because I used to sell my body and strip that I was supposed to give them a play. But I didn't stoop to those other females' level and because of that I was called all types of names."

"I just wanted more for you and I didn't see the love you and Smokey had for one another. And I know what love feels like because of Forst. To think I doubted you and Smokey when the both of you shared the same feeling as Forster and I. I'm glad that you see that I'm not a hater. I just want what's best for my best friend. I'm your friend and sister. You've been through a lot and I know Smokey. Before I could judge him I had to see what you saw in him. As long as we've been friends I never heard you talk or feel about someone the way you feel about him. And I never really saw any other guy treat you the way he does. You'll always have my blessings whether I truly agree or not. My love for you is unconditional and I'm glad you feel the same way towards me. Now before I get all emotional let me hang up." Dawn laughed.

"Girl, you too? My eyes are as watery as they can be. Thanks for all the support DJ. I need to sit with you because sump'ns come up and I pushed up the date for the wedding."

"Alrighty, then let's sit and talk again."

"Alright, get your work thing on. Enjoy the day, DJ. Love you, girl."

"I love you too, Kee. Be good."

They ended the phone call. The day went by really fast for Dawn. She didn't even work a whole day. Most of it was her co-workers celebrating her being back at work. Her boss didn't mind at all, because she was in the mix of the welcome-back party too. I arrived shortly before Dawn was getting off. I took the elevator upstairs to get my fiancé. Her co-workers cheered as I entered and gave Dawn a kiss. She gave me her seat while she ran upstairs to give another lawyer some paperwork. I sat at her desk and looked around. She had a picture of Cash, Keya, her and me when we first met. There was a picture with her parents and a recent one of her and me. I was thrilled that I had seen her work area. I had no idea she had these pictures here and never thought to ask how her desk looked. Dawn said her goodbyes and hugged everyone.

"I'll see you guys tomorrow." She waved as we headed to the elevator.

"So, how does it feel to be back at work?" I asked pressing the elevator button for the lobby.

"It was good. Everyone went out of their way to make my day. I knew they had love for me, but I didn't know how much. I'm so grateful for such nice co-workers and I am blessed to have a boss like the one I have."

"Guess what?" I asked.

"What Baby?" She answered using her sexy voice.

"Cash went to visit his father today," I said.

"Are you serious, Forst?"

"Yep, and he said it went well. He and I are going to pick out some rings for Stacey," I said getting excited like I was the one doing the proposing.

"That's what I'm talking about. I hope his attitude changes along with everything else."

"You know what? I think he's already working on it."

"Oh, now you guess what?"

"What?" I asked and hugged her from behind while making our way to the car.

"Keya called me to let me know that she pushed her wedding date up. Isn't that sweet?"

"Sweet?" I asked with a puzzled look.

"Yeah, sweet. Why did you look like that?"

"Maybe because you was against her getting married in a jail."

"I know, I know, but I now know Keya is a big girl and she can take care of herself. And I'd rather be a part of my best friend's life instead of criticizing her for it."

"Well, I'm not mad at her. Life is what we make it and it is definitely not promised to us."

"That's funny you mention that because Keya mentioned the same thing."

"Okay, here's what I have on our agenda for today. We're stopping at Houston's for dinner and then going by my parents' house. How does that sound?"

"Sounds good, but you know what sounds even better?"

"What? Whipped Cream on top of you?" I asked licking my lips.

"No greedy. What about our wedding plans?" Dawn asked sounding a bit peeved.

"Huh? Where did that came from?"

"What do you mean where did that question come from? Are we not engaged?"

"Yes we are, but I thought we have to empty our plate before taking that plunge."

"No, you need to clear your plate."

"Come on the day is going smoothly," I said getting a little annoyed.

"Yeah, it was until you shut down my mood," Dawn said looking out the window.

"Don't even start with me, girl. You know I'm going to marry you. But it will be when I feel we're both ready. Not just myself, the both of us. Marriage equals a whole. Don't worry, we won't be engaged for five to ten years," I said joking and reached for her hand to kiss.

"I mean, out of all of us? Keya? I can't wait till it's me," Dawn said poking her lips like the spoiled child she was.

"Do I detect my baby with a little jealous streak?" I asked.

"Not in a bad way. Can I be jealous in a good way?" She asked.

"Baby its okay to feel the way you feel, you're only human. But we both know you want the best for Keya. She's very excited and you don't want to take away her joy."

"You're right, but I feel all stinky inside. I know she's going to be so happy on her day. I'll be right there next to her. Because, Kee's my girl."

"That's what friends are for. Don't worry we will be next," I said holding her hand.

"I hope so."

"Oh babe, I knew it was something I had to tell you," I said. "You know the guy who runs the tournaments at Magenta?" I asked.

"Yeah, but I forgot his name. Why?" She asked.

"Ron Archer, in a few weeks he is having a promotional party and that is the last time we'll be partying in there."

"Why?"

"He's moving somewhere else," I said.

"When did you hear about this?"

"A few hours ago I went to the store and saw this kid I know. And he told me."

"You know we're going to have to tell Cash and Keya. We all have to be there for the last time and I don't care if the both of them don't want to see each other right now. We all have to go say our goodbyes."

"I hear you, honey."

"When is it?"

"In a few weeks, but I'll get the official date," I said and Dawn shook her head. She didn't care that she was accidentally shot a few months ago. Her mind kept going as we headed across the Hudson for dinner at Houston's. I opened the door for Dawn and we walked about a block and a half to the restaurant where a hostess greeted us.

"Hello my name is Sandra," the hostess announced with a smile. "Two for dinner, right?" She asked. We both nodded yes and she escorted us to a booth near the window. Sandra handed us both menus and asked if we wanted anything to drink while we waited. I ordered pink-lemonade and Dawn ordered Sprite with no ice. The waitress was off.

"This has a nice atmosphere."

"I know its romantic right? Go ahead you can say your man still got it." I laughed.

"Yeah my man always had it and that's why tonight, I'm gonna thank you when we get home." She said rubbing the top of her foot up and down my leg.

"Check please," I said and we laughed. Dawn perused the menu before making her choice.

"Stick around. Don't be so hasty," she said with a smile.

"I know what I want. Do you have a clue what you want yet?" I asked.

"I'll try the salmon with baked potato."

Shortly after that the waitress came over with the drinks.

"Are you ready to order?" She asked with a smile. I ordered for the both of us.

"Okay I'll have your dinners, shortly." the waitress said and left with the menus. Dawn snuggled closer so she could reach my hands.

"You're so sweet," Dawn said.

The food came. This waitress was right on point. She remembered who wanted what. Dawn told me she would give the waitress a nice tip. We laughed and enjoyed our food. We sat for a while before paying and taking off. Dawn took most of her food to go. I had finished mine. While walking to the car, my phone rang.

"They shutting the park down."

"Say word?" Cash asked.

"Word," I replied.

"Where are we gonna go to have our summer jams?"

"I don't know yet. I heard they gonna have a three day celebration."

"Oh, you know we're in there every day. I told the little shorties from around the way and they are all bugging about it."

"Maybe we should go out there and support."

"True that, true that," Cash said.

"One more thing, Keya pushed up her date to get married. Are you going?"

"Keya is cool and all, but I ain't with it. I mean, I'll let her live without me being present. It might cause some discomfort to her and ol' boy," Cash said.

"Why he's got to be ol' boy?" I asked laughing.

"You know what I'm saying. That Crab ass nigga," Cash added with a laugh. We both started laughing even more.

"You still have feelings for your ghetto girl, huh?" I asked and knew it agitated Cash.

"You know I'm gonna get you for that. I'm going to tell Dawn that your first crush was on booger-nose Sasha from back in the days. You was loving that dirty chick." Cash laughed. It was true I couldn't do anything but laugh along.

"Nah, you got that one, payback is a mother." After we had gotten our laughs out the way, Cash told me that next week he would be ready to get Stacey an engagement ring.

"How much do you got in the stash?"

"Well I spent crazy cash when I had to stay up in Connecticut. So that takes away from the center you wanted to get for the teens. But I'll get up some papers don't worry."

"No, no, no you have my goddaughter. Don't even worry about it."

"Fool what you talking about? My pops have some money saved for me. I'm saying Forst, with that I could add that on to the drug money we saved, and there's your teen center, dogs."

"Sounds good. It's like sweet music you're playing right now, Cash."

"I'm done with ho's. That's why I'm buying Stacey this ring. I stopped all this running the streets cause of my daughter. But I just can't see me working no nine to five right now."

"Yeah, we'll have to finish this conversation later."

"Tell wifey, I said put you to sleep," Cash said but I had put the cell phone to Dawn's ear so she could hear Cash herself.

"No doubt, my nigga." Dawn said jokingly.

"Ahight, you heard the misses. I'll holla at ya tomorrow bro."

"I hear you. That's right take care of home. Forst, hit me tomorrow." Dawn and I continued with our night like we were on our first date.

DREAMS COME TRUE

The next few weeks went by fast for Keya and Smokey. Their wedding was a few hours away. Smokey wore a white button up and beige pants and white Uptown sneakers. Keya had on a tight fitted wedding dress that hugged her curves. Keya asked me to wear beige pants so Smokey would not feel like the only one. I agreed. Dawn wore a beige dress. Mrs. Jordan had on a pale pink skirt suit. Te'rena had on a beige flower girl dress. Smokey's twin sisters were there along with his close friend Mike. Mrs. Jockton had on a white and black suit. Two of Smokey's friends were there along with their girlfriends. Keya looked beautiful. Her makeup had been done by Dawn and she had spent three hours in a beauty salon getting her hair done. Everyone looked wonderful. Smokey and another inmate were talking while the family was driving up to the prison.

"Man, you look sharp," the inmate said.

"Thanks man. I'm so nervous," Smokey said to the older inmate.

"I know. I sit here and just read my Bible and I don't say much, but there's not a mean bone in my body. I just lost a lot over someone else's mistake. Young blood we live and learn, sometimes the hard way. I wish you all the best," he said.

"Hey you know me! I'm Smokey," he said extending his hand

"My government is Paul Wilson Jr."

They shook hands.

"Paul Jr. would you like to attend my wedding? I know its short notice but you'd be able to meet some fine people and get some good food," Smokey said.

"Didn't you have to give the CO's a list of your guest names in advance?" Paul Jr. asked.

"Don't worry I got this."

"Alright," Paul Jr. said.

"We're going to be the first ones in the visiting room."

"Hey is what I have on, okay to wear?" Paul Jr. asked. He wore green pants with a dark blue turtle neck along with his brown boots.

"Man you look sharper than me." Smokey gave him a pound. Paul Jr. turned to the mirror and brushed his hair. He favored the old school look; the part on the side with deep waves.

There was a van packed with Mrs. Jockton and Smokey's twin sisters, it also contained Mrs. Jordan, Te'rena along with Mike, a good friend of Smokey's. Keya rode in the car with me, Dawn and Mrs. Jones.

"I just want to say thank you all for showing me unconditional love. This means a lot to me. You're all being a part of my dream coming true. Thank you all so, so much," Keya said with tears in her eyes.

"Girl, you look too beautiful to be crying and besides you better not mess up your make up until after your future husband seen you," Dawn said wiping her teary eyes.

"You do really look nice, Keya," I said.

"Thank you so much Forster and you don't look bad yourself. Oh no..." Keya shouted.

"What's the matter?" Dawn asked.

"That's my song on the radio. Can you please turn it up?" Keya requested.

"Forster you use to sing this to me," Dawn said. I turned to Dawn and sang the song I had dedicated to her years ago.

> *"...Always and forever each moment with you*
> *Its just like a dream to me that somehow came true*

And I know tomorrow will still be the same
Cause we got a life of love that won't ever change and...
Everyday love me your own special way
Melt all my heart away with a smile,
Take time tell me you really care,
And we'll share tomorrow together
I'll always love you forever..."

We sang together. Then I kissed Dawn's soft hand.

"Dag, that brings back old, old memories," Keya said.

"We're getting old," I said.

"Boy, speak for yourself," Keya laughed.

The ride went smoothly after our impromptu concert. We were only minutes away from the jail. I had passed the van with Smokey's mother and the others a while ago. We pulled over and we waited for them to catch up to us. We were in the best of moods singing along to all the old school jams on the radio. Keya didn't seem nervous a bit. She was loud, laughing like she was in the playground. Dawn's hands were sweating as if she was the one getting married. I was excited because I had never been to a wedding before.

"You all know what?" Keya asked. Everyone turned to hear what she would say. "This is my first wedding I'm attending."

"That makes two of us." I said.

"I've been to a few," Dawn said.

The conversation continued as the van pulled up. The two vehicles drove onto the grounds of the facility and easily found parking. While everyone else exited the vehicle I grabbed Dawn's arm.

"Babe we're next," I said and gave her a kiss.

"Don't make me cry so soon," Dawn said with a smile on her face.

"I love you sugar," I said.

"Love you more," Dawn answered. Then we exited the vehicle.

"Well late birds," Keya joked with Mrs. Jockton.

"You look so marvelous Keya," Mrs. Jockton said.

"That's my brat all grown up now," Mrs. Jordan said smiling.

Keya was happy her family was there but sad to learn that her stepfather

and sister couldn't make it. They were down south. Keya knew in her heart that her stepfather wasn't here because he felt she deserved more than as he put it 'a jailhouse wedding'. Keya had let it go. She knew this was true love that she was feeling. It was something she never felt before for any man.

"Shall we go in?" I suggested. We were searched as we entered the prison. No one seemed to mind the minor hassle. We were here for a good cause.

"I'm getting nervous now, DJ." Keya whispered and Dawn held her hand.

"Honey you look so beautiful, Smokey is the one who should be nervous," Dawn said.

We greeted one another on our way in. Smokey's friend, Mike and I kicked it. Dawn and Keya walked ahead of us. Both mothers spoke while the twins had Te'rena's hands. We finally got passed the security and headed for the visiting hall where Smokey was waiting. Tears began to roll down Keya's face.

"I can't even catch my breath," she said chuckling.

"You are supposed to be nervous and out of breath," Dawn joked.

Meanwhile Smokey and his new pal Paul Jr. were patiently waiting.

"Man, I feel like I need to cry," Smokey said.

"Brother you can, if that's how you feel. It's your wedding day and let me tell you this; thugs cry too. I was one of those hard rock guys. I didn't even cry at funerals for my love ones. Then I found my special someone and our day came. I was joking all the way up until she entered the room. I thought of all the new responsibilities I had to take on now. And for her I would do anything. My tears came down my face. I finally matured and was ready to step-up to responsibilities." Paul Jr. explained.

"So what happened to her?" Smokey asked.

"Man, look where I'm at. Some women can't deal with this jail shit. The CO's are rude and they assume you have to get raped, or do sexual things with other men. I mean the list goes on brother. I've been here for about ten years and not one man approached me and neither did I have any desire for one. I would be in the hole for the rest of my stay if any fag tried anything." Paul Jr. said and Smokey gave him a pound.

A correction officer alerted Smokey that his bride was now on her way. Paul Jr. checked out his gears and gave Smokey a fatherly hug.

"You alright with me, Smokey." Paul Jr. said. Smokey took a deep breath as he saw his mother and sisters enter the room first. Dawn, and his two friends, then I followed them. Mike and Te'rena were next.

"I present to you all the future Mrs. Nakeya Jockton. The preacher announced and everyone in attendance cheered as Mrs. Jordan escorted Keya to Smokey's side. All eyes were on them when Keya entered the room. Smokey put his head down. No one saw his tears falling. Keya was overcome and cried at the sight of her future husband. Smokey lifted his head up and glanced at her. Keya drifted closer to him. His head went back down but this time the tears just didn't roll but he wore the crying face. Keya was face to face with him. Smokey looked her up and down before he spoke.

"You're just how I imagined you'd look. Just like my princess." He said with a smile.

They stood facing each other. The preacher informed the guests that Smokey and Keya had written their own vows.

"Smokey you're first," the preacher said. Smokey held Keya hands.

"It didn't take me long to know you would be my wife one day. I never had any one care for me the way you have. I never shared so many secrets before and I never gave my heart completely to a woman. You are the only woman worthy of sharing all of my thoughts with, and I will continue to share moments with you in our future to come. I am blessed to have such a dedicated mother, a down to earth intelligent woman on my side. You are beautiful inside and out, you are my friend, you are half of my heart. Nakeya you complete me and from this day forward I will always cherish you through the storms, and even on sunny days. Your family is now mine as mine is now yours. I will keep you dear to my heart and leave my family to build one with you and Te'rena. I am so in love with you that it hurts and I would like to thank God for giving me such a strong sister to spend the rest of my life with. What's mine is now yours, and with that I do." Smokey said and we all could tell that he had rehearsed the lines well. I looked over at Keya and her mother and knew both were praying that Smokey was being real. As soon as he ended, the tears rolled down his face. Keya was crying uncontrollably. Smokey wiped away the tears as fast as he could.

"Now Ms. Nakeya Jones, it is your turn to share your vows with your future husband," the preacher announced. Keya cleared her throat and Dawn wiped her face. She began.

"I had a tough time in my previous relationships but when you became a friend to me and had gotten to really know you, I asked God can you be the man I've

longed for? Well he didn't answer me right away. God let my answer be known through your actions. I lay next to you one night and I thanked God for sending you to my rescue. I say rescue because you're the Prince who rescued me from other heartaches that would of came my way. You helped me find myself when I was down. You keep my spirits high. You told me to believe in myself and all things are possible." Keya may have been nervous before but she knew what she wanted to say and did. She paused as the tears flowed.

"Take your time baby," her mother shouted realizing that there were no dry eyes in the place. Keya dabbed at her face before she continued.

"I am a very lucky girl and the way you make me feel can not be put in words. I thank you for believing in me and taking my daughter in as your own. Smokey you complete me, emotionally, physically and financially. And I'm pledging to you that I will continue to do the same for you as long as God allows my mind and body to do so. I love you with my mind, body and soul. Every ounce of love I have in my heart I place it in your hands this day. I look forward to getting older with you. I look forward to expanding our family. I am the female version of you....Smokey, you are my soul mate. And with that Mr. Smokey, I declare that I will forever be yours. I do."

"If there's anyone here who wishes for these two not to be joined in Holy matrimony this day, speak now or forever hold your peace." The Preacher said. Smokey looked around, jokingly daring anyone to object. Everyone laughed. "Smokey, being the head of household and your wife. All men should love their wife... Ephesians five verses: twenty-three through twenty-eight of the scriptures tells us that: 'He that loveth his wife loveth himself'."

"Amen," we all shouted as if we were in a church.

"Keya, as the church is subject unto Christ, so let the wife be to her own husband in everything. And let no one come between you and your husband... repeat after me. 'I, Emanuel Jockton take you Nakeya Jones to be my lawful wedded wife to have and to hold and to cherish until death do us part'." Smokey repeated each word then slipped the wedding band with diamonds all around it on, Keya'a left ring finger. Her face glowed.

"Now, Nakeya repeat after me: 'I, Nakeya Jones take Emanuel Jockton to be my loving husband to have and to hold and to cherish until death do us part'." Keya repeated each word then placed the ring on Smokey's left ring finger. Smokey hugged her and whispered in her ear.

"You won't regret marrying me while I'm in here."

Dawn and everyone else joined in with hugs congratulating the newlyweds.

"I give all of you Mr. and Mrs. Emanuel Jockton," the preacher said aloud.

There were cheers and tears. It was a beautiful moment. Throughout the ceremony Mike and I were busy taking pictures. After Smokey kissed his bride the rest of the family and friends came over to share their blessings. Pictures were taken and Keya threw her flowers. One of Smokey's twin sisters caught it.

"Don't be getting no ideas, no time soon." Smokey warned.

"Yeah, yeah, yeah you're so overprotective," his sister responded.

"Please, Te'rena is going to have it worst. She'll be escorted everywhere she goes when she's a teen." Smokey said and held Te'rena close. She smiled at him.

"You's a married woman now." Mrs. Jordan shouted quoting a line from the Color Purple.

"Girl look at your hand. You look like you're up there with Whitney Houston with that rock." Dawn noted.

"I can't believe it myself," Keya said.

"Can I get another kiss from my wife, please?" Smokey interrupted.

"Oh you're such a show off," his mother said.

"Don't hate, don't hate, it could happen to any of you," Smokey joked.

"Let's take these flicks and then chow down on whatever food is here."

I took pictures of Smokey and Keya kissing, the preacher, along with their parents and Te'rena, then all the men along with the groom. After that I took pictures of the women and the bride. Later we all sat down and Smokey's mother blessed us with a prayer and we ate. Smokey smiled and was eating heartily along with the rest of the family. Then he asked to be excused with his lovely bride. Smokey got up first and then took Keya's hand. They moved to another table. Te'rena was about to run over to them until Mrs. Jordan explained to her that they needed a few moments alone. The other guests didn't mind, we continued to eat and talk.

"It's going to be real hard to let my wife go home alone. You know if we were going home together I would tear your ass up in the bedroom. I will start by undressing you, then kissing you from your feet up. I would stop at your goodies for at least an hour before I get up in it. Then I will turn you around and start from your neck down to

your butt, there I would at least spend thirty minutes before I put the sausage in the oven," Smokey said.

"Hmm, that sounds good." Keya mumbled smiling. "Yeah but before you put him in I will finish undressing you. By sitting you on the edge of the bed and massaging your calves and feet while he is in my mouth." Keya smiled and put his middle finger in her mouth.

"Girl you don't know what you're starting under this table." Smokey laughed.

"You don't think I'm not tickling down there?" Keya asked mischievously. They both reached over the table to kiss.

"Can we go in the bathroom real quick?" Smokey asked. Keya started to laugh. "I'm serious. Call the CO over here." He said to Keya. She signaled to CO. He came swiftly.

"Yes ma'am," he responded. Keya pointed to Smokey.

"You see we just got married and I wanted to know, if there's any rules in taking my new wife into the bathroom for thirty minutes?" Smokey asked.

"Thirty minutes? What happened to you undressing me, then working your way from my toes to my head?" Keya interrupted. Smokey laughed.

"Babe, that's when we're home, now can we live for a few minutes?"

"I didn't hear that was against the rules." The CO smiled and winked.

Smokey dragged Keya to the bathroom while looking over at the family. We were busy sitting having an after meal discussion. No on was paying any attention to the newly-weds. They proceeded into the bathroom. He kissed Keya on her neck. That was her weak spot. He kissed her shoulders and she went crazy. Keya massaged and rubbed her husband from his back down to his butt and his hardened package. Smokey worked his way down passed her shoulders. He figured she would be ready to ride him while he sat on the toilet seat. Smokey pulled the toilet seat down and laid some paper towels on it before he sat down. He then took Keya's thong off and lifted her dress up. Keya climbed on him like she was about to ride a horse. Before she could sit on top of him she whipped out one of her breasts and put it in his mouth. Smokey slowly sat her on his love muscle and her eyes rolled back. His head whipped back. It had been a while since Smokey had her good loving. Keya wouldn't work him like she usually did because it had been a long time for her.

228

"I love you so much," Keya whispered in his ear and pulled out the condom.

"I love you too. But what the hell is this?" He asked looking at the condom. "What does it mean?"

"I'll have to write to you and explain..." She said going down on him.

After awhile he was screaming and quickly whipped on the condom. He slid easily in her.

"Agh...oh I'm coming Keya!"

"Give it to me Smokey." Keya answered. Chills ran through both their bodies afterwards. "Keya baby-girl that's the best you've ever been." Smokey said and kissed her putting his tongue in her mouth.

"You're telling me," Keya said. Her legs were stiff so Smokey stood up and held her while she was still on top of him. "Ooh I love when you pick me up like this." Keya whispered.

"You haven't seen nothing yet." Smokey responded then slowly lowering her to the floor. "Hold your dress up while I wipe you off," he added. Keya did just that. Then Smokey wiped off. "I'm going to leave out first because I know you have to touch up some more areas." He said and gave her a kiss as he eased the door open. The other guests weren't really worried about them, but as soon as they saw Smokey they asked for Keya. "She's in the ladies room," he responded. I smiled and gave him a pound because I knew exactly what had gone down.

"You're my idol." I said jokingly. Smokey laughed he knew what I was talking about. Smokey sat next to his mother and thanked her some more for all her help up to this point. The visit was almost over and Smokey made sure he talked with each of us thanking us personally for supporting him and his wife.

We started making ready to head back to the city.

"Let's give the newlyweds these last few moments." I said and everyone agreed. We all said our farewells to Smokey then headed out. Paul Jr. shook all the guests' hands and he too gave Smokey and his wife some privacy by heading back to his cell.

"Kee you know I am so glad that everyone that came believed in our decision. I just want you to know that if no one came it wasn't about them anyway, it's about us. If I make you feel good and take care of you there shouldn't be anything negative out of anybodies mouth. How do they know what's right for you? Only God can judge us.

I hear stories in here about childhood sweethearts that rekindle but the women are afraid because of what people think. Most people feel men in here are desperate. Okay maybe some are but its all for love. Topics in here isn't always about sex. I say that to say its only you. It doesn't matter what other people think. I love you and thanks for that quickie. I owe you a longer one."

"Like I told my best friend, if I found love and its a few hours away then I'm going for it. She knows you are the only guy who hasn't hurt me. Or use me. You're here temporarily and you support me mentally with conversation and letters. Emotionally I can always share with you anything. Physically I know you can hold me down. Financially I never asked anyone I dealt with to help me with her. But you just jumped at the chance to include my daughter. And I love you even more for that. I've never been so happy with anyone else. Now don't get me wrong I did love my daughter's father. Then he played me but that's a different kind of love. I wasn't floating like I am now. When I'm home I only think of you and all our memories. I love to visit you because the ride up here gives me a piece of mind from the fast life at home. I'm glad you made me your wife. So many females don't even get asked and they're been in a relationship for ten years with three kids. And if they did get a proposal they never get married. You have a lot financially and I don't, so for you to trust me till you come home is touching as well. I won't let you down." Keya gave him a long goodbye kiss.

It was very hard for Keya to leave Smokey even harder for him to see her leave.

"Kee, I'm going to call you tonight at our house," he said solemnly.

"I'm glad to be your wife," she said blowing kisses at him.

"And I'm your husband, don't ever cross me," Smokey replied.

Keya gave up on wiping the tears from her eyes as she made her way outside. The fresh air felt good against her face. She could smell the scent of her new husband on her body. Everyone cheered Keya when she entered the car. Her eyes were still red from crying. Dawn asked her mother to sit up front with me while she comforted her best friend.

"I want him home now," Keya cried.

"I don't even know how this must feel for you. But girl you are a married woman now. You have a husband, girlfriend," Dawn said hoping to cheer her up with that truth. "You look so beautiful and your celebration isn't over with yet." Dawn mentioned.

Keya was looking out the window until Dawn said the celebration is not over.

"What's that suppose to mean?" Keya asked.

"Well your husband knows all about your surprise," Dawn said.

Keya looked at Mrs. Jones. She shrugged her shoulders. She wasn't telling either. Keya tapped my shoulders.

"Don't tap me you know the rule and there is no way I'm getting in trouble with my fiancée and her mother."

Smokey and his mother had arranged a reception for Keya and Smokey at her house. Many of the family members that Keya had not met would be there. They were left behind to prepare the food and decorations. Smokey and Keya would have plenty of gifts to share when he was released.

I drove and jammed to a Bobby Brown CD when my cell phone vibrated. I answered it.

"Hello," I said.

"What up boy? How did the wedding go?" It was Cash.

"We're on our way home now and Mrs. Smokey is in the car." I joked.

"Put her on," Cash demanded and I passed the phone back and Dawn took it. I looked through the rare view mirror and told her it was for Keya. Keya was in shock.

"Hello," she said.

"Congrats, shortie."

"Thank you, Cashmere. That's real big coming from you."

"Oh, it's all good. Long as dude treats you right and you let him know that I'm still your baby daddy then we're cool."

"Cash, I see you haven't really changed a bit. And I thank you for your concerns. Smokey knows everything, he also knows about the loss of our child, so relax, buster."

"Where is Te'rena?"

"She's riding in the other car with my mother and in-laws."

"Hmm! Look at you with your in-laws and all that. It's all good shortie enjoy it. You heard?"

"I got you Cash. Good looking out." Keya handed the phone back to me.

"Cash, where you at?"

"I'm in the crib why, what up?"

"I'm on the road that's why."

"I called to tell you that I got one hundred and twenty G's from my dad's account he saved all that for me. You know I'm bugging right now. That's all going to Sydney's schooling and whatever else she needs. Stacey is going to put a hundred of it in a bank account for Sydney. She'll be good if anything. I gave Stacey five G's and the other fifteen G's for our wedding. I know I might have to spend more but that's all good. Sounds fair, right?"

"That's hot right there, my brother. Do it just like that. I'm gonna hit you later, Cash."

"Thank you, I feel safe again once you ended the call," Mrs. Jones said.

"That was Cash and he was excited about some good news."

"I know who it was," Mrs. Jones said. I drove to the Jockton's house where everyone was waiting for the new bride and her family. Keya's stepfather was supposed to be there with her little sister. He told her mother that he did not agree with Keya marrying this guy in jail but she is still his little girl and he'll part take in anything else. Keya thought they had gone down south but they hadn't. Smokey planned to call his mother's house later to see if his wife liked her surprise.

FRIENDS... LIFE...

It was hours away before me Keya, Dawn, along with Cash had to get dressed and head over to the park for the last time. I was waiting for Cash because he took Stacey and Sydney to visit his pops. He wanted Stacey to show her beautiful ring that I had taken Cash to pick out from the diamond district in Manhattan. Stacey was six months pregnant and she was expecting a healthy baby boy. She told me that every night Cash would talk to his son through her stomach. I remembered joking with him about having a little him around.

"Forster, please get the door, it's Keya." Dawn shouted from the kitchen.

I ran sliding to the door and opened it.

"Hey old married woman." I joked greeting Keya with a kiss on the cheek. She really did appear tired, worn and older.

"My husband is working me from that jail. And to tell you the truth I'm glad he's in there. If I got to spend the rest of my life with someone I'd rather have a year or two by myself. This is the best decision I made yet. Most Sundays Te'rena and I go to church and come back to peace and quiet until you-know-who calls. Then mom has not been well and Te'rena and Smokey starts running their mouths. All he talks about is that stupid barbershop. In a way I'm glad his phone calls are down to thirty minutes." Keya complained.

"Well dig, Mrs. Newlywed and her issues. I'm sorry to hear your mom isn't

doing well. You know Smokey gonna be a man in jail or out," Dawn said.

"I'm kind a glad he's in jail, for real. I love my husband to death but he works my nerves about what his wife should and shouldn't do," Keya said then laughed. "Girl, give me hug. What's up? Don't get married till he goes to jail," Keya said laughing.

"Next time we visit him, I'm telling Smokey," Dawn said jokingly.

"DJ, are we ready or what?"

"Well, are we feeling grouchy today?" I asked Keya.

"No Forst, and don't mess with me because you're a man," Keya said and slapped Dawn's hand in agreement.

"Sweetheart, go in the room you don't want no 'Waiting to Exhale' type party up in here." Dawn said and slapped my butt as I walked into the bedroom.

"Girl, I'm so glad we're alone. Why I found out I was pregnant?" Dawn whispered. Keya jumped up and down with joy.

"I'm gonna have me a Godchild. Heavenly Father, thank you. I'm gonna be a Godmother." Keya began dancing and singing.

"Shush!" Dawn cautioned.

"Why, Forster doesn't know yet?"

"He knows, but its very shaky up in here right now. I wanted to get married before the baby comes and he planned for us to get married in another two years. What's the damn difference?"

"Man, pride and damn ego. He's got new responsibilities and now you're trying to throw another hard one at him." Dawn stood quietly thinking. Then she spoke.

"I didn't think about it that way."

"DJ, men are a lot slower than we are and when it comes to the old ball and chain, then fatherhood, they cannot think straight, okay?"

"Kee, I hope you're right."

"And you know something some men be getting scared when their women tell them about p-word. They feel their freedom gone. Even though we had about twenty minutes at the altar, I wanted more. It is such a beautiful thing to commit to one another. It could be hard too now, don't get it twisted."

"Hmm..."

"I guarantee he'll come around soon and let you know what he feels. But let him live. Don't mention nothing else about marriage or the pregnancy right now. He knows you are with child now and he'll take it from there. And besides give it up to God and leave it there."

"I'm not going to say anything else about it. And I'm not telling anybody else I'm pregnant since he ain't telling anyone."

"Now how selfish is that? You two are adults, so act that way."

"Okay relationship expert," Dawn said with mock attitude.

"Where is that slow-ass Cash?" Keya asked changing the subject.

"He went to visit his pops in jail. Afterwards he's going to drop his daughter Sydney off to Miss Carroll's house. And I guess he'll head over to Magenta."

"Okay DJ, are you in his mind?"

"Kee, did you know Cash and Stacey got engaged?"

"I didn't know that. Well, that's good if he don't cheat on her."

"No honey child, Cash been faithful to her for this past year. He's really growing out of his nasty ways."

"I wish them all the best," Keya said flippantly.

"Dawn," I shouted from the bedroom.

"Excuse me, Kee," Dawn said and rushed to the bedroom.

She saw me standing with my hands on my hips.

"What're you some kind of super-hero?"

"Come give your daddy some good loving." I said playfully. Dawn burst out laughing.

"You're such a stupid boy, Forst. We've got company and I'm not doing that with you right now."

"Yeah, I bet you if Keya's husband was home and we visited them, he would have a quickie," I said.

Dawn smiled and agreed. She dropped to her knees and got into it. When I was finished handling my business, she spoke.

"What about me?" Dawn asked with urgency in her voice.

"That's nothing to me," I said and turned Dawn on her back and started munching on her cookies. The sex was great. We were both satisfied even though it was only a quickie.

"I need little more quickies more often." Dawn said then kissed my cheek.

"Wimp," I said.

"Why are you calling me a wimp?"

"Because your juices are on my lips," I answered.

"If I wanted to taste it I would have been a lesbian. Now I leave that up to you to enjoy," Dawn said then went into the bathroom. I followed her right in.

"We need Jesus in our life, so we could stop sinning." Dawn paused as she soaped the hand towel.

"Church?"

"You heard me, woman."

"I'm not saying it in a bad way. I just didn't know that you wanted to go to church on any regular basis."

"I've always wanted to go back."

"In that case, I'm ready when you are." Dawn said with a huge smile spreading across her face.

"Babe, I did enough negative things to know that there is nothing else out here. And God has so much more in store for us. All we have to do is come to him and receive it. And I don't want to be like some people and wait until I get in a car accident or shot, you know? I have a good job, Cash and I stopped all that street hustling. I lost a lot of homeys because of drug dealing or just wanting to hang out on the block. Most importantly I have you."

"Oh baby, that's so sweet. We should go to church soon."

"I'm going to hold you to that," I said as Dawn cleaned herself.

Meanwhile, in the living room Keya got herself some juice and turned on the television. Keya always felt at home with us. Dawn joined her in the living room.

"What y'all up to?"

"Hey girl," Dawn smiled.

"I mean did you two rabbits have enough?" Keya asked sarcastically.

"Ha, ha, ha," Dawn laughed and the telephone rang. "I got it," she shouted. I wasn't trying to pick up the phone anyway. "Hello," she answered.

"Are y'all ready?" Cash asked.

"Just about, where's Sydney?" Dawn asked.

"She's in the car with her mother. Oh, did Forster tell you I'm having a boy?"

"No that bum did not. Congratulations Cash," she shouted into the phone. Keya's ears perked up.

"I'm going to call y'all when I drop Sydney to my Miss Carroll's house. You better call that slow ass married woman."

"Oh, she's ready," Dawn said and hung up the phone excitedly.

"What's up with you, DJ?"

"Oh, Cash and Stacey are having a boy." Dawn answered forgetting that Keya and Cash had lost their son.

"That's good. I wish them the best," Keya sadly said.

"Keya, I'm sorry, honey. I'm just happy for them because they're engaged and now they're having a little boy. I didn't mean to just blurt it out like that to you."

"You didn't do nothing wrong. I mean life goes on for the both of us and I'll have another son soon."

Dawn excused herself and walked into our bedroom to let me know that Cash was on his way. When she entered the room I was laid out across the bed wearing only boots and jeans. I was sleeping. She laid her body across mine and kissed my cheeks.

"Wake up baby." She whispered in my ear.

"I'm up," I said lazy-eyed.

"Cash and Stacey are going to be here soon." I nodded.

She didn't bother me anymore and continued to get dressed. Keya was ready to go. She had to meet up with her in-laws later. They were going food shopping. Shortly after Dawn had gotten dressed, the doorbell rang. Keya jumped up to answer. She looked through the peephole. It was Cash and Stacey. She took a deep breath before opening the door.

"Dawn its Cash." She shouted. "Hi, how are you?" Keya greeted Stacey.

"Hey girl, what's good?" Cash asked and gave her a kiss on her cheek. "This is my fiancée, Stacey. Stacey, this is a good friend, Mrs. Nakeya Jockton," Cash said with a smile.

The ladies shook hands. Dawn came running out the room and headed straight for Stacey so she could rub her stomach. Then she gave Cash a hug.

"Cash, that was quick. I thought you were going to call us after you dropped off Sydney."

"Miss Carroll was waiting downstairs. You know she's crazy over that girl anyway. Then Stace didn't want to leave her." Cash said while Stacey shook her head.

"Cash, you know that I don't like being without my daughter."

"Well come in and make yourself at home. I just woke up Forster." Cash came in the bedroom to greet me. He was not into staying around the ladies alone. The girls went straight into their girly talk. Cash walked into me as he entered the room.

"Wake up punk ass."

"I'm up. Why is everyone stressing?"

"Boy, it's time to make moves. Stop playing. I ain't staying out there with these women." Cash said and sat at the end of the bed. I laughed with my eyes closed.

"Alright sucker, I'm up," I said putting my shirt on and went into the bathroom to wash my face.

When the girls saw me entering the bathroom, they cheered me on. Cash stayed in the bedroom watching Scarface. It was playing on the DVD player. I was in the bathroom for about ten minutes then I came out.

"Ladies, let's go to the bathroom before we leave." Dawn suggested. Stacey was first. As soon as the bathroom door closed Keya went over to Dawn and spoke about Stacey.

"I guess I could see why Cash would want to settle for a woman like that, huh DJ?"

"Why do you say that?"

"She's feminine, pretty, classy, and independent. That's everything I wasn't back then."

"Kee please, you are all of the above too. Plus you have your dream husband I don't care if he's doing time or not. Smokey takes very good care of you and Te'rena and he did the same when he was out. Later for Cash, and his big-head," Dawn said. That put a smile on Keya's face.

"Ahight, let's roll out," I said.

Stacey, Dawn, Keya and Cash all headed to the cars. I secured the crib. I went with Cash while the three girls rode with Dawn.

"Yo Forst, member when we met Keya and Dawn?"

"Do I? They were the only true fly girls in the park that night and they were the best dancers."

"Yeah, they were dope."

"I swear I knew that I wanted to be with Dawn from the first conversation we had. I didn't realize back then that I'd found my soul mate. And to top it off we didn't see each other for years and we lived in the same borough. That's crazy."

"I'm not going to front I thought Keya and I was going to do it real big. I mean sticking by one another in a ghetto fabulous way. Feel me?" Cash was laughing. I joined him.

"Time has flown by. We can't front," I said.

We were leading the way to Magenta. Dawn and the girls were not far behind.

"Yo Cash, them girls running their mouths and driving like it's a Sunday."

"Who do you think going to be in the park, Cash?"

"What do you mean who's going to be there? Everybody is, fool. This is the last summer jam on the court. All week long, they've been having basketball tournaments. People we cool with will be there. I didn't even bring my gat. A brother must be changing his ways right?" Cash and I chuckled.

"We're grown men. Don't be scared now," I said while slapping Cash a pound.

"I ain't scared. It's just me without a gat is kind a new to me, Forst."

Keya, Dawn and Stacey were kicking it in the car. They were laughing as she drove.

"Kee you are a real fool. How are you going to say your husband is a bird, when he's already locked up?" Dawn asked while still laughing.

"I'm not saying he's a bird like he's bummed out or nothing. I'm saying he's a bird like a jailbird," Keya said and wiped her eyes because the tears rolled down her face from laughter.

"Ooh! DJ, turn the volume up on that song." Keya interrupted.

"Girl, Bobby Brown was the man then and still is in my book," Keya said as she sang along to Tender Roni.

Before long all three were singing along with Bobby Brown. Minutes later they reached park. Cars were lined up two blocks deep before reaching the park. With all this traffic, both drivers knew they had to find parking a few blocks away. They found parking three blocks away. Dawn and the girls got out and walked to where Cash and I were standing.

Cash kissed Stacey and rubbed her stomach. We started our trek for the last time to the courts. Cash and I were giving daps to all the old school guys we knew coming up. We hadn't seen most of them in years. Keya and Dawn were reminiscing

while telling Stacey how they were in the dance contest back in the days. Throngs of ghetto celebs swarmed Magenta. People were everywhere on the basketball court. It was a tight squeeze but we made our way to the center court. Once we reached the middle the rush of the crowd was less.

The deejay opened the festivities with Big Daddy Kane's, *Ain't No Half Stepping*. It was off the hook from that point on. Everyone was dancing, singing and prancing around. Stacey, Dawn and Keya were busy mingling. Cash and I were kicking it with old school cats. We chatted with cats from elementary and junior high. Things were going better than anyone expected.

I saw a black Mercury Sable creeping. It came to a stop alongside a row of cars double parked next to the basketball court. The car was tinted black and people around began fearing the worst, kept their eyes on the vehicle. It had stopped suspiciously and none of the windows came down. The doors did not open. Almost every local drug dealer was paranoid at the shady happening. Minutes later the passenger door opened and all worries were put to rest as a chick came out the car. The crowd went back to raising their drinks in the air. The smell of smoldering weed filled the air and touched off the excitement as the deejay continued to spin vinyl from the golden era of rap.

"Wow, shortie can I get those digits?"

One guy approached the unfamiliar female who exited the Mercury Sable. She wore red spandex suit with flared legs at the bottom and flared sleeves. She carried a silver bag, and she had a mean walk. Her legs moved swiftly but slow enough so that everyone could see how bow legged she was. Her waistline was small and her buttocks protruded. Her perky breasts bounced up and down as she made her way through the crowd. She bobbed her head to the beat as she squinted. She was sexy but I had never seen her before. The men and young boys were trying to kick it to her. She smiled without responding then walked swiftly away. A tear rolled from her eyes when she saw the man that shot and killed the love of her life. She stopped and all her tears came down. While clutching the silver bag, she made her way silently to where I was. Then she pulled out a silver nine millimeter. She stopped, aimed and fired twice. The bullets exploded in the back of her lover's killer. I watched helplessly as the explosion occurred and the crowd scrambled to get out of the way. Pandemonium broke loose as people stampeded pushing others over. She just stood there gripping the nine, crying uncontrollably then disappeared into the midst of the frantic crowd.

I had my eyes on the girls and began looking for Cash. I was hoping he was not looking for the girls or me. I dragged Dawn and Stacey away from the commotion. Frightened, Stacey began to hold her stomach.

"Where is Cash?" She shouted.

"Forster will find him, he always does," Dawn said. I assumed someone had let-off a couple of rounds in the air like they always do so I really didn't panic. I glanced over by the deejay booth. I didn't see Cash. Then from nowhere and through all the chaos I heard a voice yelling.

"Cash's been shot!"

My whole body went numb as I pushed past the crowd. I was trying to get to the area as quickly as possible and rudely pushed women and men. I didn't care I just wanted to get to my man. I reached the area where people had surrounded someone lying on the ground. My stomach did loops and my heart raced.

"Lord please don't let it be Cash, please Lord." I kept repeating in a low voice as I moved closer. It was too late. Someone had a grudge to settle and did. I saw blood gushing from Cash's body staining the hardtop. I lost it. I held both arms above my head and wailed loudly. Tears came pouring out. "Nooo God! Oh my God! Yo, move the fuck back." I yelled. My eyes were cloudy from sweat and tears once I realized that Cash was on his stomach, not moving and bleeding. I took another look and dropped to my knees in front of my fallen buddy. "Yo, don't just stand around call paramedics!"

Damn near everyone pulled out a cell phone at the same time. The crowd then cleared a little bit and Stacey, Dawn and Keya headed to where the small crowd was. Neither one of them knew who was shot. They had heard gunshots and knew someone had been shot. When they were closer, Keya and Dawn were still ignorant of who the person was. Stacey looked in between the legs standing around and saw me on my knees. She stopped in her tracks and screamed loudly. Keya turned when she heard Stacey fall to the ground. She passed out. Dawn ran over to the small crowd. Her eyes immediately filled with tears. She thought that Cash and I were hurt. When she got closer she saw me on my knees. I was covered in his blood.

"Oh, my God, no Lord, not Cash." She sobbed.

Dawn didn't know what to do. She walked over to me and pulled on my shoulder. Then fell to her knees. She said nothing. Her emotions flowed with the tears running down her face. I cradled Cash's upper body in my arms. Blood was everywhere.

I hugged Cash while we waited for the EMS to arrive.

It seemed like forever but the EMS came. They rushed over to Cash and checked for his pulse. "We got a pulse, but it's low, so let's go to work on him." I got up from my knees to assist.

The EMS worker rushed over to Stacey who had passed out completely. I couldn't go in the ambulance with Cash. Dawn and I took their car while Cash's car remained parked. Keya went in the ambulance with Stacey. They headed to Jacobi Hospital. I was crying uncontrollably and Dawn was trying to console me. She did as much as she could while trying to keep her eyes on the road. Dawn had never seen me bawling. I was miserable with boogers running down my face and all. I didn't care about anything except for my brother's life.

I telephoned Miss Carroll to let her know to meet us at the hospital. She dropped the phone and began to scream.

Stacey had an intravenous needle in her arm. Both she and the baby were okay. In the ambulance the EMS worker was dealing with the gunshot wounds. Both ambulances got to the hospital and rushed Cash and Stacey into the emergency room. Before he left, the doctor informed Miss Carroll that Cash's lungs had collapsed and they were successful in reviving him. He promised to update us as progress was made.

"We'll do all we can to help him. You cannot accompany him any further," the doctor said. They wheeled Cash in on a gurney and for about five anxious hours we waited in the reception area while they kept him in surgery. There were no further updates.

Stacey was up crying while the nurses, Dawn and Keya tried to calm her and get her to eat. Miss Carroll was in the waiting room area leaning on me. My eyes were closed because I had a pounding headache. It wasn't long before a nurse came out and told Miss Carroll that someone would be out to talk to her soon.

"How is my son?" She asked.

"He's in critical but stable condition," the nurse replied and rubbed her arm.

The atmosphere in the room felt lighter as a huge relief came over us. I got up and went to Stacey's room to let her know how Cash was doing. I walked the bright hallways with many things flashing in my throbbing head. Tears continued to roll down my face. I whispered a prayer.

Stacey was sitting up on the hospital bed. Dawn and Keya were right by her side helping her eat. As soon as Stacey saw me she began crying.

"Forster, I want Cash. I should have been with him," she continued. I walked over to the bed and hugged her.

"The nurse just came by and told us he was in critical but stable condition."

"Oh that's not too bad," Dawn said. Keya nodded solemnly in agreement.

"He's alright thanks to God. Now you better be eating cuz you know if Cash finds out you're not feeding his son, he's going to pull those IV's from his arm and come crawling down here." They all laughed more out of relief than what I'd said. "And besides, that's my Godson in there. So please eat and now that you know Cash is doing better, he'll need you to be better as well," I said trying to make sense of a bad situation. Just then my cell phone rang interrupting the conversation. "Excuse me." I said then answered the call. "Who's this?" I answered.

"It's me, Craig," the guy replied.

"What up money?" Craig was one of Cash's little soldiers.

"How's Cash?" Craig asked.

"He's stable now, we'll know more in a minute." I told him.

"Yo, bust it, I know who shot Cash. So what's good?" Craig asked.

I was still shaking when I walked out the hospital room.

"As soon as I hear from the doctor about Cash, we're going to get our peoples together then get those niggas!" I said determinedly.

"What niggas homes?" Craig answered.

"You heard me," I replied.

"Nah man, it wasn't no nigga it's some freak," Craig replied.

"A what?" I asked emphatically.

"A bitch shot Cash," he said. I was stunned as I heard him continuing. "Bust it Forst, it gets better. This bitch is Boobie's baby mother, Lacresia," Craig said and his answer set my heart on fire.

I almost dropped the phone. I knew Lacresia, she was Boobie's ride or die girlfriend. For the life of me, I couldn't see anyone riding on her. Not even for my man, my best friend and brother who was in the hospital fighting for his life. I wouldn't allow that retaliatory action to take her out.

"Leave her. I'll handle this one," I said.

"Whatcha mean dogs? Nah man, we got dudes right now ready to shoot up

her whole family," Craig said.

"Yo, you not hearing me or what?" I asked angrily. "I got this, so let it go. And if anyone touches her or her family, I'm coming after you."

"What's up with this bitch that we can't get at her?" Craig asked.

"Its personal, trust me. I got this, ahight." I said then ended the call. I did not want to go after her. I knew she already fled New York. She knew Cash's clique was tight and besides that, Boobie taught her well. I went back into Stacey's room without discussing the phone call.

"Did she say anything about his condition?" Stacey asked.

"Nah, the doctor is about to come out and explain all that. I'll be back to let you know what's what, ahight?" I kissed Dawn's forehead and rubbed her belly. "How're you doing, honey?"

"I'm okay, just a little hungry. How're you holding up?" She asked with tears in her eyes.

"I'm still here." I said. "Kee, how you, girl?" I asked.

"I'm good, thanks for asking, Forst," she said.

"Y'all know Cash is stronger than most people and he's not going to give up because that ain't even in him. So let me go out there to his mother. I'll be back. And Ms. Stacey, you better eat," I said with a smile and made my way back to the waiting area. I ran into Miss Carroll walking toward me. "Ma, where are you going?"

"The doctor told us that we could see Cash."

I didn't hesitate. I got on the elevator with her. He was on the seventh floor and the police stood in front of his room. No one was allowed admittance except family members. I walked in the room first pausing then leaning over to where his head was. I winced when I saw him close-up. Cash looked different with tubes in him. As soon as Miss Carroll saw him she started crying hysterically. A nurse rushed to assist her. I sat beside Cash and listened as the doctor explained his medical condition.

"Cashmere has lost a lot of blood and his lungs have collapsed. The first bullet pierced his chest cavity damaging some tissues and the second bullet hit his spine," the doctor explained. "At this time there are no movements in his limbs. He maybe paralyzed from the waist down. It's too early to tell."

Tears were coming as I listened and realized that once Cash regained consciousness, he was not going to be happy with the diagnosis. He had fought for props on the streets and received repect. Now he would have to deal with the fact that he was paralyzed. Sometimes we reap what we sow.

True story or my name ain't Forster Brown...

The end

ACKNOWLEDGEMENTS

God has been better to me than I've been to myself. Through God anything and every-thing is possible. Keep him first.

My dad, Alonzo Henegain, you're the best person in the world and I love you always. Thank you for having my back. To the person who changed my life and the way I see myself, God has blessed me with the most precious thing, my son Joseph. I love you so much it hurts. Thanks for bringing a new meaning and smile to my heart. I love you mommy. Shout out to my family, especially my sisters Wanna Seignious, Champagne and the rest of the Seignious. Shout to all my nieces and nephews.

A special shout out to my ACS fam. You guys have been there for me. I love you all, Ms. Berridge, Gloria McFarland, Omogo, and all the rest, thanks.

Shout to Lanette R. Brown, my girls Neffie, Eva Gray, Kharifa my buddy. A special shout out to my friend for twenty years who is now my husband. Our love grew with time though things didn't go the way we planned in our hearts back then. It was meant for us to mature and grow through experience. I love you Malik. You're my soul mate. My brother-in-law, Armeen, you've been down from Elementary school. We should've lis-tened (smile). Your voice is beautiful. I can't wait until you blow for the rest of the world. Stay focused. Love ya big sis Keisha.

Jason Claiborne, Anthony Whyte, Tamiko Maldonado and Joy Leftow, the poest, I appreciate the tireless effort of the Augustus Manuscript team. Go hard or go home.

I've listened to the following artists, Life Jennings, Music Soulchild, Yolanda Adams, T.I., Toni Braxton, Heather Headley and the old school artist.

Though I really didn't want to mention my close, close friend this way, I told him I got him this time around. I didn't want to add you like this. When I heard you were called home I knew it wasn't because of no one else, he's the truth and he's real. I miss our laughter. I miss your over-protecting ass, most of all I miss your saying 'I love you K'. RIP to my nephew, who had such a bright future ahead. Isiah Henegain AKA Zay-Zay we miss you.

To all those who lost a loved one, remember the good times and love those that are here. If you're upset with a family member, take the initiative to squash it. Life is short. Give all your problems to God because the battle is not yours.

Keisha Seinious

KEISHA SEIGNIOUS

[LITERALLY DOPE]

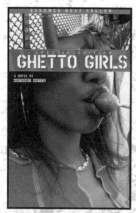

GHETTO GIRLS
AUTHOR // ANTHONY WHYTE
ISBN: 0975945319 // $14.95

GHETTO GIRLS TOO
AUTHOR // ANTHONY WHYTE
ISBN: 0975945300 // $14.95

GHETTO GIRLS 3: SOO HOOD
AUTHOR // ANTHONY WHYTE
ISBN: 0975945351 // $14.95

A BOOGIE DOWN STORY
AUTHOR // KEISHA SEIGNIOUS
ISBN: 0979281601 // $14.95

BOOTY CALL *69
AUTHOR // ERICK S GRAY
ISBN: 0975945343 // $14.95

**IT CAN HAPPEN
IN A MINUTE**
AUTHOR // S.M. JOHNSON
ISBN: 0975945378 // $14.95

Expressing the widest possible range of the urban experience...

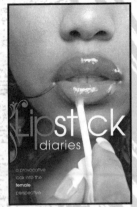

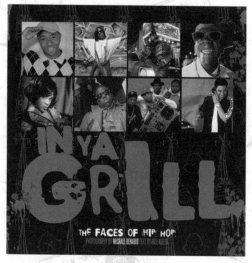

IN YA GRILL
THE FACES OF HIP HOP

PHOTOGRAPHY BY **MICHAEL BENABIB** TEXT BY BILL ADLER

"Its like a hip hop encyclopedia, its all you need."

-DJ **Kid Capri**

In words and pictures, **In Ya Grill: The Faces of Hip-Hop** depicts and defines the music that has changed the American cultural landscape forever. More than 250 images by photographer Michael Benabib, accompanied by the text of writer Bill Adler, tell the story of hip-hop from 1987 to the present. Included are artists such as **Tupac Shakur, Biggie Smalls, Snoop Dog, Public Enemy, Salt 'N Pepa, Sean Combs, Queen Latifah, LL Cool J, and Mary J. Blige** performing, recording, and relaxing at clubs, parties, and on the street.

Produced By **Watson-Guptill Publications & Augustus Publishing**

Augustuspublishing.com / Info@augustuspublishing.com

ORDERFORM

Make All Checks Payable To: Augustus Publishing 33 Indian Road Ny, Ny 10034
Shipping Charges: Ground One Book $4.95 / Each Additional Book $1.00

AUGUSTUS
PUBLISHING

Titles	Price	Qty	Total
Ghetto Girls (Special Edition) / Anthony Whyte ISBN: 0975945319	14.95		
Ghetto Girls Too / Anthony Whyte ISBN: 0975945300	14.95		
Ghetto Girls 3: Soo Hood / Anthony Whyte ISBN: 0975945351	14.95		
A Boogie Down Story / Keisha Seignious ISBN: 0979281601	14.95		
Booty Call *69 / Erick S Gray ISBN: 0975945343	14.95		
If It Ain't One Thing - It's Another / Sharron Doyle ISBN: 097594536X	14.95		
It Can Happen In A Minute / S.m. Johnson ISBN: 0975945378	14.95		
Woman's Cry: Llantó de la mujer / Vanessa Mártir ISBN: 0975945386	14.95		
A Good Day To Die / James Hendricks ISBN: 0975945327	14.95		
Lip Stick Diaries / Various Female Authors ISBN: 0975945394	14.95		
Spot Rushers / Brandon McCalla ISBN: 0979281628	14.95		
Hustle Hard /Blaine Martin ISBN: 0979281636	14.95		
Crave All Lose All / Erick S Gray ISBN: 082307885X	14.95		
In Ya Grill: The Faces of Hip Hop ISBN: 082307885X	21.95		
Subtotal			
Shipping			
8.625% Tax			
Total			

Name

Company

Address

City State Zip

Phone Fax

Email

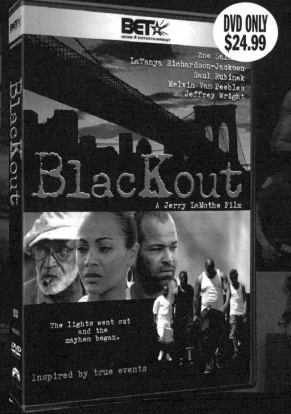